The Touch of Inno

Broken Lives

'Made In Birmingham' IV

By

Michael Layton & Stephen Burrows

Dedications
Michael Layton: To my wife Andry for her unswerving support, all of our supporters on *'Bostin Books'* Facebook page, and to fellow *'Brummies'* wherever their journeys take them in the world.

Stephen Burrows: To all those who fight child abuse, whether in the Police or elsewhere.

Our special thanks also go to two former colleagues Debbie Menzel and Jean Wachala.

First Published: 2020 by Bostin Books

Other books by Michael Layton and Stephen Burrows

Joint:
Historical Crime Fiction:
Black Over Bill's Mother's – A Storm is Coming
Keep Right On

Non-Fiction:
One in For D & D – a little book of police slang
It's A Blag – police tricks and funny stories
Reporting for Duty – West Midlands Police (The first twenty-five years 1974 – 1999)
Top Secret Worcestershire
The Noble Cause
Walsall's Front Line – Volume 1 (1997-1998)
Walsall's Front Line – Volume 2 (1998-1999)
Ta-Ra A Bit, Our Kid – a little book of 'Brummie' slang

By Michael Layton

Non-Fiction:
Hunting the Hooligans (With Robert Endeacott)
Tracking the Hooligans (With Alan Pacey)
Police Dog Heroes (With Bill Rogerson)
Birmingham's Front Line
Violence in the Sun
The Night the Owl Cried - A Taste of Cyprus (With Androulla Christou-Layton)
The Hooligans Are Still Among Us (With Bill Rogerson)

By Stephen Burrows

Historical Fiction
Pretty Thing

—

4

Author Biographies

Michael Layton QPM joined the British Transport Police as a Cadet on the 1st September 1968 and, after three years, was appointed as a Police Constable, serving at Birmingham New Street Station. In 1972 he transferred to Birmingham City Police, which amalgamated in 1974 to become the West Midlands Police, where he eventually reached the rank of Chief Superintendent in 1997.

On retirement from that Force in 2003 he went on to see service with the Sovereign Bases Police in Cyprus, and then returned to the British Transport Police in 2004, initially as a Detective Superintendent (Director of Intelligence), and then in his last two years as the Operations Superintendent at Birmingham, where he continued with his passion for combating football violence, until finally retiring again in 2011.

In the January 2003 New Year's Honours List, he was awarded the Queens Police Medal for distinguished police service.

Since retiring from the police Michael has been a self-employed consultant specialising in crime and community safety and done work for several Train Operating Companies.

Stephen Burrows joined West Midlands Police in 1983, working in Birmingham, Wolverhampton and Walsall. He performed a wide variety of roles in ranks up to and including Detective Superintendent. These included uniform command, complaints and discipline, (including internal and cross force enquiries) and CID command, (including Serious Crime Investigation, Child Protection and Head of Intelligence).

In 2002 he transferred to Warwickshire Police as Chief Superintendent (Area Commander), and then became Detective Chief Superintendent, (Head of Crime) for the Force, a post held for five years. He was trained as Senior Investigating Officer, in Kidnap command, and all levels of Firearms Command amongst other skills. He retired in 2013 following thirty years' service, eleven of which were spent at Chief Superintendent rank. He currently works for The Home Office in the field of Communications Data.

Chapter List

Chapter One

'Little Bo Peep Has Lost Her Sheep'

Disparate lives, distant places. Fate, luck and circumstance forge our paths. We step forwards through time, knowing nothing of each other, and caring little, but sometimes we converge, and change each other forever.

***

It had been a good war. Europe lay in ruins, filled with the displaced, the homeless, the refugees. Whole societies shattered, families torn apart, conventions trashed. The Nazis had started it, but the Russians had paid them back in kind – and more. Casual murder, rape, cruelty, inhumanity; the spectre of death loomed large across the whole continent. To the victor the spoils, and he was on the winning side.

War had freed him, forged him, given him wings. He was flying high, feeling the warmth of the sun. No *'Icarus'* he, no plummet back to earth. He had plans, he had skills, he was ruthless, he had desires to be fulfilled. War had provided the means, but now it was ending, and thoughts must be given to peacetime. Order would be restored, laws enforced. He would be misunderstood in a peacetime world, his promising career threatened. A new way of achieving his needs was required.

Twice he had been moulded. Public School the first. He had been a victim then, of bullying and more. An all-boys school; a beautiful Victorian country house, set alone on a secluded estate. But there was no beauty within. Abandoned there by parents with better things to do, money to be spent, fun to be had, they could easily afford the cost of removing him from their lives and assuage their consciences by labelling it, 'a good start in life'.

And later, it would prove so. The contacts made, the things done, the lessons learnt there, stayed with him for the rest of his life. A member of a privileged group, 'one of their own', the bonds were strong, nurturing him, protecting him, and later looking to him for leadership.

At first there had been horror for a young boy all alone. The older boys were cruel, the regime harsh. It was a self-perpetuating system. The Prefects treated the new boys, 'the fags', like slaves. Some were better than others. Most Prefects did it because it was expected, and had been done to them, but a few enjoyed other delights. Bullying, and the infliction of pain and torture, and darker and more damaging, the fulfilment of sexual needs. In some the two combined.

And what of the teachers, *'the Masters'*? They were a similar mix to their wards. But even the good ones adhered to principles of child-rearing handed down from Victorian times. *'Seen and not heard'*. Cold baths and exercise. It was all *'character-forming'*, had built an Empire, *'made a man of you'*. And blind eyes were turned. After all, what was the harm of a spot of *'fun'*, much in the ways of the Greek scholars and their students from another time where academia and not so forbidden love had mixed freely. Boys became men. They had to learn what it was all about, and there were Masters and pupils only too willing to play the mentor.

He had been eleven years of age when he had first been made to perform oral sex on a Prefect, who had beaten him first; not because he needed to force him into submission but simply because he enjoyed sadomasochism: twelve when a Master had bent him over a desk, pulled down his shorts and pants, and administered not the expected caning, but a *'rod'* of a different type. He suffered in silence. It was the norm as far as he knew, and who could he tell, who would believe him, or care?

By fourteen he was enjoying it, by sixteen, a Prefect administering it; now one of a trusted circle that included Masters. He grew in size and strength, a mainstay of the rugby and cricket teams. His father was proud of him and knew him not.

By eighteen he had found his escape route from the family that had abandoned him, one they would endorse. They could boast about him, and still be rid of him in order to continue their glittering progress amongst the social elites.

That was the second forging of him. It began with officer training at Sandhurst Military Academy. There was a well-established conduit from the school to the Army. There he found both a sanctioned means of leaving home, and a familiar-feeling institution, full of possibilities to further his interests.

The Army built upon the foundations the school had begun, but added something they could not, a killer instinct, and a machine to support it. He excelled from the start, a star pupil, earmarked for greater things. He went to war in 1939 as the youngest Lieutenant in the British Army. Pulled from the beaches at Dunkirk, decorated for doing what he enjoyed second-best – inflicting pain; promoted several times and disgorged from the landing craft onto the beaches in Normandy, a Major.

He survived, not through cowardice or hiding behind his rank. He was lucky, he believed the Gods favoured him, he had an unassailable confidence, and no bullet found him. The men loved him. An officer with guts, not afraid to get down in the mud, fight with them. They allowed him his 'little eccentricities' because he kept them alive and visited vengeance on their enemies. And luck was with him once again. God, if he existed, clearly favoured him, forgave his vices, perhaps even endorsed them? The Germans began to collapse, determined resistance became the last thrashings of a dying regime; the race across Europe bestowed upon them the glow of glory, righteous warriors of freedom.

Who would begrudge him a little 'fun' on the way? Others indulged their own particular tastes as they went. Theft, rape, murder. They were the conquerors, and before they reached the borders of Germany, they were the liberators, welcomed everywhere. A smoking, shattered, continent and its peoples lay at their mercy. Desperate people, surviving at any cost.

It might cost a little food, safe conduct, protection, but everything was for sale. And if not for sale, who would stop him indulging himself? In Germany they could take what they wanted, as punishment for the Nazis. They weren't as bad as the Russians though. They were British after all.

He returned to England a hero.

***

Lives apart.

It was only a small advert, and he didn't usually bother with the newspaper, but his mother had left the *'Gleaner'* outside when she went back inside the shack to cook, and he was idly flicking through it.

It was a hot afternoon, but the wooden decking was shaded, with a slight cooling breeze. The shabby armchair was a welcome relief after hanging round the dusty streets, looking for something that would pay, or something, anything, to do to break the boredom.

Seventeen years-old and bored stiff. His whole world encapsulated in the backstreets of Kingston, Jamaica. Life lay before him, and right now, the prospects did not look good. The neighbourhood was hard and he had been raised poor and tough. Anything that paid poor wages was as good as hard labour, and if it paid well, it was criminal. If you were going to do hard labour either way, the temptation was to follow the money and hide the fact from his mother, Evadne an ardent Christian who loved him unconditionally.

He was already getting hardened to it; both

'Bud' and he had grown up the hard way, tempered to steel by the streets, handy with their fists, and people, the wrong type, were beginning to take notice. He knew that soon they would be getting offers, work of a kind that meant selling your soul to people he wanted to avoid. Bud felt the same, they had known each other forever. Played together in the dust, same class at school. They trusted each other. They needed to escape. 'Ses' was actually short for Cecil, whilst Bud had picked up his label from an American they had come across in Jamaica who had insisted on calling the young man 'Bud' at every opportunity – it stuck.

Evadne was the anchor holding him in Jamaica. He loved and admired her. She had raised him alone, scraping along by working endless hours, cleaning or crop-picking. His father had been killed in the war, fighting for the *'mother country'*, the family's reward for his ultimate sacrifice a telegram from the King, and a life of poverty. All that remained was the piece of paper, framed upon the wall, a few faded photographs and faster-fading childhood memories

Bud and he discussed it endlessly. They both had dreams and none of them involved *'sweating their bollocks off'* doing manual labour for bugger all, or the alternative, which led to prison, or worse. It was easy for Bud. He didn't get on with his mother, and his father was long gone, but Ses was hung on the horns of a dilemma. He wanted out, wanted excitement and adventure, to see the world, wanted his own life, but he knew what that would mean to his mother.

13

He vacillated, mused, talked, but did nothing, and the days in the sun floated past. He was nearly a man. He would soon have to choose his path, but he knew he was putting the decision off, lying to himself that he had plenty of time.

The advert might as well have been in neon lights.

'Passenger Opportunity

To United Kingdom

Troopship 'Empire Windrush' sailing around 23rd May

Fares: Cabin Class £48

Troopdeck £28

Royal Mail Lines Limited. 8 Port Royal St'

Ses read it ten times, and ten times more. Excitement and a sick feeling in the gut mixed. A moment of truth, a moment of destiny. He could turn the page so easily, stretch back on the porch, or he could rip it out and show Bud.

*

The ship crested the waves. It had been rough at times, and there was plenty of vomit about, but the passengers were a happy group. A lot of them played instruments and there was singing, mainly Gospel, but also the songs that their forefathers had learnt, mixed with the influence of American music from the radio, music that would soon take over the world when it became the roots of *'Rock and Roll'*.

They had stowed away. Neither of them had the passage money. Evadne had offered it, but Ses had refused, full of guilt. It was bad enough that he was abandoning her, she could keep her hard-won money. There had been plenty of tears, but she understood. 'Same as his father', she said, 'full of that 'wanderlust'. And look where that had got him, she added, 'a box in the ground'. He had promised to be careful, go to church every week, write home, and one day, when he had made his fortune, to come home and visit. He had promised, filled with love for her and good intentions, and had added that he would bring her to England once he was 'set up'. He meant it too.

There was a mixture of families and young single men like Ses and Bud travelling, full of hope. But they stuck together. They were all literally, 'in the same boat', voyaging to a new life in a new land that was welcoming them with open arms. The land of plenty, the 'mother' of civilisation'. Their King and their rulers, needed them, had asked them to come, and a good life was promised

*

The origins of Jamaicans coming to the United Kingdom started with the arrival of the ship the *'S.S. Empire Windrush'* on 22nd June 1948 at Tilbury Dock, in Essex.

The ship had made the 8,000-mile journey from the Caribbean with four hundred and ninety-two passengers on board from Jamaica, Trinidad and

15

Tobago, and other islands. It marked the beginning of a policy of post-war mass migration which was designed to deal with shortages of workers, both skilled, in professions such as nursing, and unskilled.

Until the Commonwealth Immigrants Act was passed in 1962, all Commonwealth citizens were granted the status of British citizenship with full rights of entry and settlement under the British Nationality Act 1948. As America started to tighten its laws on immigration Great Britain seemed to offer a brighter future.

*

They walked down the gangplank, gazing at the London skyline. A new land for them. Everyone had their best suits on. Most had just one suitcase, battered and tatty, and several had musical instruments in their hands or slung over shoulders. They had made it to Paradise and smiles were wide and frequent. But there were also nervous glances at each other, seeking the comfort of comradeship and shared experience as they took in the harsh docks and felt the English 'summer' for the first time.

They were mustered together and taken into London, to Clapham South Deep Air Raid Shelter, where the requisite papers were issued, and dispersal to areas with the greatest shortage of semi-skilled workers began. Many found their way to the Midlands, and worked in furnaces and forges, whilst others took jobs as porters and cleaners – low-paid jobs that few white workers would take on. A sizeable number of the new arrivals were taken on by British Rail, who specifically recruited from migrant workers.

In due course an estimated 172,000 West Indian born immigrants made their way to England, looking for a better standard of living. Many of them had served in the British Armed Forces during the Second World War, and regarded England as the *'Mother Country'*, with more than 5,500 West Indians serving as ground-crew with the RAF in the UK as a result of the Overseas Recruiting Scheme in 1940.

*

Ses and Bud had been plagued during the voyage by worries that they would be sent home once their 'stowaway' status was discovered, but quickly realised that they were no more or less than a consignment of goods to be delivered and processed. Their Jamaican papers were inspected, and British ones issued. None of the bored-looking officials seemed bothered, none of them interacted on a personal basis, it was all forms to be filled and official business to be completed – just numbers in a sea of other numbers.

The new arrivals spent a few nights on camp beds before being split up and allocated trains to various destinations. Ses and Bud stuck together and made it very plain that they were not to be parted. When it looked like they might be, they said they were brothers by different fathers, and nobody asked further questions. Nobody was bothered. There was a process to be gone through, more 'immigrants' were en-route, and jobs were waiting.

They had no idea where Birmingham was, or what it was, but a few days later they emerged from a smoky railway station into an equally smoky city. A steady drizzle fell. The glittering image of the 'motherland' was being rapidly tarnished and the stares of people passing were not welcoming.

Ses saw a child point and exclaim excitedly, "Mummy, mummy, look at the black men."

The woman looked, then looked away and hurried the child on. Ses caught a shadow of fear cross her face. She never saw his broad and welcoming smile.

They had been given an address, a 'boarding house' in Trafalgar Road, Moseley. They were to attend their new jobs in a week with Ses on the railway, and Bud on the buses. Their new life had arrived without any sign of the adventure they had so desperately craved.

They didn't know how to get to Moseley, so they walked, asking directions as they went. Some passers-by wouldn't even stop when they approached, hurrying past, eyes averted. Those that did try to help spoke with a strange, nasal accent and in turn seemed to find the newcomer's English impenetrable. Two hours of seemingly endless grey city tenements and bombsites, its noise and traffic impressed upon them that they were in an alien land. Kingston was fading like a golden-hued dream. They saw signs saying *'No Irish, No Blacks, and No Dogs'* in the windows of many homes where rooms were available to rent, impressing their 'difference' upon them. They would soon find out what a 'colour-bar' was.

Their lodgings were in a large Victorian terraced house divided into 'rooms'. The landlady was a fearsome-looking Irish lady of considerable size and loudness of voice who laid down the rules with the threat of eviction for any transgressions. In time though, they learnt that under that rough exterior, Briony had a warm heart. She knew what it was like to be abandoned in a strange land, having arrived from the poverty of Ireland before the war and lost a husband to it, just as they had finally scrimped enough money to buy the house she now let out to survive.

Just one room with a shared bathroom, a double bed and kitchen facilities was now home. Ses and Bud shared everything – their financial worries, their love of goat curry and dumplings, even their women.

Weekends were for spending the contents of their pay-packets, and having fun, and they started to regularly attend local dance halls, in particular the Moseley and Balsall Heath Institute. Always immaculate in suits and wide brimmed hats on nights out, they were both good dancers and popular with some of the young white girls.

Ses tried to keep his promises to Evadne, but life had other ideas. For starters, there was no church to welcome them, and any Christian feelings they arrived with were tested to breaking point and broken, lying forgotten as the first few years passed in a stew of work, prejudice and seeking the things young men want.

It was inevitable that at some stage conflict would emerge, and one night both men were badly beaten by a gang of white men who took exception to *'darkies'* touching their women. They gave as good as they got, but it had a dramatic effect on their mentality, and fuelled resentment, which grew as the place they thought would be home was starting to feel like nothing more than an open prison.

Whatever they did to try to fit in with their new lives; they were always shown to be different, but not in a special or good way. Good enough though to do the jobs nobody else wanted, they felt like they were just a necessary evil. People still stopped and looked as they walked around. Not many other black faces in a white world, and nowhere for them to mix with 'their own'.

There was one mystery that they remarked upon to each other, a mystery unresolved, although they unknowingly met the answer over a decade later. Sometimes they would see another dark face in Moseley, a boy, big for his age. But this boy was with a white boy, and even more astonishing, a white woman. The woman still bore the signs of prettiness, and wasn't old, but a sense of 'wear' hung about her, and the beginnings of a face drawing in towards its bones. Ses and Bud were intrigued enough to try and work it out, constructing several stories, but they never got close to the truth. They would not have believed it either. They never knew that their lives had brushed another's who would one day be important in theirs.

As the *'Fifties'* and their *'Twenties'* rolled

onwards, their attitudes hardened along with their knuckles, and survival on the streets once more required the fighting skills they had tried to escape. They both decided to refresh their combative skills and joined a local boxing club. Ses discovered he had some skill and was quite successful on the local circuit until he got too old, earning some extra money by fighting 'legally'.

It was as if fate was pulling strings, drawing them back towards the life they had tried to escape.

***

Separate lives.

Ses and Bud didn't know it when they saw the 'mysterious' family in Moseley village centre, but Robert Docker was also an outsider. People stopped in the street and stared at him, and he had borne the brunt of plenty of nastiness in his young life. He had registered the new, dark faces, but they meant something different to him than to the white, gawping, denizens of Moseley, and they made his life harder to bear.

It was so unfair. None of it was his fault. He struggled to believe in God, despite the constant efforts of school to indoctrinate him. Had he any faith, he would have believed that the Devil had cast his net and claimed Robert Docker for one of his own early in life.

He was torn and anguished. Had been since he realised he could think. He loved his mother but also hated her at the same time. He had once loved his brother Joe before things had changed forever. He just hated his stepfather, and with good reason.

Hated his mother because he was a bastard, and that was her fault. He knew that everyone thought she was a slag, his school 'mates' loved to tell him so. Few adults said it out loud, but he could see it in their eyes, the way they spoke to her, treated her. And the proof was there, plain to see. He and his brother Joe, especially Joe, a walking, breathing, growing reminder that she had gone far beyond the acceptable. Children from a one-night stand was one thing, and deserved ostracism and condemnation, but Joe was another.

But he had once loved her beyond anything else. Already that feeling was being corroded by the acid of years and experience. He was young and wanted to love his Mom, and it was tearing him apart, her abandonment of them to the mercy of his stepfather, Richard.

His hatred of that man was pure, undiluted and more bile was added every day of his life. The irony was that Robert was a boy who had to grow up quickly, and by the age of ten he understood that 'Dad' had every right to feel aggrieved. After all the love of his life had cuckolded him in the most public of ways, whilst he languished in a Japanese prisoner of war camp, starved and tortured.

But Richard's punishment of Mary Docker was endless and varied, and unjustly extended to her sons. Made worse when the only child he conceived with her died, leaving him to bring up another man's brood. Robert suspected that Richard was probably

22

mad. It frightened him, because he knew that Richard was capable of anything when in one of his drunken rages, and his sober, cold 'tortures' were almost worse.

And that was why he had once loved his brother. 'Big Joe', his protector, his twin, his soulmate, his constant companion. Loved the way he coped with the affliction he bore. Stoic, resolute, noble even. Joe acted as if he wasn't different, an oddity. Wasn't pointed at in the street. Wasn't the butt of all the jokes. Wasn't black.

Finally, the young Rob hated Joe merely because he existed. The visible and constant reminder of his mother's sin. The cause of the bullying and beatings that Rob endured at school and at home. His situation was bizarre and ridiculous. His mother had been with a black man and borne twins as a result, one black, Joe, one white, him. He juggled the opposing poles of brotherly love and hate within him, and they changed all the time.

Love and hate. Hate and love. A maelstrom of emotions in a young and formative brain. A unique set of circumstances forging a unique character. Robert Docker was already vowing that he came first, and once he was old enough, nobody was ever going to beat him again, whatever it took.

***

Separate lives, but a similar beginning:

A wartime romance in bomb-torn London. Two people who would never have met, never have loved, never have parted, but for the war. 'Pulling together' with victory in sight, shoulder to shoulder. Fighting for country, he in the Army, she in a factory. Snatching comfort from each other in adversity. Live for today as tomorrow we may die. Comradeship becomes more. A seed is planted.

Then *'Juno'*, *'Omaha'* and *'Sword'*. Names that once meant nothing, known only to a few. Wading waist deep from the landing craft, struggling with equipment and gun through the undertow. A beach that should be redolent of children's cries of joy, families in the sun.

The tracer searching and finding. Another bundle of torn flesh and clothing floating in the surf. Another fatherless child. 'Juno', 'Omaha' and 'Sword' now epitaphs.

*

They were the salt of the earth, the 'Eastenders'. They had survived the blitz, shown 'backbone', defied Hitler. Mr. Churchill and His Majesty had been proud of them.

Victory should have given them their share of the spoils, but life went on the same, despite voting out Mr. Churchill and giving Mr. Attlee a chance. Despite Nationalisation, the National Health, everything pretty much went back to how it was before. The rich got richer, the poor, poorer. The struggle to survive carried on remorselessly.

They wanted, but Britain did not deliver. First it was austerity, Britain broken by the war, then 'you've never had it so good'. But the 'Eastenders' didn't feel they were having anything much. They were tough, resilient, so they would take what they deserved, sort themselves out. They were the 'Eastenders'. They turned inwards.

The war was consigned to history, although its effects lingered on in a triumphant but economically shattered Britain. Its people, the scions of a rapidly fragmenting Empire began searching for a new way, a new place in the world.

By 1955, the fragile fabric of peace crafted at the end of World War Two was fading, replaced by a new kind of conflict.

A 'Cold War', had begun. The United States, and Soviet inspired and supported Communism, faced off, now with fingers on nuclear buttons. The Warsaw Pact and NATO were the new adversaries. Korea had been torn asunder and Vietnam was divided into a Communist North and Republican South. That tragedy was yet to unfold.

In America, a black lady named Rosa Parks boarded a bus in Montgomery, Alabama, and sat on a *'Whites Only'*, seat. A man named Martin Luther King led protests and bus boycotts, the genesis of the black civil rights movements. Meanwhile, in England, West Indian immigrants continued to arrive in London in greater numbers, *fuelling* resentment, and more. The term 'colour-bar' becoming common.

A 'Class War' was also fomenting, with Trade Unions flexing their muscles to the extent that in May, a 'state of emergency' in Britain was called, due to a national dock strike.

In the midst of all this conflict an unstoppable new force was being born, ironically a fusion of black and white culture, one that would arrive from America, and become all - pervading. It would set a flame in young hearts and lead to the term 'teenager' being coined, followed by the consumerism of the young. Late in that year a film called *'Blackboard Jungle'* was premiered in London, and *'Bill Haley and his Comets'*, *'Rocked Around the Clock'* as *'Teddy Boys'* stalked the streets.

In 1950 he had been six and frightened. Abandoned. Firstly, on a Normandy beach by the father he never knew. Then by a mother, if that was the right label for someone that saw him as a burden, an embarrassing reminder. Doris Foster, once pretty and lively, now bitter and marked. What man would look at her twice now?

They were called *'latchkey kids'* – given a door key and left to their own devices. At six, he was filled with fear. Of the bigger kids, the bullies. Fear of having nothing to eat. Fear of being left alone, fear of the streets, of what happened there.

By 1955, there had been changes. Eleven years old, but he had survived - on his wits. He was neither big nor tough enough to mix it physically, but he had a talent. He could spot weaknesses in others, work out what 'made them tick', and he was clever enough to exploit what he saw. Setting the playground gang leaders against each other, rather than him. Making himself useful in exchange for 'protection'. A bit of spying here, some false information there.

At sixteen there were more changes. As he matured, he realised that he was different to the others, had urges that needed to be kept hidden, or satisfied in the shadows. He was drawn into a darker circle, welcomed, first as a potential victim, then as a useful person. He moved out, never saw his mother again, and hoped she would rot in hell.

He used the contacts made on those rough streets. Combined them with the protection offered by his new friends and a little money he made, buying and selling, including his own body. He discovered that he had a natural flair for business. The East End had tempered him, made him ruthless. He could 'smell' the weakness and desire in others, and use that information wisely. He started buying people as well as things, using both blackmail and cash to get what he wanted. He recruited some muscle, then some young 'ladies' and boys.

His line was straightforward, 'Want some cash son? You be nice to someone for me and I'll make it worth your while. Just some old bloke needs some love.' Photos taken; another little favour due one day.

He saw the potential in the old wartime buildings nobody wanted. Bought them cheap, rented them out, used his money hiring 'muscle' to ensure there were no late payers or nuisances. By twenty he was a 'player', albeit a minor one. His talents had been recognised. The terrified boy was no more. He had become very useful. But he always kept his secret life separate.

***

Disparate lives:

A lucky boy, born in 1950 into a family that was 'getting along nicely thank you'. Father at the Midland Bank in Birmingham. Not yet at the top, or near it, but a future of security and steady advancement secured. Mother at home to love and nurture him. An 'only child', and thus adored and indulged. 'Spoilt' they would say. Mother would say he was clever and sensitive with a fragility that needed protection. He would probably go into a 'nice' profession, perhaps follow in his father's footsteps?

Wrapped in love in a big house in a tree lined road. Life was soft and easy, then it changed. In the year the Beatles debuted at *'The Cavern'*, and would change the world, he went to 'big' school.

It was different straight away. The 'ragging' was shared around to start with. The 'First Year' kids were fair game. It was traditional, and handed down across the years from a not so distant past when the youngsters were 'fags', slaves of the prefects. All low-key stuff. Being taken to see the 'blue goldfish' down the toilets. Caps and bags snatched and hung in trees or thrown on roofs. Just harmless fun. The new kids stuck together, knowing that they too would get a chance to dish it out one day.

Then things changed. He couldn't pinpoint an exact moment. His 'year' of three classes were drawn from both affluent and poorer areas. That background stamped its mark on the offspring. You couldn't hide where you came from. It was there in everything you did. The way you spoke, your interests, the quality of your clothes, your satchel, your packed lunch. The kids from the Council estates were streetwise, survivors, rough around the edges. They recognised it in each other, knew that others were different, saw it as weakness.

There was a leader, there always was. Human nature is raw in the young, before social convention masks its essential savagery. In his year the leader was Paul Murphy. He was one of the oldest, had only just qualified for the September intake. That meant he was bigger. He came from a tough estate and had clearly been left to his own devices, so he was confident and worldly wise. A Manchester United fan, he was already taking himself off to Old Trafford and associating with football hooligans. He told stories about being part of the fights. Probably a load of bullshit, but it added to his reputation and nobody was about to challenge him.

Like in any other animal pack, a few fights established his supremacy, cementing his reputation as the 'hardest' kid in his school year. Others were drawn to him; hangers-on began to emulate him, and soon a gang formed. Gangs need victims and their eyes naturally turned towards the 'soft', 'rich kids', inventing all manner of propaganda to justify dishing out punishment and terror for imagined 'sins'. Less than twenty-five years earlier, this type of human behaviour had been employed on a much larger scale and had led to the gas chambers.

His life became hell, or so he thought at the time, it surely couldn't get worse. He was 'taxed' of any cash he had and then more demanded, 'or else'. So, he began to lie to his parents, inventing reasons for needing money. School club fees, tuck shop, more pens and the like, and because he was loved, no questions were asked. He was beaten a couple of times, taken behind the old air raid shelters across the playing fields, but they were careful not to mark him and he dared not 'tell'. It was the dawn of the decade of 'peace and love', but not for him.

***

She was a fat baby, heavy-boned and full of giggles. It was a big family, four younger brothers and plenty of uncles and aunts. They were Brummies through and through, and the tall terraced house in Harborne resounded with their nasal ululations.

She was the only girl, apart from Mom of course, but Mom was what in those days was called 'scatty'. Empty words poured from her mouth, she forgot names, mixed them up, went on endless rambling tales of the small doings of friend's friends, or Mrs. Butler at the Post Office's mother. Mom struggled to run the house, and often things got so 'on top of her', that she had to lie on the settee, her eyes shut, with the company of the Light Programme on the 'wireless'.

The children learnt to fend for themselves, and the sole daughter learnt how to cope with brothers. It was an experience that would serve her well later in life.

She experimented with various techniques and observed the results closely. Sometimes being feminine worked, sometimes being 'cute' did. Other times she needed her wits, or to play dumb. And the final resort was to be one of the boys. It all worked; the skill was working out which one to apply to whom and what situation.

By the age of ten she had easily outstripped her mother in handling the world and its occupants, but had also learnt scorn for the weakness of her only female companion. She loved her father dearly. He was a gentle giant of a man who worked for the Council, sorting out problems with the housing, but he worked long hours to feed and keep his brood, and was always too tired to do anything other than eat his tea then slump into his accustomed armchair with a library book.

He devoured books, and sometimes the daughter thought he might prefer those worlds of imagination to the real one, with her in it. But she adored him, felt safe with him. He was always kind, never shouted, and her wiles had long ago been put to use in placing herself as his favourite in the family. She was his 'princess' and she wished he was home more often.

The 'trouble' began at one of the family 'get togethers'. Dad had no real relatives, but Mom more than made up for that, with three sisters. They took it in turns to host gatherings, punctuated by drinking, singing, games of cards, or peering at the tiny television screen in the corner, for those who could afford them.

The girl was thirteen and had begun to develop, especially 'up top'. She was self-conscious about her body and very aware that her male classmates, and older men, were beginning to concentrate their gazes well below her eye-line. She had unconsciously started to fold her arms as a shield, although the attention was not unwelcome, and made her aware of another power she would have over men.

One person in particular began to pay her extra notice, Uncle Jim, married to the youngest sister, Beryl. In his early forties, he had been in the RAF and still sported a moustache and a rakish demeanour that contrasted with his dowdy wife, who looked much older. Family legend had it that he was still 'a bit of a lady's man'. He acted and dressed the part, never lacking the latest clothes or cars. The girl was already old enough to wonder why they ever married. They didn't seem close, no children and nothing in common as far as she could see.

It had begun with little comments about her 'growing up fast', comments with double-meanings and a wink, seemingly innocent, but she had an idea what they meant, and she couldn't help but like being the focus. Girls are nothing if not vulnerable to doubts about their looks, and his compliments did wonders for her self-confidence.

As to the subject that lay beneath the comments, there had been no 'birds and bees' talk with either parent – they still thought of her as a little girl, and the topic was subject to an unspoken taboo at home, but between them, the girls at school had pooled their fragments of knowledge and arrived at an understanding.

The rest of the family seemed not, or pretended not, to notice her uncle's behaviour, or if they did, it passed without comment or approbation. 'It must be ok then', thought the girl.

As time passed, she noticed that he would always sit next to her, or be there right by her. There were 'accidental' brushes of contact and the smell of his cologne. Hugs of greeting lingered a little too long, and on the previous family meeting, his hand had wandered down her back when they hugged on arrival, and pulled her close. Just for an instant, so short it could almost be her imagination, but she knew it wasn't and thought about it for days afterwards.

It was the Boxing Day family meeting. The relatives took turns to host, and this year it was at Jim and Beryl's, who had the biggest house and the most money, and liked to show it off. Accommodation for the night had been offered and accepted by her parents, so they could 'make a night of it'. When she asked why the others hadn't been invited to stay, her Mom had given a look so smug that the girl resisted an impulse to knock it off her face,

"They weren't invited. You know I've always been closest to Beryl, and Jim and your Dad have always got on. Besides the others are close enough to walk home and there are no buses we could get on Boxing Day."

Jim made a beeline for her as soon as they arrived, and this time his hand reached her bum. There was a momentary caress. It was the first time a man had touched her there and it sparked a mixture of emotions, confusion, shock, shame, and perhaps a split-second of pleasure? She buried the experience for later dissection and did her best to avoid him all evening.

Jim and Beryl had provided a fantastic 'spread', and there was loads to drink; *'Watneys'* and *'Brew XI'* beer in *'Party Seven'* cans for the men, *'Babycham'*, *'Advocaat'* for *'Snowballs'*, and spirits for the ladies. Uncle Jim proclaimed,

"It's Christmas and this lovely lady is old enough to try a drink," and gave her a Babycham. Then another. She liked the taste, and the feeling of being treated as a grown-up.

The evening wore on as the adults got drunker and drunker. Finally, the others left for home. Dad was almost asleep in his chair. She didn't begrudge him that. He wasn't a big drinker and why shouldn't he enjoy himself at Christmas when he worked so hard for them all? Mom was on another planet as usual, twittering on about some nonsense and nobody was listening to her.

At midnight, Beryl began clearing up, the unspoken sign that the event was at an end, and Mom joined her in the kitchen. Dishes began to clatter, and she could hear them laughing. Dad began to snore. Suddenly she was alone with Jim. Her brothers were upstairs playing with the joint Christmas present they had bought from home, a *'Scalextric'* set.

He was in the armchair opposite her. He was staring at her. His voice was thick with drink as he attempted a line used many times in the past with other conquests, "You're looking very lovely tonight".

She didn't know what to say – lost for words in a situation which was unfamiliar.

"Growing up fast." He smiled sweetly. A sick smile.

Before she knew it, he was beside her on the settee.

"Let me give my niece a Christmas cuddle" – not a request more a signal of his intentions.

She could smell the beer on his breath. He pulled her close, his arm around her shoulder, the hand just brushing the swell of her breast, as if by accident. She could feel his other hand on her thigh as panic set in.

"I need the loo". She wriggled out of his grasp and left him on the settee. He seemed to have lapsed into a semi-coma.

In the bathroom she composed herself, reflecting on the situation. A few of her friends had 'boyfriends' of a sort, and boys were the talk of all the girls this year, and like her peers, she was 'coming of age', in fact in the advance party of maturity in her class, and beginning to experience the ups and downs of puberty.

Her periods had started some six months before, prompting an awkward conversation with her mother who simply did not want to know, or advise, and told her to hide the fact from her father. As usual, she had no choice than rely on the gleanings of information, accurate or not, from friends, whilst maintaining the outward appearance of knowledge to avoid derision.

Having fled from the settee, she assessed herself in the bathroom mirror. 'He's right though', she thought, 'I am growing up', and not too bad looking either.

She was a self-sufficient girl and, having done a speedy review, decided that no harm had been done, and in fact she felt a little flattered at the attention of the older man. After all, Uncle Jim wasn't bad looking either, just older.

By the time she returned downstairs, the women were tidying up the lounge and Jim had apparently retired for the night. They sorted out her bed for the night, the very same settee she had recently fled, and soon the house fell silent.

She couldn't say what woke her, probably a primeval sense of another presence in close proximity. The room was dark but, as her eyes got used to the gloom, she could make out a figure sat on the armrest of the settee, could hear his breathing – fast and full of anticipation. She knew who it was.

That was when it began. His hand had been on her, on top of the blanket to begin with, then creeping beneath. The breathing got deeper. He said nothing. Later, she would be unable to say why she hadn't stopped him, but she had remained still, frozen, experiencing the sensations he aroused. He had only used one hand, but she was aware that his other hand was busy under his own clothes.

It was 'their little secret' – a secret touch of innocence. He told her so lots of times, stressing the trouble for both of them if it 'came out'. Except it wasn't little, and she had no idea why she kept it. It was complicated. Who could she tell? Who would believe her? If Jim was right, she would only suffer as a result. And then, it was fun, and made her feel so grown-up.

After that night Jim turned up after school, collecting her in his brand-new Ford Cortina GT. They met secretly. It was easy, Dad was at work and Mom never really bothered where she was or what she was doing. There were plenty of excuses to use. The deceit was thrilling. He treated her like a princess, like a grown up. Presents, trips out in the car, the flicks, cafes and restaurants. He would pretend she was his daughter.

She was crazy about him. It was surely love.

Chapter Two

'Polly Put the Kettle On'

(July 1977)

The return journey felt like an eternity as the uneasy silence closed in around the three men in the nondescript police car.

In the back seat, Rob Docker had little interest in the flashes of green, and animals grazing in large open fields. Chewing grass reminded him of the speed with which some of his so-called *'superior'* officers ruminated and made decisions. He smiled lightly at his own joke. He much preferred the phrase *'senior'* officers and indeed there were still some around who were in fact quite old, set in their ways, obstinate autocrats who gave no quarter. A known quantity.

He was anxious for them to fuck off out of his way, but equally anxious about some of the new breed that were making an appearance in 1977, ambitious and ruthless men totally focussed in their personal quests for power. Some of them would stab their own grandmothers in the back to get a promotion. He almost admired them, but if they in turn could look through a window into Rob Docker's mind, even they would have recoiled.

He could see a day coming where the *'split-arses'* might need some consideration too. But for now, they were no problem. It was a man's world at the top with few females getting anywhere near to the glass ceiling, let alone breaking it.

The journey continued, the drone of the

engine providing a colourless backdrop to his thoughts. He fixed his gaze out of the window again. But Docker had even less interest in the glimpses of drab housing estates and the odd tower block as they drew closer to home, many of them had seen better times, and were well past their 'sell-by' date. They just served to remind him of his own deprived, and often turbulent, upbringing in Birmingham's back streets. His thoughts went to Joe, as they always did in these moments; his twin would always occupy a space within him no matter the distance or circumstances between them. Joe's existence had defined him, had made him what he was, and he knew he would never be free of him.

The driver of the car knew his role well and did his best to merge into the fabric of the vehicle – a faceless man who said nothing and heard everything. All logged for future reference. The man was a survivor and with three years left to go in the job, to get his thirty-year pension, he knew enough to make sure that his position was 'rock solid'. No more night shifts or work at the 'sharp end' for him and there was plenty of 'double bubble' overtime to boost his pay as he ferried gaffers around the country on various 'jollies' and 'piss-ups' all courtesy of the job. A fellow Mason had even promised to look into the possibility of civilianising the role in three- years' time and he had been assured that he would be well-placed to give it a shot.

The man in the front passenger seat was equally silent. Deep in thought whilst sporadically flicking through endless sheaths of paper – the words seemed to swirl around, and the future strategic approach of the Force looked distinctively uninspiring and unappealing at that moment. Responsibility lay heavy on his shoulders, not helped by the fact that the back of his neck was crawling from the almost tangible waves of contempt emanating from Docker.

He had not liked the way he had been spoken to during the course of the afternoon, least of all Docker's presentation of the facts afterwards which clearly demonstrated that Docker had concluded he was a man with 'no balls'.

Chief Superintendent John Rackham shifted uncomfortably in the front seat as if Docker had just squeezed them. Normally it felt good being the boss but today was different. The fact that he disliked Docker intensely and knew that the feeling was reciprocated didn't help one bit. He didn't trust Docker, believed all the stories he had heard about him and had tried everything to avoid having him as lead investigator, but Docker had been available, and the Assistant Chief Constable had practically ordered Rackham to use him.

To his surprise Docker had proved effective, although Rackham preferred not to inspect the methods he used too closely. He was a man with a future and Docker's type tended to leave an indelible stain on a good CV if you got too involved with them. He had decided straight away to just be a figurehead. Take the credit if any were due, and distance himself from any dubious goings-on or disastrous results as best he could.

Docker badly needed a drink to cleanse the bad taste in his mouth, and his thoughts turned to his long-term mistress and confidante, Jane Smith.

"Get a fucking move on, I'm sick of looking at bloody cows" Docker snapped at the driver, who shot him a nervous glance through the rear-view mirror before complying.

If the 'prat' in front put his foot down a bit, then he might be able to satisfy both needs before returning to the place that was a poor excuse for what he called home.

He thought that Rackham was going to say something about his rather inappropriate outburst, but the Chief Superintendent thought better of it, looked back down at the papers on his lap. 'Wanker', Docker thought.

The seat next to Docker was empty, and his thoughts went to the absent John Burrell. Docker had initially been suspicious of the clever young detective but had grown to recognise that he was an asset. A good investigator, and one of the 'new breed', he was a useful cover for Docker – a man who operated in a manner that would fail every ethical 'modern policing' test. Burrell had proved himself surprisingly handy in a fight too.

Burrell was clever enough to recognise and work within the environment surrounding him, had known his place in the 'pecking order' and was well-used to practising his listening skills, especially when it came to his gaffer. Essentially Docker's 'bag man' since the football job, he had been made up to sergeant off the back of that success and was ambitious to go further. Things had been going well and the overtime had been welcome. Burrell had been looking to put a ring on Sally's finger and move into a 'police house' within eighteen months.

That would have been Burrell's second 'marriage'. He had already been wedded to Docker and had been a trusted and loyal servant.

*

As the interminable journey continued in silence, Docker couldn't help himself. The events of the day kept intruding upon his need to put them to bed by doing the same to Jane. He was surprisingly angry given the fact that he usually didn't give a shit about anything unless he could benefit in some way. This job had got to him and he didn't like that.

*

Docker had been sat having a nice brew and a goggle at Sally's tits through the office window when Rackham suddenly appeared and announced that he had to go and see the Chief Constable of the neighbouring Force and insisted that Docker was going with him. That interfered in Docker's own plans, putting him in a less than gracious mood before they even left. He suspected that he was required to be either 'cannon-fodder', a 'flak -shield' for Rackham, or to deliver some reality that Rackham lacked the guts to do himself. Whichever it was, there was no upside for Docker.

Not even their own Chief, but the boss of the 'carrot-crunchers' patch they were investigating. 'Total waste of my fucking time', Docker thought sourly, as Rackham denied knowing why their presence had been required at the rural Police Force Headquarters, which was set in tranquil grounds near to a historic market town. It was, in his opinion, the sort of place where no-one normally broke into a sweat and 'blue-sky' thinking abounded, keeping many an academic-minded person in a non-job.

It didn't take long to find out.

On arrival the unlikely partners made their way to the Chief Constable's Office whilst the driver busied himself with cleaning his windscreen, eating his 'snap' from the Tupperware container that his wife dutifully prepared each day, and taking the chance for some 'shut eye'. He had even less interest than Docker in what was going on, and was content being a 'mushroom', 'kept in the dark and fed shit'.

He too thought Rackham was a 'bottle-less' wanker, but he had a healthy respect for Docker; not of his police abilities, but of his capacity and ingenuity for making the lives of anyone who crossed him a misery. The bitter experiences of others led to the driver giving Docker as wide a berth as possible. The man was definitely not one of those soft gaffers you could manipulate with a bit of a sob story. You just kept your mouth shut with Docker and watched your back.

Chief Constable Brotherton was new in post and had the typical clean- cut, square jawed, steely appearance, coupled with an effortless 'air' of being not only superior, but bright and always right. There had still been no time yet for his 'head and shoulders' portrait to appear in a gold frame alongside the other 'great and the good' in the corridor outside, but he had already practised the preferred pose several times in a large mirror in his office.

This was a man who was short in stature and suffered from *'small man's disease'* which left him with the habit of routinely raising his body on the heels of his slightly enhanced shoes. How he had ever made the 5'8" height limit was a mystery to many and would remain a tightly kept secret.

He did however more than compensate for his height with the size of his ego.

As Docker walked past the row of imperious faces in the corridor portraits, he found it difficult to conceal his loathing for the type. These feelings were only to be compounded still further as they made their way into the Chief Constable's PA's office and announced their arrival to a disinterested blonde woman who surveyed them as if she had just discovered a rather smelly substance on the bottom of her high-heel shoes. Docker had a well-seasoned eye for short skirts and made a mental note that the one that she was wearing just about did it in terms of protecting her modesty. In different circumstances he would most certainly have considered giving 'it one'. He knew the type, however. Rank had its privileges and attractions, and 'scrambled egg' on the shoulders would be the minimum required for her to 'open her legs'.

Ten minutes elapsed and Docker's temper worsened as they kicked their heels uncomfortably in the reception area : ten very deliberate minutes – before the Chief suddenly opened his door, welcomed the Chief Superintendent by his first name and grasped his hand in a welcome handshake before quickly ushering him inside. Docker always made a habit of closely observing handshakes and this one clearly betrayed the existence of a common bond between the two men. To cap it all, Docker was completely ignored by the Chief.

Rackham, before he disappeared through the door, shot a worried glance at Docker as he was left outside without so much as an acknowledgement – a *'spare prick at a wedding',* left hanging around like a naughty schoolboy. Rackham was right to be worried; Docker had a habit of getting even.

The Chief Constable's PA stared dismissively at Docker for a second before adjusting her skirt in a pointless exercise and burying her head in her typewriter. She couldn't care less for these strangers from another Force, especially the roughly spoken one who was making her uncomfortable by boldly staring at her legs and more under the desk. Her loyalty was with the new man who had quickly displayed the virtues of *'do as I say not as I do'* and expressed his open approval of her dress sense. Their relationship had already been consummated and she saw no reason to waste time on the two strangers who were merely here to be put in their place. They had nothing to offer her whereas the man with the power, influence and rather large manhood, for his size, had plenty.

Thirty minutes later Rackham emerged looking flushed and uncomfortable, and beckoned Docker inside. Another worried look of assessment. Docker could guess what was going on and determined to make Rackham as uncomfortable as possible as a bit of justice for dragging him out on this pointless exercise.

The Chief Constable sat behind his desk, no effort made to engage on a personal basis, no handshakes, and no offer to be seated. His little speech was directed at Docker specifically.

The Chief smiled thinly, it was nothing more than cosmetic, and in a measured voice he said,

"Before you go, I just wanted to thank you for your efforts. You've clearly worked very hard to get to the bottom of this. I've looked at your interim reports and I'm quite satisfied that we've gone as far as we can with this. You've done a good job though. I'm sure that your Force will be glad to have you back. It's a shame about your officer, but these things happen – all for the best perhaps."

Docker recognised the approach. This wasn't a discussion; it was a statement of fact. The new man was having a clean sweep of the past and burying some skeletons, before putting his 'stamp' on his new Force.

Docker responded, "Thank you sir. I'm sure you know better than I do about these things. Good luck in your new post. I'll watch your progress with interest, and I'll keep the case papers close to hand in case anything comes up – you never know what the future holds."

It was a threat, and the Chief knew it, but not enough of one to pin down. He locked eyes with Docker, waiting for the man to look away, as always happened. Not this time though, and he saw something in them that made him feel uncomfortable.

Docker turned on his heel and left, just quickly enough to prevent the Chief Constable from responding, but timed to perfection as a demonstration of not-so-subtle discourtesy. The sight of Docker's back rattled the man who prided himself on control. It made him feel uneasy until he expunged the feeling by reflecting on the gulf in rank and power and the fact that he would never see Docker again. 'Fucking cocky bastard,' he mused as his mind turned to other matters.

Docker wanted to get back to Birmingham and friendlier faces. Before he took himself off to the car, leaving Rackham to make his own way, Docker had a parting word for the PA. He bent down over her as she sat at her desk, deliberately invading her space, and said softly, but in a voice full of menace.

"If you ever need a spot of cash love, give me a bell, I've got some contacts in Balsall Heath who could help you turn a few bob if you like flashing your cunt about like that. You've got the look spot-on, so you'd fit right in darling." It was trivial sport, but the shocked look on her face and the involuntary crossing of the legs gave him some small satisfaction.

During the interaction with the Chief,

———

Rackham had stood limp and ineffective on the sidelines, hoping the ground would swallow him up. 'Fucking Docker', still that was it, job finished, and their ways could part – hopefully forever.

The Chief got up to wish him well – he had enjoyed the experience of bullying the man, He knew the type, essentially decent, and indeed a gentleman, but one who did not like confrontation and did not seek it. The Chief Constable also knew the man's little dark secret and had had no compunction in letting him know that.

But Docker had rattled him, he needed to re-assert his power.

A smile passed the Chief Constables lips as the door closed. He raised his feet to the desk and pressed the intercom to his PA,

"Can you put the kettle on. Then when you're ready I've got some 'dictation' to give you."

***

Whatever the truth was of what had taken place all those years ago and in fact more recently, Docker was quite clear in his mind that too much had already been swept under the carpet, and he hadn't had any benefit out of it either.

At the start of the return journey Docker took great pleasure in providing a clinical forensic analysis as to why they should not participate in a process of winding up an investigation which still had some way to go and some justice to deliver. Whatever his private thoughts, Docker had a reputation to maintain and could not be seen to be rolling over without a fight. Besides, it was a great way of letting off some steam and proving to Rackham what a useless 'yellow' tosser he was in front of the driver, who would no doubt spread the word in the pub later. It was after he completed his demolition of the false case being presented to them that the uneasy silence had enveloped the vehicle.

Rackham was deeply unhappy and struggled to clear his mind. Still ambitious he knew that if he made the wrong move it could result in some long-term damage to his career prospects. Damage limitation time.

After a few platitudes the Chief Superintendent momentarily found an inner strength,

"Rob. I appreciate you're upset but I think you've overstretched yourself a little today. You have a bright career ahead of you, but it doesn't pay to piss your bosses off – including me. A period of reflection will do you no harm. Take a week off to get used to the idea that this is over, and I'll tell our A.C.C what a good job you've done. I expect to receive a nice letter from Brotherton in due course recognising our efforts – who knows you might receive a commendation for this one if you don't rock the boat."

That was it – Docker sat back in his seat – the silence intensified and pervaded the rest of the journey.

They arrived home and went their separate ways, Rackham hoping that his threat would put a lid on the job, and Docker already working the angles in his mind. There would always be an issue between them. Docker knew there would be a price of sorts to pay, and Docker knew who was going to pay it. But he also knew enough to let things rest for a while. There were other priorities and Rackham wasn't a big deal.

The driver was quietly pleased that he didn't have to get involved in this nonsense. Unlike his passengers he got paid overtime for yet another long day and wasn't required to make decisions, plus there was the bonus of being privy to these potentially valuable pieces of information. He knew one thing though, he didn't fancy Rackham's chances, having crossed Docker, Chief Superintendent or not.

He liked his job.

Chapter Three

'The Grand Old Duke of York'

God continued to favour him. Or did the Devil rule the earth as the old legends said? It seemed so, as the World War continued in other guises and locations, for new causes, and the work of a soldier was never done.

Firstly the 'Iron Curtain' had descended and Allies became enemies. They called it a 'Cold War', but it spewed fire too. The last thrashings of the old war helped, as new Nation States were formed, and began to covet their neighbour's possessions, or wanted to impose their own dogma.

In 1948 the 'Berlin Airlift' was in full swing following the Russian blockade of the city. He had been sent back there, and enjoyed re-visiting some of his old haunts in the West of the shattered city, finding that the savagery following the collapse of Nazism had been replaced by desperation, a state equally capable of exploitation for his purposes. He had to be more careful of course, society was beginning to re-assert some rules, but the unspoken shield of the ranked and rich still held good.

He had decided soon after the war that the military would be his home. He was good at it, rewarded with regular promotions, and there seemed to be an inexhaustible conveyor belt of conflict. Plus, the army held a proper respect for those who were blessed with birthright and money, and 'rank had its privileges'.

He had money, plenty of it. His long-absent and uncaring parents had done him a favour by getting themselves killed by a bomb. He revelled in the delicious irony of it. He had sought out battle and emerged victorious and feted, they had bought their way out of it, then died whilst 'socialising' in London whilst others fought for their freedom. By then his father was very, very rich and in truth he could have left the army and retired, but he enjoyed the killing, and the chance to further his kind of love, unimpeded by those who did not understand.

He continually marvelled at mankind's ability to go through six years of destruction and death and then look for a fight somewhere. And where there was battle, and the collapse of society, there was opportunity for him, a predator, skilled in the ways of hunting prey.

In 1950, the newly formed People's Republic of North Korea invaded the South, and once more the world powers faced off across a battlefield. His experience and reputation as a warrior, despite his now loftier rank, meant that he was lucky enough to be sent to assist the US forces in the first deployment of British troops in July of that year. From the ruins of Berlin to burning peasant villages, there were always desperate people, and boys, always boys around, scratching for survival in the dust. Glad of money and attention. Whatever their looks or nationality, it made no difference, they were the same where it mattered, and some of the Koreans were very beautiful.

But he was clever enough, and cunning

51

enough, a hunter that knew the value of hiding in plain sight, to plan for peace. He was always on the lookout for like minds. Not from the common masses, they were for exploiting, but from his own kind, those with power, influence and money.

By the time he arrived in Korea, he had the vestiges of an exclusive 'Club' identified. An inner core of four, then five, then six. A Lord, a politician or two, a couple of rich industrialists. He was the undisputed leader. None of them had his capacity for cold violence, and they both feared and trusted him to protect them.

The rules of membership were simple, and rigorous. They all had to have the same philosophy regarding the satiation of their desires, coupled with a selfishness, a sense of their superiority to the rest of society, that had been the driving force that they had used to achieve their successes. They were sworn to secrecy, even if arrested, upon pain of death, and they absolutely believed that sanction would be carried out if they betrayed the club. They paid a huge 'membership fee', knowing it would be used to both protect them and facilitate the procurement of their victims. They all owned secluded estates that could be used for club 'meetings', weekends of perverted lust. They all had their own networks, strings that could be pulled, establishments that could be used to protect, hide and influence.

Initiation involved the signing of a legal document handing over their assets if they transgressed the rules, and the application of a small tattoo on their shoulder, the letters *'OK'*.

They felt as if they were Gods amongst men, and thus called their organization the *'Olympus Club'*, but the letters were Greek. They used the names of Greek Gods in all their dealings, never their own. The warrior leader was of course, *'Zeus'*.

Using the money and power of the organisation, Zeus 'bought' others. These were not members of the 'inner circle'. Many of them did not even know the purpose of their masters. They asked no questions; and the money was good. They were 'fixers', 'muscle', those who could stymie any enquiries. A mixture of 'out and out' criminals and the seemingly respectable but corrupt. Some knew what they were doing. What it was all about. Like-minds, but without the requisite assets and power to join. They got paid to identify and provide the prey. Paid in cash and in kind. There were strict rules about not touching 'the goods' until the senior members had taken their fill, but they could have the discards. They were paid with protection for their own activities. Paid to keep all the secrets, for their own good, and out of fear of punishment.

The *'Olympus Club'*, a dark cancer at the heart of British society. The arrogance of the Gods, the ethos of the gutter and depravity, rolled into one. A complete lack of any morality was celebrated amongst them.

***

1964. In London the Krays were the 'guvnors' who ruled with a rod of iron, as extreme violence was exercised to protect 'turf' and to ensure loyalty. Transgressions were dealt with swiftly and without mercy. Rick Foster, once a frightened and weak boy, now a much-changed man of twenty, had begun to rub shoulders with the 'serious' people of his world. As an 'Eastender', it was natural. They were his role models.

He was still 'small fry' and still needed to do work for others to survive. But he had lost none of his cunning, his ability to assess and use, to see and exploit opportunities. He was young to have his own 'firm', but the foundations were there. A couple of 'heavies', a pimp, some girls and boys, and a market stall supplied with dodgy goods. They stuck with him because they could see possibilities. A young man with potential for the big time.

He was careful. He kept the big fish sweet; paid them their dues; did the 'favours' asked, never took sides. And all the time he watched, and waited, and made notes in the little black book he always carried. He used a code he had invented so nobody would know what it said if they got hold of it, because it contained the most potent weapon in his arsenal, information. Who was beholden to whom, who owed, who paid, what secret vices were indulged? Contacts, locations. A burgeoning encyclopaedia of local crime syndicates. And when the big boys fought or fell to the law or the 'dog eat dog' of the streets, he was ready. Catching the scraps from the table, filling a vacuum. Never a threat, never a competitor. A little step forward here and there. Building trust and respect.

He was doubly careful to keep himself one step away from the law. There was always an intermediary, a false name, an innocent phrase that was understood to mean more. He was 'clean'.

He took one risk only. But he was addicted. The urge to indulge his 'unnatural' desires persisted. As a boy, he had hidden it. As a teenager he had experimented with those willing, always secret and hidden. He knew the price of being found out.

As the years passed, he realised that the attraction he felt towards beautiful young boys had not matured along with him. Older men, or those his own age, exerted no pull. From ten to around fifteen years old the excitement lay, drew him, aroused him. He had two lives, hidden from each other, and from society. A small fish in two pools, hiding from the sharks, living on the scraps.

And so it was that one day he met a man in a hip but anonymous London cafe that he was wont to frequent, it being well away from his criminal stamping grounds. The man was older, roughly spoken. Rick Foster was in his usual seat with a view of the room, eyeing up the potential, and sipping a coffee. The place had a jukebox and pulled in a constant stream of the young, including those who had just stepped off the train at Euston, drawn by the bright lights and 'the scene'. Runaways, loners, new arrivals, all looking for something. Rick, or 'Jimmy' as he was known here, had plenty to offer, for a price, and rented a room nearby.

Rick had seen the man before. Had vaguely registered a potential fellow predator, but there was plenty of prey to go around.

"I've been watching you." The man spoke quietly, a trace of an effeminate lilt in the voice.

Rick looked up, wondering if this was finally the law catching up with him, but instantly dismissed the idea. He had developed a 'radar' for police officers, even in plain clothes they stood out a mile, and it would have taken years of careful preparation for this dude to carry it off convincingly. The man was so 'queer' it was as good as a sign on his forehead.

"I'm not interested, sorry." Rick spoke equally quietly but with a hint of steel in his voice. He had no desire for unknown elements to enter his safe space.

"Oh no, dear, you misunderstand, this isn't a pick-up, you're not my type either, far too butch. No, this is business. Can I sit down?" - a smile grew.

Rick took a closer look. Small and tubby, in his forties, clean shaven, and was that a hint of eyeliner? Dressed in all the latest gear, finished off with a beret, but the whole effect spoke of femininity. He re-appraised the man, there must be some well of courage in there to walk around like that. He was the opposite pole to Rick, who was now tall and wiry, worked out, and was currently fashioning himself as 'a Mod', razor sharp clothes and his blonde hair longer.

He gestured to the seat opposite, and the man sat down, holding his hand out across the table. There was a handshake like gripping a wet dead fish. Rick waited.

His visitor paused and continued, "As I said I've watched you. I hang around here a lot – good hunting ground." He gave a conspiratorial wink, but Rick remained impassive.

He tried again to penetrate Ricks stare, "I spotted you straight away. Very careful. Very good at what you do. And you don't look .... well like me. I venture that you have another life, and nobody knows about this?" He waved an arm, taking in the café and its occupants.

The question hung in the air. For the first time, Rick reacted. He leant forward and grabbed the damp limp hand and pushed it down onto the table. He kept the pressure on and saw the pain register in the man's face.

"If this is an attempt at blackmail, you've made a very bad decision." Rick was now fighting the rising anger within him and was close to failing.

Surprisingly the man smiled again, despite the pain and threat, as he responded, "I was sort of hoping that you'd react like that...Rick."

Rick remained outwardly impassive, despite the shock of the use of his real name. He released the hand and leant back, feigning relief.

"Sorry, you've got me mixed up with someone else. The name's Jimmy." Rick felt like he was losing control to this insignificant 'tool' and he didn't like it.

The man laughed loudly now, "And mine's

57

Bob, well it isn't, but that's good enough. No, this isn't anything to do with extortion, although I've heard you're not averse to using information to good effect."

Rick began to worry, his mind calculating the options. He rarely made a bad assessment, but he had prematurely dismissed this foppish clown in his mind. There was clearly something more here.

Finally, he said, "You've got my attention."

The man glanced around then leant forward conspiratorially, "There are some people I know who ask me to look out for people like you."

"And what sort of person am I?" Rick tried to see behind the man's eyes, into his soul, but nothing was forthcoming.

'Bob' looked like he was choosing his words carefully, "A survivor. Careful. Someone with potential, and contacts in the right places. And then there is your personal interest in…" he looked around, "these young people."

Rick knew better than to say anything, keeping his face impassive.

The strange interrogation continued, "Anyway, these people I know have done what they like to call 'due diligence' on you, and they like what they see. They want to offer you some business. I'm here to set up a meet and convince you that it is well worth your time to hear what they have to offer."

Rick tried to get the upper hand, "Prove it. If

you're the best they can send, I'm not impressed. It all sounds like crap to me."

'Bob' reached into the 'man bag' slung across his shoulder, produced a thin folder and slid it across the table, "I'll get us another coffee, have a look."

The folder only contained three sheets of A4 paper, but they contained all the details of his life to date, his criminal activities, and worst of all, details of his other 'interests'. There were two grainy but recognisable photographs of him with recent 'pick-ups'. His stomach churned for a moment, then he forced the panic down, regained control and began thinking. Survival, not confrontation, was his way.

Two days later he met another man in Hyde Park. A different type of customer to 'Bob'. This time no names were given or asked for. Rick accepted the business proposition put to him. He was clever enough to know when he was outmanoeuvred and outgunned. Anyway, there were several advantages to the new relationship. Better to be inside the tent of the biggest shark in the pond, pissing out.

Rick didn't know or ask the name of the organisation he now worked for.

***

Ses had never invited Evadne over to see his new life. He wasn't proud of that, or the fact that he hadn't been to church either, despite his promises. Memories of home were fading fast, replaced by an existence of prejudice, victimisation, injustice, and the loneliness of being different. The only constant was Bud, and the two were closer than ever, their bonds strengthened by their mutual reliance in an unforgiving world.

Things had got worse for them when, following a minor dispute with a white colleague, Bud lost his job.

Getting another one proved difficult as word went around that he was 'trouble'. After ten years in the country, his skin colour still marked him out. No matter what he did, had done, years of hard work and faithful service counted for nothing compared with the widespread preconceptions of his kind being violent, lazy and untrustworthy.

He was forced to rely upon Ses, now working on a building site and making good money in cash from the successful local boxing career. They were brothers in all ways bar actually sharing blood, and Ses never begrudged Bud a penny, but Bud didn't like the feeling and began, with increasing desperation, to look around for ways to contribute.

Then Ses got a letter from home. Evadne was ill, very ill, could he come? Bud was filled not only with guilt, but frustration, and anger, at a society that conspired to deny him the money to help Ses to see his dying mother one last time. Once again Ses came good in the form of cash from a fight. Bud hugged him and wished him a safe journey home, silently vowing that he would pay him back every penny he owed him one day.

Ses was too late, only seeing his mother cold and lifeless in her open coffin. Alone with her, in the close confines of the shack living area, he hugged her, wept, apologised for letting her down, and made a vow that, whatever it took, he would never be placed in the position of being a beggar needing charity again.

Days turned into weeks as he buried her and made all the arrangements to tie up the loose ends of her life. Many years had passed since he had sat on the porch reading *'The Gleaner'*, but the pace of life in Jamaica was slow and he soon discovered that not much had changed. The older criminals had mostly moved on, many permanently, to whatever hell awaited them, and his contemporaries had replaced them.

He was a novelty, something of a celebrity, one of the first 'returnees' from *'The Land of Hope and Glory'*. He lied, enjoying the attention, exaggerating how well he was doing, 'bigging himself up'.

One evening he was approached in a local rum shack by an old friend. After the hugs and greetings, it became apparent that it wasn't a chance meeting. Once a 'street friend', during the intervening years he had risen through the layers of criminality.

"Man, it sounds like you are doing good in England." The man ventured.

Ses had to continue with the lie of the life he had portrayed, "Yeah, great, best decision I ever made."

"More and more of our people leaving now, staying over there, making new lives." His visitor smiled broadly.

Ses assented. He was beginning to see more Caribbean people, particularly around the Handsworth suburb of Birmingham.

"But they still miss some things from home I hear?" his friend probed.

Ses laughed, "The sun for definite."

"Yeah that, but I'm talking food, beer, music

and smoke." The conversation was moving to where his friend needed it to.

"Yeah, especially the last" Ses was starting to wonder where this conversation was going but it didn't take long for him to get his answer.

"And it's a strange new place when you arrive, takes plenty of getting used to. Good to have a friend there to help?" came the enquiry.

Again, Ses agreed, remembering his experiences. The friend nodded, sagely stroking his goatee beard. He produced two large spliffs and handed one over. Ses had to admit it was good stuff and he had missed it.

His visitor now had his full attention, "I got a bit of a proposal Ses. A try out first, see how it goes. Could make us both some cash."

Ses lit his spliff and inhaled, "Go on, you've got my attention."

His visitor paused before following suit, "I can put together the brothers here who want to go to England, and the stuff that our people there want. You're there. You can be me man on the spot. Help new people, distribute the goods, take a cut. The beauty is that we know and trust each other, our people keep to themselves and keep it tight. No way any English nosey parker's gonna be able to get inside, no po-lice and no men from the Customs."

Ses knew what the score was and appreciated the irony. He had left Jamaica to escape being drawn into crime, but England had forced him back to it. But he wanted a better life, better things around him. They shook hands on it.

Ses and Bud did everything together, and the new enterprise was no different. Bud was easily persuaded. Ses was getting too old for the boxing and was looking to retire. He had been passed over for deserved promotions at work - who would take orders from a 'coloured'?

He was bored, with the same simmering anger as Bud at the way they had been treated over the years. Any resistance he had to 'shadowy' business schemes had been eroded, indeed he had thrown the odd fight for cash and used his pugilistic skills outside the ring, for money. The two men felt that they had been given no alternative in a blatantly unjust society and determined that they would not lie down and accept it.

Towards the end of the decade, they bade farewell to Moseley, and moved to Handsworth, drawn towards the new 'West Indian' community coalescing there. With one eye on Ses' Jamaica conversation they rented a very large, run-down terraced house with plenty of rooms.

They began in a small way, setting up weekend *'shebeen'* parties in the large empty garage in the enclosed yard at the rear of the house, selling cans of beer and small amounts of 'weed', the first visible result of Ses' meeting with his 'old friend', whilst Jamaican music from *'Blue Beat'* records played on a cheap record player. It didn't bring much money in, but it paid the rent and strengthened their connections with fellow immigrants. There were no complaints from the neighbours, who were themselves regulars

By the early Sixties they had both left the world of legality far behind. They were earning enough from selling their 'goods', charging for parties, accommodating new arrivals, including 'illegals' and 'couriers', and using their combined fighting skills for money. They were well-known in

63

the area and protected by the community.

Before leaving Moseley, they had acquired another joint interest. They met Brenda at a dance at St. Paul's Institute in Balsall Heath, and for a time she went out with both of them. The two men still did everything as a 'double act' and for a while she had sex with both men either at the same time, or sometimes separately. Brenda had a high sexual drive and even the combined efforts of the two men were sometimes not enough to quench her appetite. It was inevitable that she would fall pregnant.

Stewart was born in 1959 and 'Ses' was named on the birth certificate as his father at the age of twenty-nine years. In truth it could have been either of them and they both loved him as a son. It was a difficult birth, and Brenda learnt that there would be no more children. Brenda moved into the house in Handsworth with the child, and life carried on. She doted on her child, and fiercely protected him. He may have been 'an accident', but she loved him more than anything in the world. Her devotion rubbed off on Ses and Bud, who decided that, as either could be Stewart's father, they both might as well be.

In 1965, they all began frequenting a new club, a club for their own kind, and, unbelievably, owned by one of them, 'The Hole in The Wall' on Soho Road. They quickly found that they knew lots of the denizens of the club, including Winston, the head doorman, and it wasn't long before Ses and Bud were invited to a meeting with the owner.

Winston showed them to a private alcove and left them alone. The man was sat on his own, secure in his kingdom. He was tall and heavy-boned, athletic – Ses thought he had the look of a boxer too. He bade them sit and summoned up drinks. Once the heavy who was acting as temporary waiter left, he shook their hands and introduced himself, "Winston has recommended I speak to you, and I trust Winston. I'm Joe Docker."

Ses and Bud thought that they were meeting him for the first time and were not enlightened as to their error. Joe Docker had good reasons for hiding his past, and his family, but he recognised them, the inseparable black 'brothers' he had seen as a child in Moseley, when walking with his white mother.

After some small-talk, Joe got down to business, "After Winston told me about you, I did a bit of checking up. Seems like we are in roughly the same types of business, if you know what I mean."

They did. Joe continued, "So, we could be competitors or allies. We're brothers and I think brothers should look after each other." A cloud crossed his face and for a moment he was somewhere else.

He mentally shook himself and went on, "I think we would work well together. I could use your knowledge; your contacts and I hear you're pretty handy in a fight. I'm going places, got big plans, building a network. You two could be part of that. What do you think?"

Ses and Bud didn't need to do any of their own checking up, they knew all about Joe Docker. He had a reputation. For looking after his own, for helping the community, and for not being a man to cross. Plus, everyone working the angles knew he was well on his way to being one of the 'main men' in Birmingham, which said plenty, given the endemic hostility to those with dark skin.

It was their best offer since arriving in the

'promised land', and they grabbed it.

***

On the 24th January 1965, Winston Churchill died and lay in state in London's ancient Westminster Hall before a funeral befitting a man who was perceived by the masses as the person who had saved the Nation in its time of need. His passing was mourned by the common man and the great and powerful alike; some of them figures who had themselves occupied positions of rank and power during the Second World War but now operated in the shadows.

The world remained a dangerous place, with conflict ever present. At the beginning of February, the United States bombed North Vietnam following a Vietcong attack on an American base in South Vietnam. It was the start of a three-year bombing campaign that exceeded the number of bombs dropped in World War II in Europe & Asia.

In August, India and Pakistan engaged in a seventeen-day border war in Kashmir.

The need for Britain to maintain an interest in its ability to develop and train its Armed Forces remained crucial, and Cadet Forces provided a valuable source of recruitment - to the Regular Army and other endeavours.

***

Peter Hall liked to think of himself as a rod of iron, a man steadfast in his commitment to making sure that the youngsters placed in his charge once a week, during occasional weekend's exercises, and at their annual camp, were kept on the straight and narrow.

The boy's parents placed total trust in his abilities as Officer Commanding the local Army Cadet Force detachment to maintain discipline and to turn them out as smart young pillars of society. He 'marshalled his troops' with a great sense of pride.

In truth Peter Hall had other, darker and hidden motives, although in the mid-sixties the word 'paedophile' had really not yet been invented.

A travelling salesman by day, and not a very good one at that, he had risen in rank by the time he had reached his mid-thirties and revelled in wearing the Queen's uniform proudly displaying the three *'bath stars'* on each shoulder which denoted his status of Captain. The impartial observer wondered how he had managed it, but Peter Hall had backers. He provided a service, a 'delicate' matter, and the people he worked for had no problem in placing him where they needed him.

His role gave him a position of power and influence which sometimes extended to functions with local dignitaries and politicians – a nobody transformed into a somebody.

He lived with his seventy-year old mother in a council maisonette to the south of Birmingham, and to the outside world he seemed doted upon by one person who loved him unconditionally.

She often enjoyed the 'sport' of chiding him for his lack of a wife and children for her to shower her affections on; but he always deflected her sadness with stories about his passion and commitment to moulding future generations of young men. For the time being they were 'his life and priority' and he repeatedly reassured his mother that there would be time later to find a good woman to stand next to him. She would smile, reflecting what a sad, lying bastard he was, but never giving him any inkling that she knew what he was really like.

Peter Hall had not been born with the 'condition' as far as he knew. As a child he had been abused by his church-going father, right under the nose of his mother, who was seemingly oblivious to the weekly pain and suffering he inflicted following Sunday services, on the pretext of providing additional fatherly direction in the ways of God.

His father took his predilection for anal sex to an early grave, following a sudden stroke which left him partially paralysed and unable to speak for several weeks prior to finally succumbing. There was no opportunity for a final confession, and he did not consider it a sin, having been introduced in turn to the practices by his uncle in the potting shed on the allotment between the wars.

In time Peter Hall trod the familiar path, the transition from victim to perpetrator – an evangelist for introducing children to sex.

***

Harris Grange Army Cadet Force detachment, based in Rubery, on the outskirts of Birmingham, had a reputation for being one of the best cadet units in the West Midlands, winning cups for drill, boxing, and weapons training. In 1965, the year that the construction of the Rotunda building was completed in Birmingham City Centre, the Unit was also seen as unique.

The cadets were aged between twelve years and sixteen years, and exclusively male. At any given time, their core numbers comprised up to twenty-five local boys from the Birmingham overspill estate, with their numbers being supplemented by a special arrangement with Richmond House, a Social Services Care Home in Redditch, who sent ten of their boys every week by transit van to join the others.

Both sets of boys maintained an uneasy truce with each other, but whilst the Richmond House boys were smaller in number they made up for it with their aggressive approach and a sense of solidarity which the others could not match.

The van was usually driven by John Baxter, a residential social worker at Richmond House. Baxter presented himself as a large, overweight and ugly man who was handy with his fists and accepted nothing from his charges other than total obedience. The job provided him with a room in the main building, three square meals a day and an endless supply of other 'home comforts'.

Accompanying him would be Paul Evans, another social worker at the Home, who also held the rank of Staff Sergeant in the ACF, and was one of the adult instructors. Normally a less than confident man, the uniform empowered him, and under Peter Hall's leadership he was blossoming as a disciplinarian, feared by the boys during drill practice for the bark of his voice, and the volumes of spittle that were released from his mouth during bouts of fearsome rants should one of them put a foot wrong. As it said in the famous nursery rhyme, he would relentlessly, 'march them up to the top of the hill and then back down again'.

Richmond House took children, both boys and girls from their catchment area in Birmingham. Already vulnerable and damaged, they entered a world where the least of their worries was the institutional bullying which took place at every level of the establishment.

A number of the boys were just one step away from being sent to a borstal, as their lives spiralled downwards, and Richmond House merely functioned as a clearing house for the majority. It was a bad place, but fractionally better than some of the homes they had fled, and the institutions that many would eventually become resident in.

The boys who were nominated to become members of the ACF were carefully selected by Evans and Baxter, but Peter Hall had the final say as to whether they stayed or not, and all of them served a month's probation before the final decision was made. The others knew the score. Hall was in charge and they all fed on the scraps left by those that Hall really worked for.

Based on a system of reward and punishment, the 'lucky ones' who were allowed to stay were subjected to an initiation ceremony exclusive to the Richmond House boys.

Evans and Baxter would take personal charge of the event which usually took place on a Sunday at the home when staffing levels were at their lowest. The latest recruit would be marched to one of the communal bathrooms and made to strip naked in front of the other boys. Whilst one of the social workers ensured that the door was kept securely shut the other would deliver instructions to one or two of the other boys who would be tasked with smearing boot polish on their victims' testicles.

Once the humiliation was complete the victim would be ordered into a shower with two further boys who were instructed not to come out until he was totally clean.

The psychology of the exercise was complex as Evans and Baxter never made any attempt at touching the boys themselves but it was clearly aimed at breeding sexual familiarity between the boys with a view to creating a new norm. The reactions of the participants were closely observed as suitable prospects were assessed. The grooming process had begun and anyone that resisted was expelled from the group.

For the rest, Peter Hall and Paul Evans devised a similar initiation ceremony which took place when cadets received a promotion to Lance Corporal. Careful not to be seen to be encouraging any inappropriate behaviour, they used the Richmond House group to bring their plans to fruition.

Following the announcement of a promotion it would only be a matter of time before Evans would orchestrate a situation whereby the unfortunate newly promoted cadet would find himself trying to do drill practice with the Richmond House boys.

The exercise would always result in a ritual 'debagging' exercise, following which the contents of several large tubes of toothpaste would be liberally smeared on the boy's testicles and bottom.

Most of the boys were too embarrassed to say anything afterwards, but any protestations would be played down by Evans as being nothing more than schoolboy 'high jinks', with promises that they would be sorted out on their return to the Home.

Thus, boot polish and toothpaste became part of the sexual grooming of the boys.

All of the time in the background Peter Hall quietly surveyed this preparatory activity with satisfaction. The boys were being softened up as the main course for his masters, and himself. Those that would be 'passed up' the chain were to be groomed, cajoled, browbeaten and institutionalised until any resistance was broken.

Hall had his instructions. The 'Club' wanted only fresh meat and had the capacity to enforce their rule with extreme prejudice. He feared them, but in turn, they supported and protected him and his 'recruiters', and allowed them the 'morsels' from the table. It had proved a very satisfactory arrangement and Hall had been enjoying the benefits for many years.

There were many little 'bonuses' to the work. Hall particularly enjoyed supervising the firing of .22 rifles in the indoor range.

To the casual observer barking out orders and

maintaining strict range discipline was normal for the occasion, as was the continual repositioning of legs by Hall as the boys lay prone on the floor in firing positions.

With one leg straight and the other bent Peter Hall was able to continually run his hands over the boy's lower bodies on the pretext of achieving a better shot.

On occasions he even dared himself to straddle boys, bending so close that they could feel his breath on their young faces as he adjusted their hand and arm positions.

It was that easy and Peter Hall knew all of the subtle tricks with which to develop close contact.

There were those amongst them who sought to justify their actions by blaming the children themselves, claiming they 'wanted it', it was 'natural' and they were 'helping the boy's education', but for the likes of Peter Hall it required no such excuse; he wanted to do it and could do it – an evil man with no boundaries.

***

On the 28th October 1965, Ian Brady and Moira Hindley were charged with the Moors Murders – it was a crime against children which shocked the nation, yet it was still seen as something unusual. It simply wasn't part of the British psyche – or was it?

As the moral compass of society started to change, the following month Mary Whitehouse set up a *'National Viewers & Listeners Association'* in response to her fears that television was becoming a breeding ground for pornography. Whilst *'Coronation Street'* was perceived to be the most popular programme in the UK there were other elements of viewing to which she objected strongly.

***

By 'Third Year', the spoilt and bullied boy had reached the limits of his tolerance and endurance, and things had to change. He had begun to grow, tall and thin. Begun to learn the lessons of life. He was clever and worked his way through the options. He could not carry on like this, it had begun to affect him badly. He dreaded going to school. Had been inventing illnesses which his mother indulged, simply believing him 'sensitive' and 'sickly'. His studies began to suffer, and his grades to fall. His parents discussed it, and concluded that it was just 'growing pains', they would monitor and intervene if necessary. They didn't speak to him about it. This was an era where children got on with it. Seen not heard. Not considered to be developed enough for adult conversation. He was fed, watered, kept safe, indulged, but not listened to – or asked for an opinion.

Father was always at work anyway, determined to better himself and provide for the family, grab a bigger slice of the 'good life'. His absence left an increasing vacuum that his mother struggled to fill. Ironically, the boy began to develop the same sort of self-sufficiency as his tormentors.

But what to do? He concluded that carrying on was not sustainable. He fantasised about running away, but his rationality punctured this dream. Should he ape the others, become one of them? He didn't think he could. It was too big a climb from where he was. They would never accept him. It was too late. Anyway, he wasn't a follower.

Constantly looking for a way out, one day his eye was caught by a notice posted outside the gym, a place he had heretofore shunned.

'School Boxing Club. Beginners welcome. All equipment provided. Ages thirteen plus. Wednesdays after school. Enquire with Mr. Costello.'

Costello was the PE teacher. A large man who had once graced Moseley Rugby Team and reserved his interest for those pupils who looked like they would enhance the various sporting teams for which he was responsible. It never crossed his mind that talent could lie untapped, waiting to be developed, that bodies changed. He had his favourites; they received the focus of his attention and the rest lurked in a twilight zone out of his view.

The boy had never spoken to Mr. Costello. He took the concept home, mulled it over for a couple of days. It was scary and against his nature, but it had attractions. Firstly, he could learn to fight. Secondly it could earn him some respect. Thirdly he did not need to 'sell out' and join the gang. There was a big risk of course, that he would simply get 'legally' beaten up, but he was desperate.

The next day, at lunchtime, he nervously shuffled into the gym. The smell of sweat hung in the air, vying with traces of patchouli and Brut, and

75

winning. He knew that Costello customarily ate his lunch on a balcony overlooking the gym so climbed the wooden stairs.

He found the teacher, tracksuit clad as usual, halfway through a 'doorstop' sandwich and *'The Sun'* newspaper. Costello looked up, having heard the footsteps approaching, gave the boy a once over and a look of irritation flashed across his face. Not one of his favourites, which no doubt meant that his lunch was being interrupted for nothing.

"Yes, what is it?" he demanded curtly.

The boy nearly turned and ran for it, but he dredged up some courage from within and approached the teacher, "I want to ask about the new Boxing Club. I'd like to have a go."

Costello put his paper flat on his lap, clearly surprised, and gave the boy a longer look, "Would you. I don't think I know you, do I? Not in any of my teams or other gym clubs?

"No sir. But I'm interested in the boxing." The boy stuttered.

"Why?" Costello pushed him for more.

The boy thought quickly. This was a 'make or break' moment, "To tell you the truth sir, I haven't been very interested in the gym, but as I've got older, I want to do something a bit more physical. I won't hide it from you sir, I get bullied a bit too, and I'd like to see if I can do something to help me stand up for myself."

Costello nodded, "It's hard work you know, you need to get fit, and you'll get a few knocks, think you can put the time in and take the blows without crying?" He looked dubiously at the beanpole stood before him.

"Yes sir, I've thought it through. I wouldn't forgive myself if I didn't try." – the boy stood firm.

Costello was warming to the boy, "Ok, why not? You can always drop out if it's not for you, and we'll know pretty quickly if it's not going to work out. You'll need to get your parents to sign a consent form, and there's a fee. We are going to take the school minibus to a local boxing club. There'll just be us there for the two hours. A friend of mine runs it. He's on the lookout for likely lads to train up and perhaps go further, and he's doing the school a favour, giving us his gym and time free, so no messing about – understand?"

"Yes sir. I'll do my best." His new charge responded.

Costello signalled the end of the conversation, "See you on Wednesday after school then. We are meeting here. Bring your gym kit as usual, everything else will be provided.

As he left, the boy was surprised and pleased to hear Costello call down the stairs, "Well done, hope it works out."

His parents took little persuading, they never did. Mother was concerned about his 'beautiful face being marked', but father was, unexpectedly, all for it, confiding in his wife that this might be just the thing to 'bring the boy out a bit', stop him 'moodying around'. Might even 'make a man of him'.

The following Wednesday, a bag of nerves, he reported to the changing rooms after last bell. He hadn't told anyone that he was going, so didn't know who or what to expect.

About a dozen boys of various ages were in various states of repose on the wooden benches, less than he thought. He was relieved that there was no sign of Murphy or his main cronies. In fact, he didn't know any of them well. There were two others from his year, from other classes. Both were stockier, but shorter than him. One boy looked younger, the rest older and bigger. He sat, biting his lip, and engaged in some light-hearted banter. It was clear that others were nervous too, which helped.

Costello appeared, full of cheery good humour. He was in his element and clearly enjoying himself. They filed outside and piled into the minibus. Another first, the boy had never been on a school trip before in the vehicle.

After twenty minutes bumping along they drew to a halt in Selly Oak outside what had clearly previously been a factory or warehouse. A sign outside proclaimed,

'ACE BOXING CLUB

Beginners Welcome'

It looked rough and the boy's heart sank yet

again. 'What was he doing here?' The bus had gone quiet, so he wasn't alone in his thoughts. Then the red metal door opened and disgorged a black man and the silence intensified. He was stocky and looked tough, old to them but probably in his thirties, with a shaved head. He was wearing shorts and a singlet which revealed well-muscled limbs glistening with a sheen of sweat.

Costello alighted from the driver's seat and they shook hands as a row of surprised faces peered out at them. Who would have thought that old Costello would have a 'coloured' mate? The man opened the rear doors. A wide grin displaying crooked teeth with plenty of gaps broke the tension.

"Welcome boys, welcome. Hey, why so quiet, it's gonna be great. I'll look after you and just wait until the girls see the muscles you'll be getting, like mine." He flexed a bicep, accompanying the pose with a pantomime-style conspiratorial wink.

"Surprised eh? Get it all the time, but I don't bite, so ignore what you been told about us 'darkies' and let's get out and on with it. I'm Cecil, but everyone calls me Ses."

Ses shook hands with each of them as he alighted, engulfing their hands in his large, calloused ones, and giving them all a squeeze, measuring strength. It was quickly established that nobody was going to be challenging Ses.

Once inside they were quickly arranged in a training circuit, designed to improve strength, endurance, and basic boxing skills. Ses was

79

constantly moving around, checking their technique, joking and chatting. The boy soon relaxed and began to enjoy the experience.

He found the physical training hard, requiring his utmost determination to keep up, but was surprised when he realised that Ses was watching him hitting the punchbag, and nodding each time he connected.

"Where you learn to hit like that, son?" Ses asked.

The boy shrugged. "First time I've ever done it."

Ses stepped forward. "You hit hard for a pipe-cleaner, you put your body weight, such as it is, into the punch. That's good. Here." He made some slight adjustments and demonstrated the movement. "Try to do that. Start slow, then speed up."

The boy, clever and always diligent, complied. The 'thwack' of glove on the bag was distinctly louder. A broad grin cut across Ses' face.

The boy left the gym that night excited and buzzing.

He never missed a session after that and began to follow his own training regime between visits to the *'Ace Boxing Club'*. After a few weeks, Ses announced that they were ready to get into the ring and spar with each other. He paired them up and the boy put on the padded head guard. His opponent was a year older and the same weight class, but shorter.

The boy saw the look in his adversary's eyes and knew this was going to be no holds barred. The lad launched himself forward, arms flailing wildly, ignoring Ses' commands to "bloody box, this ain't some bar brawl."

The boy took a couple of glancing blows to the head, then tried to put in practice what Ses had been teaching him. He danced, ducked and weaved, kept a distance and began jabbing, using his longer reach to repel the whirling dervish. Gradually the intensity of the attacks diminished, and the boy heard laboured breathing. He saw an opening and punched his right as Ses had taught him. The older boy went down, and sat, partly stupefied, looking up. Ses jumped the ring ropes and stopped the fight. He checked the loser for injuries and sent him to sit down and recover.

The boy looked around and was pleased to see the others watching, some open-mouthed. That included Costello who was nodding his head and grinning.

After that, Ses 'blooded him' against gradually more experienced fighters. The boy took some hits and was put on his backside several times, but Ses pronounced himself well pleased. The boy redoubled his training efforts and took up the offer by Ses of an extra night at the gym, even persuading his father to take him, and watch. His mother got used to the odd cut and mark and they both thought it small price to pay for the resumption of academic progress that resulted.

Because the situation at school had changed.

81

Word had soon got around that the boy had been boxing. It reached the ears of those who laughed at the idea. One day he had been confronted by two of the 'gang' as he began his walk home. They had hustled him up an alley and pushed him against a wall. At first, he had reacted as he used to, and they had jeered at him. Then he had hit one of them, just once and that was the end of the matter. The other fled, leaving his crony flat out on his back. The boy was never bothered again, there was always easier meat to be had.

In time he began to represent the gym in competitions. He was quick, with a good right hand, and his height and reach gave him an advantage. One day Ses called him over.

"You getting too good for this place. I think you need something that'll stretch you, and someone who can take you to the next stage. I know just the thing. There's an army cadet place near here, Harris Grange, and I know one of the officers that runs it. He's a good man, offered me friendship when others looked the other way. They run a very good boxing club at County level and they also include some selected kids from a Home over Redditch way. Bit tougher opposition for you. I think you're good enough to take that step. Knew it that first time when I saw you hit the punchbag.

The boy loved his boxing and readily agreed. He would be sad to leave Ses behind and promised to keep in touch, but had found something that he was good at, and which lay at the root of his new-found confidence. He would do anything to follow his new-found star.

***

By 1965 a lot had changed for Rob Docker. And yet as a man, the boy he had once been remained within, informing his thoughts and actions. His childhood had indelibly stamped him. A man alone; completely selfish; a survivor at all costs, now equipped with power over others, to use and misuse as he thought fit, and he thought about it a lot.

He had left his so-called family behind, bar his uncle Charlie, who had always been there for him and was probably the only person Rob really felt anything for now. That included his wife Lilian who he hated and despised, and recently acquired mistress, journalist Jane Smith, who provided physical solace only. There *had* been one other he loved after Joe, but tragedy had struck, leaving a wound that would never heal and a resentment towards the rest of humanity that permeated his every fibre.

After the pain of parting with Joe he had joined Birmingham City Police on a whim. Three years later he reflected that it had been a good choice. He had proved himself, and the potent brew of the status he now held as a result of the uniform, coupled with his damaged and conscienceless character, was fast becoming a devastating combination. He looked for the 'angles' and opportunities for self-advancement or enrichment in every situation and was able to exploit them with the total ruthlessness of a man with no limits or boundaries.

It had been an irrevocable break. The recently

83

completed Berlin Wall was less effective than the internal barrier Rob had erected between his past and present. PC 117 Rob Docker admitted of no past, and certainly no 'darkie' brother.

Chapter Four

'What Are Little Boys Made Of?'

Sally was looking for a way out. The *'Swinging Sixties'* were in full flow and she was missing it all, suffocating in the embrace of Uncle Jim.

It had been going on for eighteen months and he showed no sign of tiring of her. Why would he? She was the only outlet for the frustrations of his loveless home life. He continued to shower her with gifts, but his fear of discovery and its consequences for both his life and liberty had rapidly limited their meetings to what she felt were grubby pawings in guest houses. He was meticulous about wearing a 'johnny', which not only looked ludicrous, but the very process of putting it on underlined what she felt was her real worth.

Her initial rush of love had switched to its opposite pole, but she was careful not to let the hatred leak out.

On the two occasions that she had begun talking about ending it, he had reacted with anger underpinned by desperation and fear. He was controlling and manipulative, and held all the cards in terms of influence and credibility. Who would believe her?

The second time, he had taken hold of her arms and pushed her against the hotel wall. He had shouted, so close that she could feel his spittle on her face. At that moment she had believed that he would do pretty much anything to keep her 'on tap', or prevent the whole sordid business coming out and ruining him.

She had returned to playing the love-struck girl and things had settled down. But she watched her friends lapping up the new and exciting teenage culture; music; cafes; parties; boys their own age, and fruitlessly turned over plans to escape in her head as she lay in bed at night.

One day at school she broke down in tears and confided in a girl who showed an unexpected kindness, hugging her and taking her for a walk. The girl told her that they had all thought she was either 'a square', unfriendly, shy, or not interested, and had left her alone, excluding her completely from their world.

Sally swore the girl to secrecy, but was no longer alone with her anguish, and now had a second person to help. Together they came up with a plan. After an afternoon 'session' with Jim, she let it slip out that she was interested in photography at school, but couldn't afford a camera. The lie had the expected result; a shiny new 35mm camera with twenty rolls of film appeared. She showed her gratitude in the expected fashion, keeping her delight at the irony of Jim supplying the means of her escape well - hidden as she finished him off with a level of expertise borne from her misfortune.

She supplied her new friend with details of her meetings with Jim. She found ways of occupying his attention at crucial moments and manufactured moments of 'inappropriate' physical contact in public, or in hotel room windows visible from public areas. They were patient and, although it took several weeks, the collection of images mounted.

Sally took the films to 'Boots The Chemists', and feverishly leafed through the prints in the paper wallets as soon as she collected them. There were the usual failures, bad exposures, missed subjects, but there were plenty of good ones.

She selected one that showed them framed in a hotel window in a passionate embrace with her wearing just her bra on top, and another of her kissing him in his car.

Sally had a rendezvous arranged as usual the next day near to school. Jim liked her in school uniform and routinely collected her in his car, lost in the melee of other parents and children.

She had decided it was too dangerous to execute the plan when alone with Jim. His reaction was unpredictable and she was scared. With her friend within calling distance, she approached the car window. Jim was surprised that she hadn't jumped into the passenger seat as usual, and wound the window down, nonchalantly putting his elbow on the sill, "Hi sweetheart, get in, we've not got all day." He ventured – still playing the 'man about town' but in truth 'an empty vessel' driven by carnal desire.

Sally got closer and handed him an envelope. "I thought you had better see this." She stepped back as he took it, taking care to keep out of reach.

"What's this then, a love letter?" His face

tightened and paled as he scrutinised the photographs. "What the hell?' He began to open the door and she took another step back.

Sally found some strength from somewhere – it was now or never, "I've got lots more, and worse. Enough to put you in jail, so you stay in the car and listen. I've got friends who know what's been going on and they are about, watching out for me, so don't you do anything stupid."

Jim stopped dead, looking around at the sea of pupils around him. Too many to know which ones, too many to intimidate. He shut the door again, as his stomach churned. In an instant the balance of power had changed, and he knew it. He had underestimated Sally and it could cost him dearly.

Sally knew that there was now no going back and delivered the 'coup de grace' , "That's it. You listen like a good boy. We are finished. I see now what you've done, what you are, just a dirty old man. You've ruined me and I hate you. You've stolen my life to satisfy yourself. You should be ashamed."

"Come off it, you loved it, you wanted it and me, you little slut." Jim sneered.

Sally was having none of it – she would not allow him to turn himself into a victim, "No, I was too young and didn't know what love was. I should have found out with someone my own age, but you've stopped that ever happening, spoilt me. My head is all over the place. You disgust me, make me feel dirty, and if you say anything else, try to justify yourself, I will just walk away and give the photographs to Dad and the police."

Jim lapsed into silence. She could see the skin on his knuckles whitening where he gripped the steering wheel. He desperately wanted to strike out to hurt her. She needed to end this, "Right. Listen to me and believe me. This is the end. You never try and contact me again. If I get so much as a glimpse of you it's photo time. Otherwise I'll keep my mouth shut. And if we are in the same room at a family get-together, which I'll do my best to avoid by the way, no contact, minimal chat, avoid being alone together. Got it?"

He said nothing.

Sally stood firm, "You better decide right now, or my next stop is the police station with my friend." She began to turn away.

Uncle Jim capitulated as he visibly spat out the words, "Ok, ok, you win. You little bitch. You're not so pretty as I made out, bit on the fat side, but any port in a storm. Go find some pimply kid who won't mind a slag."

Jim started the car and screeched away, drawing disapproving looks from some of the mothers.

Sally found that she was shaking uncontrollably, tears welled in her eyes and she started to feel faint.

Her friend ran over and hugged her, "I'm so proud of you. You come back to mine for tea and we can plan to go out with the girls. Everyone will love to see you; I've told them how nice you are and that you've been under the cosh at home but have rebelled. It's close enough to the truth."

*

Sally threw herself into her new life and recovered some of what she had missed, including having a passionate fling with a boy she had met at the 'Silver Blades Ice Rink' in town. She didn't see Jim ever again. She was old enough to cry off the family 'do's, and years later she heard from her Mom that her uncle and lover was 'retiring to the coast'.

She never quite managed to expunge him; the memory of his hands on her. The way he had used and controlled her. She often dwelt upon her own part in what had happened. Had she wanted it too – was she equally guilty? As time went by she realised that she wasn't to blame, recognised the courage and inner-strength she had shown, and found herself able to draw upon that core when faced with problems. She became very popular and valued as a source of common-sense advice, developing a maturity beyond her years that far outstripped her mother.

By the time she was eighteen years of age she had left home, sharing a flat with the friend who had supported her in her time of need.

One day, she saw a recruitment advert for police officers. It struck a chord. She hadn't ever considered that girls could join the police, but it seemed to fit. She could turn her own experiences into something positive, help others, and herself.

***

In the late 60's one of the local newspapers decided that they would like to run a story about the staff at Richmond House, describing how young and vulnerable children were being protected and integrated within society. They wanted to run it as part of their series about different careers under the banner *'A day in the life of a social worker'*.

At a senior level within Social Services the proposal was embraced eagerly as an opportunity to showcase their methods. It was agreed that a reporter would be given unfettered access to the Home for three days on condition that the identities of the children would remain anonymous, and that no interviews would be carried out with any of them without a social worker being present to safeguard their interests.

What the reporter assigned to the job did not know was that behind the scenes the whole visit was to be personally choreographed by one of the Assistant Directors with oversight for the Home, an ambitious man looking to the future.

As the date of the visit approached, a quick lick of paint here and there, a revised menu for meal-times, and strict instructions to a revitalised matron to stay off the 'sauce' for a week, would all support the feeling that Richmond House was an oasis of well-being, peace and good order.

The reporter was young and female, fresh out of University, with just six months in the job. She was ambitious to move onwards and upwards to one of the national papers. She was already bored with the lack of action in the backwaters of Redditch and was hungry to get to the bright lights of London. The assignment did however give her a few days out of the office, so she determined to make the best of it.

On the first day she was given a tour of the Home and was then briefed by a succession of senior staff. All was apparently well at Richmond House and the reporter went home feeling somewhat frustrated at the lack of insight as to what it was really like working with children in care.

Next day the reporter observed some group exercises in the grounds and was then allowed to interview two of the children, a boy and a girl, who spoke warmly about the staff, albeit the reporter found their need to constantly seek reassuring looks from their chaperone disconcerting.

On the third and final day the reporter endured yet another round of updates before one of the staff she was interviewing was suddenly called away to take an urgent phone call just before they were due to finish. She found herself twiddling her thumbs for ten minutes in one of the staff rooms but then on impulse decided to go on an unsupervised 'walk-about'.

The reporter eventually made her way upstairs and was wandering along one of the corridors when she heard raised voices coming from one of the shower rooms. She paused outside and heard the voice of a young boy pleading, "Please Mr. Baxter. Please don't."

Pushing the door open, she was confronted by

a picture of John Baxter, one hand raised, towering over a boy in his early teens who was on his knees on the floor.

Baxter had previously been introduced to her briefly and when he turned to face her he spoke quickly, "I think that you are in the wrong place young lady. This room is for males only. Young son here has been a bit of a naughty boy and likes to test us a bit." He smiled and, with one hand, pulled the boy to his feet and propelled him past the reporter towards the door, through which he made a hasty exit.

The reporter was somewhat taken aback, even a little frightened, as Baxter stepped closer and invaded her space. She could feel his breath on her face and smelt alcohol. It was time to withdraw.

Baxter escorted her back downstairs to the room where an anxious social worker was waiting. This had not been in the script. The reporter made her excuses and left – she had a story to write up.

Within twenty-four hours the editor of the local newspaper was leafing through a document which was troubling him. He had read the reporter's account several times and it was potentially explosive. Headed *'The truth behind the closed doors – a day in the life of a child at Richmond House',* it was nothing like the congratulatory spread that he had been expecting. He was out of his depth and was still editor of a 'tinpot' local paper because during a lacklustre career he had never looked for controversy and lacked the guts to 'make waves'. Taking a deep breath, he came to a decision and picked up the phone.

Within four weeks the reporter had been head-hunted by one of the daily national papers and, after receiving a glowing reference from her editor, she said her goodbyes to her provincial colleagues. For his part John Baxter received a written warning for inappropriate behaviour in relation to the consumption of alcohol whilst on duty and went on to continue working with children. The local newspaper received several lucrative advertising contracts and the *'Richmond House story'* was quietly consigned to the editor's waste-paper bin.

*

At the beginning of 1971, a meeting was held between senior police officers and social workers from Richmond House to discuss the impact that some of the residents were having on the local community. With a new local police commander in situ, who was keen to meet his performance targets, the meeting focused on the number of children going missing and the inference that some of them were engaged in crime whilst on the run.

Over tea and biscuits, the custodians of child welfare discussed developing a joined-up multi-agency strategy to reduce the scale of the problem – and the problem to all those present was clearly defined as being the youngsters, not the system they inhabited.

During the meeting, the local police information collator provided details of the persons who had gone missing during the preceding twelve months. Most had been found within hours, but one of the *'Misper'* files remained open. A fifteen-year-old boy was still officially listed as missing.

Described as a 'hard nut' who was a nuisance, one of the senior social workers informed the meeting that he had it on good authority from staff at the Home that the boy had made no secret of the fact that he wanted to get to London. His police file did indeed confirm that one John Baxter had informed the officers who had filled the forms in of this fact. His disappearance warranted no further discussion and six months later the papers were filed with no new leads. The boy's disappearance remained a mystery to all, bar one person who would not be seeking to enlighten anyone any time soon.

After some self - congratulation and mutual 'back-slapping' celebrating a good job done, two of those present were nominated to produce an action plan and it was agreed that nothing further was required.

A plan was duly produced, and quickly consigned to gather dust with a host of other plans on the shelves of 'busy people', who made conscious decisions not to look beneath the veneer of respectability at Richmond House.

The reign of brutality perpetrated by John Baxter looked set to continue.

***

Peter Hall had regular sales clients which frequently took him away on overnight trips to Sheffield. If he pushed hard on the first day to conclude most of his appointments, he liked to indulge his thirst for being among boys during free time on the second - and where better than a local swimming baths.

He had visited the premises on a number of occasions just to get the 'lay of the land'. His technique within the Army Cadets was a combination of bullying and grooming in equal measures, but this environment required a different and more subtle approach.

He was a patient man, a tactician who applied caution towards all of his activities. Peter Hall had no intention of letting his cloak of respectability slip. He had a position of power to protect, which provided a steady pool of youngsters that he could *'harvest'* at will for his sponsors and himself.

On this particular day, he had timed his attendance for the after-school swimming club where about twenty boys and girls, of mixed school-age, were to be found in the pool.

He slipped effortlessly into the water and surveyed his prey through the plain glass spectacles which were nothing more than a partial disguise, whilst at the same time keeping one eye on the life-guard who looked bored to death and was rather more focussed on the older female swimmers.

It didn't take him long to spot a boy, aged about eleven years, with bright ginger hair, who swam slightly detached from the main group. The boy looked miserable and lonely and occasionally suffered from a dose of excessive splashing which was specifically aimed in his direction, with shouts of *'ginger nut'*. A predator always favours those isolated at the margins of the herd, a reject among the favoured – perfect.

Peter Hall circled his prey until he was in speaking distance, almost touching distance but not quite. He was aroused by the proximity of the situation and struggled hard not to show it. The water concealed some of his state of excitement, but Peter Hall was focused on the end game.

"Looks like they're playing you up a bit" he smiled broadly and indicated to his tormentors. Hall worked hard to keep his Birmingham accent in check.

The boy looked perplexed and didn't respond but Peter Hall persisted, "You swim well. Don't let them bully you."

The boy stumbled with his words, "My Mom will be picking me up soon. I just ignore them."

"Well done son that's the spirit,", Hall responded, and without looking for a reply swam off to the area closest to the changing rooms, which were to be found at the end of a corridor, where he waited.

Five minutes later Hall's patience paid off as the boy started to climb up the steps to leave the pool; he was close enough to feel the drips from the slender boy's body.

Hall followed the boy discreetly to the changing area with its rows of cubicles painted white, with half doors that had no bolts on them. Those few that were occupied clearly displayed the bottom halves of dripping legs as people struggled clumsily with wet trunks and over-sized towels.

Hall took the cubicle next to the one selected by the boy and eagerly removed his trunks. Totally naked now he kept the door slightly ajar.

Wrapping a towel around him he chose his moment carefully when the room was empty, swiftly exited his cubicle and pushed the door of the next cubicle open.

The startled boy froze as Hall pushed his towel to one side to reveal an erect penis;
"Would you like to hold this?"

The boy was petrified with fear but there was no escape as he was backed up against the wooden bench in the cubicle.

Hall said soothingly, "Don't make a noise and I won't hurt you. Just sit on the bench quietly whilst I do what I need to do and then you can go home."

Shortly afterwards Peter Hall left the cubicle after warning the boy not to leave for ten minutes. He gathered his clothes, moved to another cubicle at the other end of the changing room and changed quickly.

By the time that the young boy had found the courage to leave the cubicle and raise the alarm Peter Hall was well on his way, heading south for Birmingham. He had taken a big risk but was feeling exhilarated.

***

Three months later Hall was again in Sheffield when

he decided to 'chance his arm' and make another visit to the swimming baths.

Notwithstanding the risks, his desire to be close to young boys was frequently overwhelming.

Once again, the fake glasses were put on and, on this occasion, he decided to wear a swimming cap to hide his hair as far as possible, whilst he went through the motions of swimming several lengths.

Peter Hall surveyed the busy pool looking for his next prey and it didn't take him long to realise that this was not going to be his lucky day.

In the area occupied predominantly by young swimmers from the after-school club were two lifeguards, on either side of the pool, and they were clearly being very vigilant. On more than one occasion he felt that one of them, a female, was paying him some attention.

Hall started to feel uncomfortable. He was used to being in charge of situations and this wasn't to his liking. He fought the urge to leave immediately and swam a few more lengths before climbing at a leisurely pace from the pool and heading for the changing rooms. With a growing sense of alarm, he imagined an uncomfortable sensation of eyes on his back, his movements were being followed – it was time to go.

Hall changed quickly and headed to the car park where his Hillman Hunter car was parked some distance from the entrance. Again, he consciously resisted the urge to look behind him.

Unbeknown to him, the alert lifeguard had slipped on a jacket and followed him out at a respectable distance. She was aware of the earlier indecency offence and something about Hall hadn't felt quite right.

As Hall reversed carefully out of the parking space and accelerated slowly away, she stood obscured from view in a bus shelter and wrote down the registration number of the car on a scrap of paper. Within the hour she had passed the details to the local police.

Time would tell if Peter Hall had made a fatal mistake.

*

Peter Hall's mother sat listlessly in the chair that was once routinely occupied by her dead husband. These days she was prone to 'farting' quite frequently and each time she did she imagined that it was the closest that she would ever come to shitting on the memory of the man she had detested so much.

She stared through the living room windows, looking for some signs of life, but knowing that all that she had to look forward to was the postman calling, or the odd Jehovah's Witness, the latter of whom got short-shrift for daring to set foot on her doorstep. This was her 'citadel' and they could keep theirs.

She was the epitome of bitterness at the hand that God had dealt her. A useless tool of a husband who couldn't keep his cock in his pants, and a son who used to like to parade around the house in the Queen's uniform as if he was somebody – somebody grand.

She knew better and had to work hard to hide her contempt for her son, but she needed him as she got older.

As she tweaked the front window blinds for the umpteenth time that morning a police car drove into view and parked outside, the lone officer straining his neck to look at the house numbers.

She watched as he sat for a few moments and appeared to be studying a sheet of paper, before finally leaving the vehicle to walk slowly up her path to the front door.

His was the frame of a men who had seen better times, made more pronounced by the 'beer belly' which had been cultivated over some years as the practice of having 'a couple' after the end of each shift had become more of a requirement than a habit.

At first glance it looked like his tunic was suffering from a dose of dandruff but mostly the white flecks came from the 'fag ash' which constantly fell from the cigarette which seemed to his colleagues to hang permanently from his bottom lip, and brought with it a wretched cough in the winter months. In the job he was an archetypal 'old sweat'. Seen it, done it, ducked it, if possible. A man who lived on past glories, most of which were fiction or heavily embellished – an absolute legend in his own mind.

The officer had put his helmet on to provide some semblance of authority but the look of disinterest on his face said it all as he knocked the door.

Mrs. Hall made her way slowly to the front door, stopping just once to pass wind again, the arthritis in her hips kicking in, the constant pain a reminder of the miserable life that she led.

"Does Peter Hall live here my luv?" The officer enquired as she opened the door.

She responded with a warm welcoming smile – totally false yet who was he to know any different, "Yes, but he's out at work. I'm his mother. Come in constable and I'll put the kettle on."

The officer never declined a cup of tea, even though his nose twitched somewhat as he negotiated his way through some rather strong farmyard aromas. He settled himself down into a chair at the kitchen table as she busied herself.

Mrs. Hall made the sort of tea that you could stand a spoon up in, and by the time that three sugars had been added it was a bit like drinking treacle.

With the pleasantries out of the way, the officer told his story and she listened intently as the details of the incidents at the swimming baths in Sheffield were outlined.

"So, you see Mrs. Hall" the officer concluded, "we have a vehicle registration number and the number plate is registered to your son."

Mrs. Hall paused over her tea, "What date did you say that this was officer?" She spoke quietly but convincingly.

The officer picked over the details again as Mrs. Hall quietly allowed herself to give way to yet further flatulence, which did not escape the officer's nostrils and added to his desire to get this 'bag of rats' over and done with as quickly as possible.

He wouldn't normally be in a rush as whilst he was tied up with this enquiry they wouldn't be able to allocate him to another job but the smell was starting to get to him and he was in danger of gagging. Suddenly this cushy little job wasn't quite so appealing.

Mrs. Hall decided to help him out, "I think that you have had a wasted journey officer. That day was the anniversary of my dear husband's death." She paused and allowed a small tear to well up in her eye. "Peter took me to the grave that day. We always take flowers every year so there is no way that he could have been in Sheffield."

Mrs. Hall was an old lady and everyone knows that old ladies don't tell lies; the officer swallowed everything that she said and due to his inherent laziness did not even bother to look at her husband's death certificate. Neither did he take her up on the offer to have a look at Peter's room as Mrs. Hall yet again delivered an unwelcome and unseen cloud of gas.

Peter Hall had yet again had another lucky escape – case closed.

The officer left with a piece of Mrs. Hall's favourite home-made cake wrapped in foil, and drove off, content that this had merely been a case of mistaken identity. He was pleased to get some fresh air. A brief police pocketbook entry would deal with the anomaly. In any event this was an 'Out of Force' enquiry which didn't have any bearing on the local crime figures and one which no-one would lose any sleep over. Once his pocketbook was complete it would be consigned to a badly managed archive in the damp basement of the station never to see the light of day again.

The pictures of Peter Hall in his Army Cadet uniform which Mrs. Hall had shown to him, had satisfied his curiosity and confirmed that this was an upstanding man who was doing his bit for the community.

Mrs. Hall watched him go, shut the door firmly and made her way slowly upstairs – the forced smile no longer present as she 'huffed and puffed' her way up.

Her son had always made it clear that she was not welcome in his room and that was fine by her when he was at home.

As she entered she knew what she was looking for – she had seen it many times before.

Inside the wardrobe she found a battered brown suitcase which was partially hidden behind his neatly hung clothes.

She lifted the case onto his bed, which was

always made up with military precision, and flicked the catches open.

Mrs Hall had known for years that her son was a 'kiddy-fiddler', but it was a secret that she kept from the world, and from him.

She sifted through well-thumbed magazines portraying young homosexual love, and photographs of boys at Harris Grange, and other locations.

Every now and then she paused to examine the face of a young boy, many of them wearing Army Cadet uniforms, stood next to her son – proud in his uniform, his brightly polished 'Sam Brown' adding pomp to his image – in control, yet a complete fraud.

She tried to imagine what the boys might have been really thinking, not through some form of guilt but through morbid curiosity.

Mrs Hall put everything back in its place and returned the suitcase to the wardrobe – she felt cold – it was time for another cup of tea and a return to her husband's chair where she reflected that in this life it was survival of the fittest. She needed Peter, and the kids would get over it in time.

She retreated into her sad world – the window awaited.

*

In 1970, at the age of seventy-five, Peter Hall's mother suffered a severe stroke at their home, and she was hospitalised for several weeks.

Hall continued to play the dutiful son, and juggled his time between the Cadets, his job and the Queen Elizabeth Hospital where she had been fortunate to have been placed in a private ante-room off one of the wards.

He had been told that her condition was such that she had only a matter of weeks to live. Although the stroke had induced extensive paralysis she still retained the power of speech although as time passed her voice got weaker.

As predicted by a friendly nurse, he got a telephone call during the early hours of one morning to say that she was close to death and that he should attend the hospital.

As he sat at her bedside holding her right hand gently he watched her life slowly and painfully ebb away. His mother was not for slipping away quietly in her sleep and was fighting the growing darkness every step of the way.

Peter Hall tried to reassure his mother that all would be well and that he was sure that her husband, his father, was watching over them to keep them safe.

His mother's eyes narrowed and she found some hidden strength to pull him towards her. The softly spoken words hit him square on, delivering a knock-out punch that he had not seen coming. "Don't talk rubbish. I know he was up your arse every Sunday, and if you want to know why it's simple – I told him to, in fact I encouraged him to. The last thing I wanted was his filthy hands on me, so you were the answer."

She fought for breath. "All that you need to know Peter is that I never loved you – I know what you've been up to with those boys – you're just filth like him – like father like son......." the last words petered away as she lay back deeper in her pillow and died without once looking at him again.

She died happy, knowing that she had inflicted maximum pain on him.

Chapter Five

'Sticks and Stones'

During her recruit training Sally Jones often talked with her new colleagues about why they had joined. Nearly all of them said it was because they wanted to do good and help others. They looked at her slightly askance when she put forth that she wanted to lock up lots of criminals and make their lives a misery. If victims got helped as a result, then that was all good, but Sally was in the punishment game.

Sally was by no means used to the bright lights of any city, let alone Birmingham, but she was no naive eighteen-year-old - courtesy of 'Uncle Jim'. Anybody that saw her as weak because she was young and female quickly found that she knew how to hold her own and would not tolerate being anyone's plaything.

Her new career began with a selection process for Birmingham City Police, and a medical, and then she faced the final hurdle – a thirty-minute interview with a stern-faced female Superintendent with grey hair, in her fifties, who looked pretty scary. Sat in her office in Newton Street, there was not the faintest trace of a smile from the senior officer throughout the ordeal, as Sally was probed as to why she wanted to join.

Finally, the officer announced that Sally would be accepted but with one condition, "If you get married you have to leave." Sally had no problem with that, it was the last thing on her mind.

She was told the starting pay-scale but reminded that she would not be on the same pay as her male colleagues – after all they put themselves in harm's way and deserved more. Sally would be making do with 90% of what her male colleagues got.

There must have been something about her that the interviewer liked, perhaps she glimpsed a fellow soul, because she was offered the job and dispatched to the clothing stores to pick up her uniform. This consisted of a belted tunic and peaked cap, white shirts with studs that cut into your throat if your neck was too big, black lace-up shoes and black nylon stockings with seams in the back. Definitely not fashionable! No handbag was issued and no truncheon. You got so many of each item and no more.

Clutching the pile of clothing, she made her way home by train and spent the evening trying to get to grips with how to wear a uniform, and used to the imposing image looking back at her from the mirror. Whilst she had not yet accumulated one shred of police knowledge Sally was already feeling proud – she was where she wanted to be, and at 5'10" tall she stood head and shoulders above most of her female colleagues.

Her next challenge was to navigate the twelve-week initial training course run on military lines and held at the District Police Training Centre at Ryton on Dunsmore. Sally made two friends and they supported each other as the daily ritual of room inspections were carried out before breakfast. They were required to complete a bed block with blankets and sheets encased within another blanket in perfect symmetry. Get it wrong and the drill sergeant would throw it across the room onto the floor and bark furiously at the officers standing to attention at the foot of their beds.

Sally was in an all-female block and whilst the day-time classes were mixed, their block was strictly 'out of bounds' for male officers. A female sergeant instructor conducted regular checks to make sure that this code of conduct was observed. This was a place of study and discipline, not somewhere for course romances.

The study regime was monotonous, as student officers learnt police definitions in 'parrot fashion' until they could recite them in their sleep. Physical Education sessions were equally traumatic, and non-swimmers faced a 'sink or swim' situation. As a non-swimmer Sally was literally thrown into the deep end and observed curiously from the side by the swimming instructor as she furiously 'doggy - paddled' gasping and choking to the side of the pool.

But Sally had experienced and overcome a lot worse. The weeks flew by. Soon it was the 'end of course Ball', where the female officers wore long glittery dresses and the men dinner jackets, most of which were hired and made them look faintly ridiculous, with a hint of children dressing up in their parent's clothes. It was all very formal with course photographs being taken at the start of the dinner, but as the evening wore on, 'dickie bows' were ditched, and some student officers got the worse for wear. Sally knew instinctively when it was time to leave and avoided the embarrassment of anyone declaring their undying love through an alcoholic haze. The married ones were normally the worst, as she knew from bitter experience!

She was posted to the Policewomen's Department at Steelhouse Lane Police Station and joined eleven other officers, one of whom was a sergeant. A female Inspector came to visit them from time to time, but for the most part they were left to their own devices.

Most of them were probationers like her and there was a high turnover of staff as the 'no marriage' rule, which wasn't changed until the following year, took its toll. After that was consigned to history it was immediately replaced with, 'if you have children you have to leave'.

Sally quickly learned that much of her job revolved around kids, and usually the ones with the 'snottiest noses' and longest 'candles' emanating from their nostrils that you could find. Whenever a male officer brought a child into the station the first instruction given was to send for a policewoman – they acted as accessories for their male colleagues, some of whom regarded the 'split-arses' with disdain, the rest as a potential source of easy sex, unless they said, 'no', in which case they were clearly 'dykes'. Indeed, to some of the men it seemed as if they were surrounded by 'lezzies' as their unwanted attentions were rebuffed. The police service had a whole vocabulary of its own for name-calling and the crueller the better for many.

Sally was routinely bored, but occasionally found the excitement that she sought when they were allowed to patrol the streets in pairs looking for homeless women sleeping rough in public toilets. Four times a year she worked nights with more experienced officers, but after twice escaping from the clutches of female officers who thought that she might want to explore the other side of her sexuality, using one of the beds in the ante-room in the policewoman's office, the novelty wore off.

As Sally became more experienced, she found that she enjoyed searching prostitutes and taking rape statements, it felt like 'real' policing. On one occasion she was instructed to take a statement from a female who had been abducted from Manchester and forced to work as a prostitute on the streets of Birmingham. Having escaped from the clutches of her violent 'pimp' she sought refuge at the police station and was met by a male officer who point-blank refused to deal with her complaint and announced that she had 'got what she had asked for'.

Sally was furious with the officer and tore into him in front of the victim. The officer laughed it off, but Sally had made an enemy. She felt for the victim and determined to do her best for her. She still bore her own scars, her motivation for joining, and it was seared deeply within her that sexual abuse was abhorrent in any form and should be challenged.

Sally became an advocate for the victims of domestic violence and child abuse at a time when the former was thought of as a 'civil matter' not for the police, and the latter was deeply hidden under a stone that nobody wanted to lift. In a job where conforming was the means of survival, even for the men, Sally began to be resented.

A week after the altercation, the male officer made his move with revenge in mind. As Sally entered the front office, he announced to two of his male colleagues that Sally had not yet received the seal of approval by way of a 'station stamp' on her bottom.

This was an initiation ritual that was normally reserved for female newcomers, but she had never been subjected to it. There was something about her that had to date given them pause for thought.

There was nothing subtle about the process as officers would manhandle their victims across a desk and lift their skirts up before stamping bare flesh with the stamp. Designed to humiliate and reinforce the pecking order in the male dominated environment, most female officers suffered it in silence. After all it was just a bit of harmless fun wasn't it?

Sally was a different proposition. She marched straight up to the officer, and the look in her eye caused him to take a step back. She was big-boned, but in perfect proportion and as she was by now a strong swimmer her shoulders were wider than his, "I'm having a period you moron but if you want to give it a try I promise you that you will not only bleed yourself if you lay a hand on me but you'll get something back in return stuck down the back of your trousers. It should fit nicely in your arse."

She could see the indecision in his eyes. He was tempted to call her bluff; he even moved his arm towards her. She grabbed it. He found that she had a surprisingly strong grip.

She touched the ring on his finger, "Married aren't you? I've heard you talking about her. I'm sure she would be horrified at some of the things you've said. Irene isn't it - works on the make-up counter in *'Rackhams'*? I bet she'd be interested to know all about our affair and how you hate her. And that's what she'll hear if you don't fuck off right now."

The man pulled his hand away and looked to his colleagues for support, but the balance of power had changed, and it seemed that they were making a swift re-appraisal of his intended victim. Swearing under his breath he made an excuse and was gone.

On other occasions Sally was tasked with her other female colleagues with collecting female shoplifters from the city-centre stores. They were not allowed to fetch them in full uniform and were expected to don a felt hat from a collection in a bag in the office before they went out onto the streets. It was a pointless disguise that didn't sit well with Sally. The officers, working in pairs, would walk their female prisoners back to Steelhouse Lane with nothing more than the power of speech to protect them. If any of the prisoners struggled, they simply stuck with it and gritted their teeth. Sometimes it was a long way back.

Sally easily passed her probationary period and was later temporarily posted to Belgrave Road Police Station due to staff shortages. It was there that she met the man who seemed to be the first real love of her life, a police sergeant on one of the shifts who was kind, helpful and considerate. Always immaculately turned out, he took Sally under his wing and helped her through some challenging moments as she was launched onto the streets with nothing more than a radio and no knowledge of the area.

Not long after her arrival, Sally once again found herself facing the prospect of an unwanted initiation ceremony as she took a break during a late shift in the large station canteen area, part of which was occupied by a full-size billiard table.

Sally was not one for playing 'boys' games', but when the three male members of the shift who were also having a break offered to pair up with her for a doubles match, she felt obliged to participate, as the newcomer.

The difference was of course that dressed in trousers the men had no difficulties when it came to taking awkward shots whereas Sally struggled to retain her modesty and was only too aware that every time she bent over the table to take aim with a cue three pairs of eyes were riveted to her bottom.

114

She realised the tactical error and was already regretting her actions. Feeling flustered she started to miscue her shots badly, much to the amusement of her colleagues.

Finally, as she was taking another shot one of them neatly side-stepped behind her, grabbing her waist with his left hand whilst holding his right hand over the hand she was holding the cue in and pinning her face-down on the table. She could feel his hot breath on the back of her neck as he held her in a vice-like grip and whispered, "I'm good at getting my balls into the hole Sally. Just stay where you are, and I'll show you."

As Sally struggled his grip only got harder, whilst to her right a second officer was holding up a station stamp – it had been a set-up and the third officer was already holding the canteen door from the inside so that they wouldn't be disturbed.

The officer with the stamp closed in on her and started to tug her skirt upwards. She could feel that the man holding her had become aroused and the sight of more stocking legs being revealed was only adding to his excitement.

He was a large and powerful man and in deciding that he wanted to get a view from the front he made his mistake. As he attempted to turn her round to lift her onto the table Sally managed to free her hand holding the cue and to swing it around, striking him behind the ear. It wasn't a heavy blow, but it stung the officer who clutched his head and said coldly, "You're going to get your arse stamped 'plonk', and maybe a bit more – make no mistake about it."

Sally took the only other course of action available to her and screamed as loud as she could.

After what seemed a lifetime but was probably just seconds, the canteen door burst open and the sergeant – her 'knight in shining armour', appeared. He didn't need to ask what was going on.

He promptly ordered the three men out of the room and sat Sally down. All of the storybooks would have had Sally bursting into tears at this point and finding solace in the arms of her rescuer. This was not to be the case however and initially Sally vented her anger with her own choice of swear words and demanded that action be taken.

It took half an hour for the sergeant to persuade her that such a course of action would be a catastrophe both for her personally and for the three officers, all of whom were married. He assured her that he would deal with it personally and that he would arrange for her to move onto another shift, 'rocking the boat' would only end in tears as the men would stick together and claim that it was simple banter that had been exaggerated.

Word quickly spread around the station that Sally was a 'frigid cow' who should be avoided at all costs. That suited her just fine and ensured that pranksters would pay her a wide berth in future.

Within weeks Sally started to date the sergeant, who quite quickly managed to reach the parts that a station stamp was never going to be able to. Sally unexpectedly discovered that she was in love with the man who was an experienced and considerate lover and within six months they were engaged to be married.

The wedding was a traditional affair at St. Peters in Harborne, with a police guard of honour outside the front entrance, wearing white gloves and holding up wooden truncheons underneath which the happy couple passed.

They moved to a police-house in the middle of a semi-circle of similar accommodation in a quiet cul-de-sac off War Lane, and for the first four weeks Sally was the happiest that she had ever been as her husband showered affection on her.

For the second time Sally had let what she thought was 'love' cloud her judgement. Her new husband was a divorcee who needed to have a woman in his life to control. Sally had known of his previous marriage but had been led to believe that he was the innocent party in the proceedings and that his former wife had left him for another man.

The reality was that he had in fact been caught out having an affair and visiting prostitutes. Old habits died hard as the novelty of a new wife quickly wore off.

Sally was smitten and initially didn't question any unexpected absences from the house. They were now working at different stations and it was relatively easy for him to come and go as he pleased. He also had a close male colleague who used to cover his back, and both of them developed a propensity for 'fishing trips', although what they were actually looking to catch was not something that you could find in a river or canal.

Sally was no fool, and very observant; little signs began to add up to a pattern that raised her suspicions. She began to wonder whether he was in fact just like the rest of them. After one excursion Sally started to ask some difficult questions and her husband snapped and struck her across the face. This was not the act of a man under the influence of alcohol but a very deliberate one designed to start the process of grooming Sally to become compliant and subservient.

Sally was shocked and ready to fight back; it was the first time a man had struck her in anger, but she allowed herself to be placated as he apologised profusely and promised that it would never happen again. He explained that he was under a lot of pressure at work and that he needed her to support him and to understand his needs. Passionate sex followed, and the matter was swept under the carpet until the next time. In truth, Sally didn't want to confront the possibility that her second real relationship was abusive and heading for disaster.

On the second occasion he didn't have an excuse as she was struck from behind and felled to the floor. Sally was again ready to take him on when he burst into tears and again begged for forgiveness. After being consigned to the spare room for a night, life continued, but she told him it was the last time. He thought differently.

The third and final act of the tragedy came when Sally announced that she was late for her period and concerned that she might be pregnant. If she was expecting signs of joy and happiness she was to be mistaken as he flew into a rage and accused her of trying to trap him. This time Sally was prepared for his next move and as he advanced on her with fists raised, she kicked him hard in the testicles. As he went down writhing on the floor Sally looked at him with contempt and declared, "I love you. It will never happen again."

With that she went upstairs, packed a suitcase,

and left the house, never to return. She stayed with a girlfriend for a few days before finding a flat to rent and asking for a transfer from a less than helpful local Superintendent who had clearly been briefed by her husband. It was even suggested that she might want to consider her options in terms of her policing career, but Sally was made of sterner stuff – she would not be leaving the police service. They could not even enforce the 'pregnancy rule', it proved to be a false alarm - one that she gave thanks for as it had proved the 'true colours' of her spouse.

Sally Jones was now 'damaged goods' according to the 'grapevine', which quickly embellished the facts, the truth being lost beneath a veneer of male chauvinism and the desire to pass on a good story, but she faced down any hint of challenge. Some of the worst offenders were in fact her female colleagues who refused to believe that her husband could be anything other than the caring gentleman he portrayed in public. She must have been a poor wife. Sally felt pity for his next victim.

Not long after arriving back in the city-centre at Digbeth, Sally did however make a name for herself following an arson attack on a multi-storey housing block on the outskirts of the Division. She was one of the first on the scene and remembered the advice that one of her instructors had given - that many arsonists chose to stay within the vicinity of the scene of the crime so that they could get their thrills by observing the actions of the emergency services.

It wasn't long before she noticed a female doing precisely that. Something about her didn't feel quite right and when Sally challenged her, she was told in no uncertain terms to 'fuck off as it was just a fire'. It was in fact a fire which was to claim the life of a six-month-old baby.

Sally had an aversion to being sworn at and her observation skills revealed the smell of petrol emanating from the woman's coat sleeve. She promptly arrested the woman on suspicion of arson – she had indeed found her offender.

On arrival back at the station, as she tried to lodge her prisoner, she found the cell- block swarming with CID officers and the prisoner was promptly transferred to their custody. She didn't even sign the custody sheet as the arresting officer and subsequently got no thanks or recognition for her efforts.

Fortunately for Sally her actions had been noted by a uniform inspector who had a quiet word with a friend – a 'forward-thinking' senior CID officer. He made it his business to keep an eye on her progress.

For the time being men were most definitely off the agenda as she buried herself in her work.

***

Richard Brent was an academic at heart and longed for a return to the days of his youth when he was a committed student who enjoyed books more than the company of fellow pupils. His ambition had been to become a teacher, but that had quickly faded with the onset of polio.

Initially his parents had put his fever and sore throat down to a bout of influenza, but as muscle stiffness in the arms and legs set in, a visit to the doctors soon confirmed their worst fears.

As the months passed by, Brent suffered from bouts of severe fatigue, and muscle wasting, but the worst symptom was his inability to sleep. During the hours of darkness, he regularly lay struggling for

120

breath as the demons he fought left him exhausted.

Brent's illness, coupled with his struggle to find his place in the world, blighted his life, but the effects of the polio ensured a relatively quiet passage through the Second World War after he was excluded from being called-up for service.

He watched many of his peers spending their last few days on leave at home prior to being posted, strutting around, chests puffed out in their khaki battledress. He was torn between contempt for their uneducated approach to life and jealousy of their vibrant health and the hero-worship they drew by the mere act of putting on a uniform.

He knew that his physical disabilities marked him out for sympathy at best, and contempt at worst, but he understood better than many of them what they would soon be facing. The art of war, killing and death, was one of his favourite studies, and pain was a very familiar companion.

Both of his parents died suddenly in the 1950s, following an outbreak of influenza, and he was left to inherit the family home in Birmingham, such as it was. Still in his thirties, Brent fell into a solitary life, his only distractions being some voluntary work among the young at his local church, and a developing interest in politics.

He cut a lonely figure with no close friends and certainly no women in his life. Not one had ever shown any interest in his frail figure and he had stifled any feelings in that direction.

Brent drifted without purpose for years, but in 1961 his life changed direction when he became aware of a vacancy for a senior care worker at Avon House Children's Home in Stratford Upon Avon.

On impulse he applied for the job, which

offered residential accommodation and the opportunity to breath in fresh country air every day.

Brent was able to get a glowing reference from the vicar at his church who extolled his virtues, despite his disabilities, working with disadvantaged youngsters, changing the direction of their lives for the better and bringing them closer to God.

He was also able to get a reference from a local politician, Ernest Page, a rising star in his party, and someone that Brent had canvassed for in local elections. In addition, Page had offered to speak to a close friend 'Charles' who he said was a man of considerable influence in the local area.

Richard Brent enjoyed the novel feeling of having friends, and following an interview with the management of the Home he got the job.

On the day that he arrived at Avon House his life changed forever.

*

Avon House was an old Stately Home, set in its own grounds, that had seen better times. Unable to pay inheritance tax, the last owner had turned the building over to the Local Authority, who in turn had created a Children's Home, taking children placed into care from their catchment area in Birmingham.

Visitors were treated to the sight of a long and winding tree-lined drive up to the main building, with large areas of greenery and woodland, through the middle of which ran the River Avon. It could have been a beautiful oasis for the children in the middle of 'Shakespeare's country', but it was far from it.

There had been several Wardens in charge of the home, none of them particularly successful, and the incumbent towards the end of the 60's was no different. The man had conducted his duties with an air of indifference. He was looking forward to further years of leading a pleasant life, until a fatal heart attack, brought on by his 'forty a day' habit, presented Brent with an unexpected opportunity.

With the patronage of Ernest Page, and local MP Charles Redmund, he got the job as Warden, being the sole applicant. He was now a man of power, and in their debt.

*

Richard Brent always carried a twelve-inch wooden ruler in his inside pocket and wasn't afraid to use it for the most minor of transgressions. He had acquired a taste for corporal punishment as the life of pain he had endured was now transferred to others.

He was however well-respected within the local Warwickshire community and regularly held fund-raising events at the Home for the elderly and infirm, to which were invited local dignitaries and politicians. These included his patron Charles Redmund MP, who had a house nearby and used it for constituency visits at weekends when he was up from London.

Brent's position also brought him into contact with the local police as some of the residents were prone to going missing as they attempted to escape from the countryside of Warwickshire for the bright and more familiar lights of Birmingham. He was an expert at both filling out *'Missing Person'* reports and dishing out the appropriate punishment when they were eventually returned by the police, who routinely treated the children as nothing more than a *'pain in the arse'* – more like troublesome offenders, and certainly not victims.

For the boys, the punishment meted out generally involved the removal of all lower clothing as Brent indulged his masochistic tendencies.

Brent also actively encouraged partnership working, a totally new approach in the 60's, and was subtly encouraged by his sponsors to build links with and support Richmond House and the Harris Grange ACF wherever possible.

Thus, it was that Peter Hall, John Baxter, Paul Evans and Richard Brent found themselves wedded to each other in a common cause. Puppets on long strings.

*

Brent was keen to please his benefactors, and when it was proposed by Ernest Page that it would be a good idea to open the doors of Avon House for Army Cadet Camps he enthusiastically agreed – it would be another piece of good publicity for his work.

An open space well away from the main buildings was identified in the grounds, where large tents which could hold up to ten cadets each were erected, whilst officers were quartered inside the Home. A number of other cadet units were invited to attend the camp and with open fires and food served in aluminium mess-tins, the emphasis was on experiencing outdoor life.

Peter Hall stage-managed the event, and on the first day all of the cadets were paraded in front of the main building for a formal inspection by none other than Charles Redmund MP and Councillor Ernest Page. The local press was in attendance and some positive media coverage was guaranteed.

The inspection party was completed by Captain Hall, and the parade was brought to attention by Staff Sergeant Paul Evans, complete with red sash, who was suffering from both an adrenalin rush and panic attack at the same time.

Redmund and Page passed along the lines of the assembled cadets, exchanging pleasantries with the officers present, but paused when they reached the section of ten cadets from Richmond House who had been formed up on their own.

The two men spent some time talking to four cadets in particular, following which Redmund made a short speech to those assembled, extolling the virtues of the staff and highlighting the invaluable personal support they gave to the youngsters. The reporters present scribbled away furiously, eager to promote such pillars of the community.

Finally, it was time for the 'VIPs' to stand on a small podium as numerous youngsters with 'two left legs' completed a march-past, following which they bid their farewells.

At the conclusion of the event, the four cadets who had been spoken to were taken to one side by Hall and informed that they had been specially selected to serve at a VIP dinner at the end of the camp weekend.

During the course of the event, various drill exercises took place as well as races between different units over a makeshift assault course erected in the grounds. To the casual observer this was the perfect setting for youngsters to develop desirable team and 'character - building' skills whilst in safe hands.

On Sunday afternoon most of the cadets were packing up to go home, but the Richmond House section were selected for a speed-march around the grounds. More by design than luck they had trailed behind their fellow cadets in all of the events and had been the butt of constant ridicule from their peers.

125

The forced march was Peter Hall's punishment for letting the side down.

As they were led off by Evans, who pedalled alongside them on a bicycle, Hall said his goodbyes to his fellow officers and before long the grounds had been cleared, except for one large marquee type tent that had been used as a canteen..

John Baxter duly arrived in the van from Richmond House to take the boys back and sat in the vehicle by the river waiting for their return.

Thirty minutes later the marching party arrived back at the river, breathless and red-faced. Hall was waiting whilst Baxter looked on – his physical presence always a factor in ensuring compliance. Hall went through the charade of chiding them for their lack of competitive spirit and then got down to the real business, "You lot stink like the armpits of some old *'prossie'*. Strip off, get in the river and be sharp about it. Last one in answers to Mr. Baxter."

The group needed no second bidding, and with alacrity shed their 'battle-dress' uniforms. No-one wanted to be last.

One or two attempted to enter the freezing water wearing underpants but Hall bellowed, "Pants off – are you men or mice!"

Eventually they stood shivering in a huddle in the water until Hall ordered them out one by one, but only after each of them had immersed their bodies fully.

Evans lined them up on the river bank and Hall went through another inspection process, but on this occasion he wasn't looking for flaws on brightly polished belt-buckles as he used the end of his 'swagger stick' to humiliate the boys with comments about the size of their manhood's.

Finally, they were told to get dressed and six of the boys were ordered into the van and driven away by Baxter.

The remaining four boys, previously selected by Redmund, were led off to the solitary tent where they were shown four sets of Number 2 dress uniforms and told to smarten themselves up for the dinner, where they were to wait on the tables.

As the boys prepared themselves for the evening to come there was no sense of excitement, just quiet resignation. They were under no illusions as to what was to come but having been subjected to systematic violence and abuse, they were conditioned to it and did what was necessary to survive.

The table and chairs were already in the tent but white tablecloths were laid over the Formica, and just before 8pm a lavish buffet was delivered on silver platters by outside caterers who laid the food out and left. Bottles of wine and port were added to the table which was set for five places. Lighting was provided in the form of several large candelabras of candles which cast flickering shadows across the tent.

At 8.30pm Peter Hall entered the tent, accompanied by Ernest Page, and placed the boys, one in each corner of the tent, and brought them to attention. Five minutes later Brent and Evans brought two strangers to the tent, who were accompanied by Charles Redmund. Both newcomers were immaculately dressed and commanded deference and respect from those assembled.

Brent was not invited to stay, and left immediately, whilst Evans, still in uniform, took up a position at the entrance to the tent, the flap of which was closed. Performing sentry duties was not to his liking but he knew that he was in the presence of some of the powerful men who underpinned his position and he was not about to argue.

One of the newcomers took a seat at the head of the table and beckoned for the other four to take a seat. The boys were brought forward to the corners of the table and stood waiting. The man said little as he picked at the food and occasionally indicated to one of the boys to fill his wine glass.

At 10pm sharp the man at the head of the table banged his glass down sharply just once and announced that 'officers and gentlemen could now stand down.'

Page, Redmund and Hall briefly joined Evans outside, before Hall drove them the short distance to the Home in his Land Rover, leaving the two men and four boys behind.

After settling Redmund and Page down with a drink, Hall returned to the tent, ready to transport the strangers to their vehicles, which were parked well away from the home. After performing this service, he returned, full of anticipation, and collected Page and Redmund. It was their turn.

At the conclusion Evans was summoned and ordered to take the traumatised boys back to the Home in the van, whilst the men gathered themselves and made one last toast to conclude the evening. Hall, Redmund and Page quenched their thirst with the remains of the alcohol. Sodomising children was indeed hard work.

By 10am next morning Brent had arranged for the tent to be removed and with it all trace of the previous night's crimes. A few miles away four boys suffered in silence, nowhere to go, nobody to tell.

***

After their introduction to Joe, Ses and Bud had expected to be working the door of the 'Hole in The Wall' club, but it quickly became apparent that Joe had other ideas, bankrolling an expansion of the drugs and people importation business. Joe was very careful and kept them at arms-length, but he looked after them well and they had no cause to complain, they knew the score.

They were the figureheads, the enforcers, and the fall-guys if it all went wrong. They had finally 'made it' in the land of their dreams, but had come full-circle and back to the life of crime they had so assiduously tried to avoid all those years ago

By the late Sixties they were hardened operators, veterans of 'turf wars', vital cogs in the organisation, and the new decade brought with it the final step in their descent towards corruption.

Conflict with the police had been growing, as the Caribbean community began to consider Handsworth as 'home', and transfer their culture there, rather than conform to the diktats of a society that discriminated and isolated them. They stuck together, and it was rare for anyone to 'break ranks'.

Joe Docker had become accustomed to hold court in the snug of a 'back-street' pub in the depths of Handsworth and tonight was practising his listening skills. Behind him Ses and Bud sat quietly at a respectable distance. Joe had already briefed them, and their job at that moment was simply to keep their mouths shut. In the background the sound of dominoes being slammed onto bar tables confirmed that they were in safe territory.

The man seated opposite Joe shared his colour, his age, and his outlook on life, but as he sat bolt upright showing due deference to Joe, it was clear that this was a man seeking help from the recognised 'top – dog', Handsworth's black 'Don'.

A drugs dealer by choice, the man told his story.

He operated through a network of street sellers, a couple of whom were also entrusted with acting as protection for his brother, who made all their bulk purchases of cannabis.

Some three months previously a new supplier had appeared on the scene. He had slowly ingratiated himself with the man's brother and subsequently supplied on two occasions several kilos of quality cannabis at a good price.

The handover of the drugs had gone without a hitch and everyone had been happy.

A week ago, the supplier had offered a much larger consignment of drugs and finalised a price, venue, time and place in Lozells, for delivery.

At the agreed time, the dealer's brother had turned up with two other young men and the drugs, contained in a rucksack, were handed over by the supplier who casually lit a cigarette before taking his payment.

At that point all hell broke loose as police officers, carrying short pick-axe handles, burst out of the back of a large white delivery van which had been parked nearby.

To the shouts of *'Police, Police'* the chase was on, as the drugs dealer, his henchmen and the supplier did a 'starburst' and tried to run off in different directions.

The end result was that the brother of the man sitting before Joe had been arrested together with both of his henchmen. They were directly linked, by several officers, to the drugs in the bag, which had been abandoned at the scene, and they were now looking at doing some serious time in prison for conspiracy to supply controlled drugs and for assaulting a number of the arresting officers following a violent struggle.

Her Majesty's Prison Winson Green awaited the three men; however, the supplier had made good his escape.

Joe knew what was coming, but nevertheless asked the question, "And your point is?"

"It was a set up!" the response came back.

The man went on to explain that the presence of the police at the meet made it abundantly clear that someone had 'grassed them up' – the question was who?

The answer to that had come from an unexpected source after a local teenager had divulged that during the chase, out of curiosity he had followed behind the supplier, and the officer chasing him, who appeared to slow up once they were out of sight, and then gave the 'thumbs up' as the supplier turned and waved at him before disappearing.

The lighting of the cigarette had clearly been a signal to the waiting officers.

Joe Docker sat back in his chair and reflected. Whilst this situation did not represent a direct threat to his own business it was nevertheless not good to see the police winning on his own doorstep. Far worse was the fact that a 'brother' had been 'turned', and that required action. That type of cancer had a habit of spreading, and if it wasn't cut out it might just start causing problems for his own business empire.

Finally, he broke the silence and said, "What do you want from me then?"

"I want justice for my brother Mr. Docker, I want justice."

After a discussion about what Joe expected in return the man had departed. Joe sat down with Ses and Bud and made it clear in simple terms what he wanted in terms of an outcome. This was serious business and he gave them the option to walk away from the proposition. Neither hesitated and after shaking hands they went their separate ways.

***

For some time, Joe had drawn Ses and Bud into the darker side of his business. Whilst they had both made very good drugs and people traffickers, he had quickly recognised that they had qualities and an edge which would be useful for 'special work'.

The two men had accepted the contract but showed no signs of bravado or self-importance. They would perform their task through a sense of loyalty to a man who had supported them unequivocally through tough times – it was just business and certainly not personal. These were men who had dealt drugs, handled stolen property and held their own in many fights - it was however to be the first time that they had killed anyone.

During discussions between the three men some consideration had been given to the notion of the death being made to look like a suicide or accidental. Finally, Joe decided that for the message to go out loud and clear to any other 'would be' informants this had to be seen as nothing less than cold-blooded murder. He knew that this would result in a lot of police activity in the area for a while, but he calculated that it would be worth the heat.

It took them two weeks to find their target in a pub on the Lozells Road, huddled together in a corner with a group of low-level dealers. He was 'holding court' and clearly held some sway as he paid for all of their drinks. There was a heavy smell of 'ganja' in the air.

Ses and Bud settled down in another corner watching and waiting.

After an hour he got up and said his goodbyes before making for the toilet at the rear of the premises. It was an outside construction, separate from the main building, with just one cubicle and a metal urinal that ran along its full length inside. The smell of decades of stale urine encrusted into the structure did nothing for its appeal and the odour from the closed cubicle merely added to the sense of decay. Not a nice place for a man to die.

As the informant stood at the urinal with an unlit roll-up cigarette drooping from his lower lip, he was conscious of movement behind him.

As he half-turned to see who was there, Ses entered whilst Bud stood in the open doorway of the toilet facing outwards.

Their target turned to face the urinal, intent on finishing the job in hand.

He heard the click of the flick-knife opening but as his brain started to register danger it was too late as one hand reached over his shoulder and gripped his mouth firmly shut to prevent him screaming. At the same time with his right hand Ses slashed the man's throat from left to right inflicting a fatal injury.

As blood spurted from the open wound the man collapsed onto the floor, arms flailing, choking to death on his own blood – life ebbing away as he slipped into unconsciousness.

Bud joined Ses, and together they dragged the

corpse into the cubicle and propped it on the toilet seat. Closing the door, Ses gave Bud a leg up in order to reach over the top and lock it from the inside. They were intent on buying some time – with luck their victim would not be discovered for some hours.

Ses rolled his blood-stained coat up and tucked it into a bag which Bud had been carrying. The knife went back into his pocket and the two men left through an alleyway next to the pub – in the darkness their luck had held.

Within an hour they had found their way to a 'safe house' where both men burnt all of their clothing on an open coal fire, washed themselves down thoroughly in a tin bath in the kitchen, changed and headed to a 'shebeen' in order to alibi themselves. On the way, and a good distance from the pub, the murder weapon was placed down a drain after being carefully cleaned.

It had not actually proved to be that difficult for either of them to kill – they had crossed the Rubicon.

Back at the pub, the alarm was raised as a customer spotted blood spreading across the floor of the toilet from the cubicle.

As predicted a major enquiry followed but with no witnesses, a closed community, no forensics and no suspects, it went nowhere. And who really cared about an 'immigrant' anyway?

***

In 1971, Shirley had been at Avon House for twelve months, the product of a mother who had succumbed to alcohol abuse, having been involved in a long-term violent relationship with Shirley's father.

Social Services had placed the child on the 'at risk' register some two years previously, but had struggled in vain to keep the family together as a unit. Finally, Shirley's mother had disclosed that at the age of thirteen years Shirley was receiving some unhealthy attention from her father, whose efforts at cuddling his daughter were going beyond normality. Shirley had found herself placed in care with restricted access to her parents, who lived in the Northfield area. Having spent some time in transit at other Homes she had finally been placed at Avon House.

She had not adjusted well to life at the Home and despite everything still loved her mother. She frequently went missing, with the sole aim of heading back to the family home, and unless intercepted en-route she would usually be found watching TV in their living room, oblivious to the fact that it was her parents who were calling the police to come and get her. Shirley's love was not totally reciprocated.

Shirley had become expert at jumping on the trains at Stratford railway station without paying for a ticket and then jumping off before reaching the stations with ticket barriers in central Birmingham. A bus journey would complete her expedition and she wasn't averse to a bit of shoplifting for food to eat on the way – if nothing else Shirley was a survivor.

Each time she went missing the staff at Avon House would report her absence to the local police station where they maintained a *'Misper'* file containing her photograph, next of kin details, and records of the dates she had gone missing and when found. They in turn would advise Birmingham City Police and request a visit to her parents. It all created unnecessary paperwork, and wasted time, leading to Shirley becoming a well-known and unpopular figure in local police circles.

Every time she was returned to the Home she was told off by the staff and frequently by Richard Brent in person. As Warden, he saw Shirley's refusal to comply as a direct affront to his authority and his resentment grew over time. His state of mind was not improved when he subsequently received an admonishment from the new Director of Social Services, who had come from outside the area and had a reputation for being both 'squeaky-clean' and was terrified of anything that could stain his unblemished march up the ranks. Brent received growing criticism for his inability to manage a regime where residents did not routinely abscond. It was made very clear that his future career prospects depended on improvements being made. "Good news is what I want to hear Richard, good news and more good news. I expect change and soon."

When an appeal to Page to 'pull some strings' was rebuffed, Brent pondered the situation and then delivered an ultimatum to Shirley, "Enough is enough young lady – next time you run away you can expect to suffer the consequences. It's a promise." The stage was set for a battle of wills.

Sure enough, Shirley went on one of her trips again shortly afterwards, and after being returned one afternoon she was confined to her room, had her day clothing removed, and was left in her pyjamas.

Shirley was left sulking alone for two hours, and as the day staff departed leaving a skeleton staff on duty, Brent made his move. Shirley was a disruptive child but never showed violence towards anyone and was always compliant with staff. Brent intended to exploit this aspect of her character to the full.

Although not normally at the Home during the

evenings, he had remained until there were fewer prying eyes about before having her brought to his office. He dismissed the female care worker who brought her in and quietly locked the door behind her as Shirley sat on a chair in front of him.

For fifteen minutes Brent persevered, talking quietly to Shirley from behind his desk, almost pleading with her to abandon her efforts at running away. Shirley for her part was polite but determined and would not give in. She had not asked to be put in the Home and would not willingly stay.

Finally, Brent's rising anger got the best of him, "Before you leave this room Shirley you will promise me that you will not run away again otherwise, I am going to punish you."

Shirley sat looking at him – there was no response.

Brent persisted as his hand went to the central drawer of his large desk and he edged it open, "I will hear the words Shirley or you will be punished" – a short cane was removed from the drawer and placed on the desk in full view of Shirley who swallowed before replying, "I can't Mr. Brent. I won't."

Richard Brent ordered Shirley to bend over the chair, and as fear set in Shirley complied.

Brent delivered one short sharp stroke of the cane to the girl's bottom and repeated the question. Each time there was a negative response he delivered another stroke as Shirley bit into her lip with the pain.

Brent realised that he was aroused for the first time in years. He became carried away in the moment. He hooked the cane into the top of Shirley's pyjama trousers and pulled them down to reveal the extent of the damage. He ran one hand over the bright red weals on her bottom before pressing the question again – Shirley remained silent, violated and humiliated but not broken.

Brent used the cane again, striking her hard several times across her back. Every strike reinforced the overwhelming thrill filling body and mind. Self-control was long gone as he used the child's body as a toy to be played with, and his hands strayed further.

Finally, Brent struck Shirley hard again several times on her bottom with the palm of his hand and ejaculated, before throwing the cane onto the desk and ordering the girl to pull her trousers up and to sit down.

As Shirley sat struggling with the pain, and his excitement dissipated, replaced with the chilling realisation of what he had done, Brent sought to justify himself and shouted at her, spittle issuing from his mouth, "You asked for this Shirley. It's your fault and you are to blame – certainly not me. If you run away again, you'll be back here for more. You need to do some thinking in your room."

Outside someone silently stepped away from the doorway and disappeared into one of the adjoining rooms.

Brent escorted Shirley back to her room and told her that she would get her clothes back the following morning. He stressed that if she said anything, no-one would believe her word against his and more and worse punishment would follow. He then left for home and a stiff drink – exhilarated and worried in equal measures.

Left on her own, Shirley sobbed uncontrollably for a while before examining the extent of her injuries in a mirror. The door of her room had not been locked and after recovering her composure she peered around it and was surprised to find that a tray containing food and a drink had been left outside. Avon House was not known for waitress service, but Shirley was ravenous and was grateful for the anonymous kindness.

Shirley waited for the duty social worker to settle down for the night before stealing some clothes from a pile of washing in the downstairs laundry room. She crept silently from the Home, dreading that at any minute she might be discovered, and stepped out into the darkness.

This time she knew that simply going home was not an option. She made for a shelter in a park near to the river and shivered the hours of darkness away. She was safe at that moment but not secure as she pondered her next steps. A young mind suddenly aged and very determined.

***

Shirley sat lonely, dishevelled and isolated in the reception area of a police station in Birmingham. She had used the little money she had for a bus which had disgorged her at Digbeth Coach Station. It had taken her all of the morning to reach it and, close to tears, it had taken her a full thirty minutes to pluck up the courage to go inside and present herself to the office constable who stood peering at her from the other side of the counter.

The 'old sweat' was upset as his afternoon TV viewing had been interrupted to listen to this tale of woe from the young girl. Unlike many of his colleagues, who had performed years of sterling duty on the streets before finishing their careers as full-time station officers, he was an exception to the rule, yet another legend in his own mind, with an ego to match, he was a liability on the streets and had simply been put in there out of harm's way.

He had lost no time in labelling and dismissing the girl before him, he had seen it all before, the product of some 'one-night stand' who would no doubt be pregnant herself before she was sixteen.

He listened to her story and the allegations of assault with growing impatience before giving her his opinion in the sternest voice he could muster, "You're in the Home to do as you're told. The staff there are trying to help you and you should be grateful to have a roof over your head. If you play up, you should expect to get a clip around the ear. Now that's the end of it so bugger off and don't waste any more police time or you'll find yourself in one of my cells."

Shirley blurted out, "But you're supposed to help me. I need help."

The officer peered at her over his glasses, "If you are still here with your 'cock and bull' stories when I get back from making a cuppa I am going to arrest you, put you in a cell and call the Home. Now clear off."

Shirley turned, tears welling up in her eyes, an increasing sense of desperation rising within her, as she made for the door. Just at that point, Sally Jones, who had been out on an enquiry, walked in and they virtually collided with each other in the foyer.

Immediately sensing the girl's distress, she stopped Shirley in her tracks, "Hold up luv, what's wrong?"

In the background the office-man mumbled, 'She needs her arse tanning coming in here trying to cause trouble," before retiring to his desk and the ageing TV.

Sally ignored him, she had the measure of the man and held him in contempt. She knew what his views were on women and even more so women in uniform. She couldn't give a toss what he thought and was more than a match for the fool, who by now was mumbling something about 'split-arses'.

Shirley was close to hysterics and pleaded with the Sally, "I need help please – I can't go back."

Sally took her gently by the hand and led her upstairs to the office where she sat her down and put the kettle on. The fact that Shirley winced in pain as she sat did not go unnoticed.

Through sobs Shirley gave up her story to the one police officer likely to do something about it.

The first phone call Sally made was to a female CID officer whom she knew personally and was confident would not be swayed or influenced by Richard Brent's position of authority. The next call was to a police surgeon who was called to the station and catalogued the numerous cane marks that Shirley had received across her bottom and back. She had literally been lashed 'black and blue'.

Finally, arrangements were made for Shirley to be taken to a 'place of safety' to a location that was known to just a few individuals.

Some hours after Shirley had been taken away in safe hands Sally Jones went back down to the front office where the office man was dozing pleasantly in his chair, the TV on low in the background on the desk. He looked up, "How's the little slapper doing then. Don't tell me that you've fallen for the little brat's lies. Soft tart."

Sally swiped the TV from its place on the desk and watched it drop to the floor with a satisfying crash as the tube disintegrated. She knew no fear, and towered over the man in his chair, "Shut your face you useless fucker. If you say one more word, I'll be making a phone call to the Chief Superintendent to tell him how you neglected your duty today and how you failed an innocent girl who was crying out for help."

The office-man exploded, "You fucking dyke – you wouldn't dare!"

Sally smiled, "You just try me. Watch your back. If your dick was as big as your mouth, you'd be a lucky man but from what I've heard it isn't. It looks like you need to get the broom out to sweep this mess up." She turned on her heel and left the office. She had police work to get on with.

***

Things moved swiftly and deliberately so. The two female officers knew that if they sat on the allegations there was every chance that 'complications' would set in. For a start it was off their patch and should have been handed over. They decided to throw caution to the wind.

It was a Saturday afternoon, so most senior police officers on the area were off duty. After enlisting the services of a male officer from one of the shifts they made straight for Avon House where they found the duty care worker. Some of the children at the Home were wandering around the grounds and looked on with curiosity but stayed well clear. Engaging with coppers was not the done thing.

The female detective took the lead – she was a smooth operator who exuded confidence and had a natural air of authority. If that failed, the tactic of outright intimidation was always an option. Sally watched closely. Within minutes they were standing in Richard Brent's office studying the accolades on the walls, framed certificates praising the efforts of a man who had dedicated his life to the vulnerable.

Although tempted to start searching the room, the detective resisted the option. She wanted any evidence found to be legally obtained, and corroborated, and the presence of the care worker would add weight to that.

Wasting no time, she gave strict instructions to the worker to make a phone call to Brent indicating that there had been an accident at the Home and that his presence was required. After parking the police vehicle at the rear of the premises they sat and waited.

Brent had a house in the grounds and whilst irritated by having his weekend interrupted, he made his way to his office within fifteen minutes. His joints were giving him hell that day and he was already struggling to gather himself after his savage attack on Shirley. He had been hoping for a period of calm, and the opportunity to justify his actions to himself.

As he entered, he was startled to see three police officers in his office, but fought back his fear in an effort to portray a figure of authority. The care worker looked on tight-lipped, feeling uncomfortable with the situation, but equally intrigued.

The detective introduced herself and the other officers, "Mr. Brent I understand that you are the Warden here?"

Brent responded calmly, "Yes that's right officer. I was told that there had been an accident. What's going on?"

The officer responded, "Actually Mr. Brent it's more like an incident. We are investigating an allegation of indecent assault against a young girl called Shirley. One of your residents I believe."

Brent felt his breathing become laboured, the butterflies starting to fly around his stomach, "Ah, young Shirley, a bit of a habitual liar I am afraid. A very troubled young girl that we have had lots of problems with. In fact, we have reported her missing again since yesterday. Is that, not right?" he looked towards his colleague in the room for support.

The detective raised her hand to indicate that she was not looking for a response. "We are investigating serious allegations which have been made against you Mr. Brent......"

Brent interrupted. "But that's preposterous officer."

The detective raised her hand again, "Mr. Brent, can you tell me what you have inside your jacket pocket please?"

Brent glared at her, he was being looked upon with contempt by a woman of all things, and he didn't like it, "What on earth are you talking about?"

The officer persisted, "Mr. Brent, if you don't show me what you have in your inside pocket, I will arrest you, following which you will be searched anyway so it's a matter for you."

Brent reached inside and produced his wallet before being prompted, "And the rest please Mr. Brent." The officer knew that she was taking a gamble.

From inside his pocket Brent removed a twelve-inch wooden ruler with bevelled edges, well-worn, which to the untrained eye appeared to have some red marks engrained in the wood.

The officer both saw and smelt blood, "Before we go any further Mr. Brent, I would like you to show me what you have in your desk drawer?"

Brent made one last effort at regaining control, "Do you have a search warrant officer?"

She smiled at him through gritted teeth, "No we don't but I am quite happy to sit here with you whilst one of the officers gets one if that's what you'd like to do. Should take about an hour I suppose. We could have a cup of tea perhaps whilst we wait?"

Without speaking Brent walked slowly to his desk and opened the drawer – inside was a shortened cane.

Brent was arrested and taken to the local station. Upon arrival he was allowed to make one call to a friend. There were not many choices.

Richard Brent later sat in an interview room with his solicitor who could think of at least a dozen places he would prefer to have been on a Saturday evening. The 'brief' was well-known to the local officers and whilst he was an absolute gentleman to their faces, he had a reputation for being something of a slippery customer.

The female detective had played everything straight down the line and was confident of a result. She took the lead whilst Sally sat making notes in her pocketbook. About ten minutes into the questioning there was a tap at the interview room door and a member of the local CID, Detective Sergeant James Hargreaves, poked his head around the door.

The officers turned from their chairs, irritated that the *'interview in progress – do not disturb'* sign had been ignored.

Hargreaves beckoned them outside, like a schoolteacher summoning his pupils, and made short work of the conversation, "Good to see you both. I'm James Hargreaves. I've been asked to take over this case by our Head of CID. As you well know this one is on our Force jurisdiction. You've done a really good job, but I'll take it from here thanks."

Clearly Brent's 'friend' or his solicitor had made some phone calls – there was no way out of the fact they were 'trespassing' in another Force area.

Another CID officer stood uncomfortably shuffling his feet in the cell block corridor waiting to go into the interview. He likewise could think of better places to be and didn't like shafting his colleagues, but he knew his place and avoided eye contact with the female detective who was visibly flushed.

Sally and the detective knew it would be futile to protest, passed their paperwork and exhibits over and left the cell block to lick their wounds and find the nearest pub.

Hargreaves asked his 'bag-man' to wait in the corridor whilst he went inside and shook the hands of the solicitor warmly, addressing him on first-name terms. Things were looking up for Brent.

Fifteen minutes later Hargreaves summoned the officer in, and an interview took place during which Brent admitted administering corporal punishment using the cane and nothing more. He was charged and bailed purely with assault, albeit suspended from his post pending the outcome of his court case.

***

Brent's solicitor was confident that his client would be acquitted and at his initial appearance at the magistrates court Brent pleaded 'not guilty' and elected to go to trial at the Crown Court.

Brent duly appeared at Warwick Crown Court, but on the day of the hearing fate took a sudden turn as the sitting Judge was taken ill and rushed off to hospital.

As confusion reigned for a short time the expectations were that the trial would be adjourned, however a visiting female Judge became available at short notice to stand in and the proceedings were set to start at 2pm.

Prior to the jury being sworn in, the Judge addressed both counsel and the defendant in the court and made it plain that having read the case papers it was abundantly clear that the indictment was not an accurate reflection of the allegations which should be put to the jury. Despite protestations from the defence barrister she insisted that a charge of indecent assault should also be added.

The jury were duly sworn in.

The prosecution case was outlined and Shirley was brought into court in the company of a social worker to give her evidence – she was a star witness in every regard, compelling, clear in every respect, and above all believable, as the hushed court and the jury hung on her every word.

The defence barrister chose not to cross examine Shirley, and as the court proceedings were adjourned for the day he went into a huddle with his client and the solicitor.

Next morning the court proceedings recommenced and as the police officers in the case prepared themselves to give evidence the defence barrister made an application for the charges on the indictment to be put to Brent again.

Richard Brent then pleaded guilty to both counts having been advised by his defence that the very worst sentence he would get would be a suspended sentence given his previous good character.

Brent was ordered to take a seat in the dock whilst Hargreaves was summoned to take the stand in order to read out Brent's antecedent history. The officer misjudged the atmosphere in court and made a mistake by stressing how co-operative and apologetic the defendant had been whilst in custody.

The Judge visibly frowned at him over her glasses before dismissing him from the witness box and listening to mitigation from his counsel.

To add insult to injury she asked for the two female arresting officers to be brought into court and publicly praised them for their professionalism.

Hargreaves glared at the busybody women from the city who had poked their noses where they weren't wanted and caused him such a problem.

Finally, the judge ordered Brent to stand. By now the man was shaking and needed to steady himself by holding onto the handrails of the dock. He had a bad feeling about what was to come.

There was no mercy shown in the summing up or sentence by the Judge;

"This was without doubt some of the most depraved and wicked behaviour imaginable, inflicted on a young and innocent girl who will be scarred by the incident for the rest of her life. You are a disgrace to your profession. On the first count of indecent assault you will go to prison for three years. On the separate count of assault, you will go to prison for two years, the sentences to run consecutively making a total of five years. But for the fact that you have no previous convictions it would have been longer. Take him down."

Brent swayed as he faced the prospects of five years in prison and had to be assisted down the steps of the dock to the cells below by two burly police officers.

Outside the court, Shirley, who had been waiting with the social worker, hugged the two female officers whilst Hargreaves slid past them and headed for a phone box outside the court. He had some explaining and damage limitation to do and he wasn't looking forward to the next conversation.

The Judge's words of praise for the two officers never reached the ears of any senior officer and the case was closed.

***

Charles Redmund had a busy schedule. Elections were always at the back of his mind and the constant need to create opportunities to 'press the flesh' were uppermost in his thoughts. However, his luncheon appointment with the new local Director of Social Services was a must.

Redmund had gone out of his way to forge a good working relationship with the man, showing support for his endeavours at being seen as something of a pioneer in the way in which youngsters in the care of the Social Services were supported.

The Director had given a number of presentations at international conferences and was already a key member of an influential Government Working Party on the subject of childcare. He and Redmund were men on the up in life.

The purpose of their meeting was for the Director to confirm that a robust review had taken place following the arrest of Brent, which had revealed nothing more than that this was a man who had experienced a temporary loss of control, totally out of character.

The terms of reference defined by the Director, which was conducted internally by one of the Assistant Directors, had been carefully crafted and narrowly defined. Above all, no taint from the case would be allowed to get anywhere near his own 'august' person. This aligned precisely with

149

Redmund's concern that no wider investigation into the Home should be conducted.

Brent had helpfully declined an invitation to assist with the review in any way from his prison cell and had kept his mouth firmly shut.

Shortly after being incarcerated he had received a visit from a nameless young man with a London accent, who had reassured him that he had not been abandoned and that there were people who would watch over him in prison and financially support him when he was released. It had all been a terrible mistake and it was time to move on. The stranger stressed however that the price to pay for this was silence – for life. There was something about the man that left Brent under no illusion that the alternative to keeping quiet would be unpalatable.

Shortly after the report was published, Brent was moved to an open prison. Academia duly returned to Brent's life and he spent his days as the prison librarian.

Redmund insisted on paying for the meal and at the conclusion stood up and shook the Director's hand warmly, "Well done. It would have been a great shame to have tarnished all of your good work due to actions of one man. Next time you are down in London let me know and we can have lunch in the House."

Chapter Six

'There Was A Crooked Man'

The thing about power, even for a big fish in a little pool, is that it can bring with it complacency, and Ernest Page was fast developing this flaw, a dangerous one given his proclivities. In his professional life he had future aspirations to become the Mayor of the City of Birmingham, and had developed a reputation for achieving results. To enable this, he had constructed a network of 'fixers' around him, some of whom were paid with 'favours' and some occasionally in cash. They included businessmen, bankers, magistrates, members of the clergy, and crucially a couple of 'friendly' police officers with rank who could 'pull strings' when necessary.

Likewise, he in turn was 'looked after' by much bigger fish every month to ensure that their interests were best served.

His wife wanted for nothing and together they regularly attended official council functions. Although there was not much between her ears, she was an attractive woman, some years younger than Page, who doted on the man, a man who was made undeniably more attractive by being a 'somebody'. They were childless, but Page had addressed this by buying her two miniature Yorkshire Terriers to shower her affections on. To the outside world they were a successful, happy, and contented couple.

In his 'other life' things could not have been more different. He had told his wife that he was a member of a secret committee which was required to meet regularly during evenings when matters of state were discussed. This ensured that he had free rein to come and go as he pleased, and whilst much of Page's unlawful sexual activity was centred on the Cadets, he had also developed a taste for the risky enterprise of unprotected sex with men in public toilets. Page was addicted to the thrill and felt himself to be untouchable.

It was mid-afternoon and Ernest Page had finished his council business early. The sun was shining, and he had decided that a trip to the infamous public toilets at Stonebridge Island, on the way to Coventry, would be a nice end to a productive day. It was a forty-minute drive away, but predators are driven people and Page was, among many things, a predator. It was also far enough away, and visited by travellers from far and wide, to afford him a degree of anonymity.

He parked his car up in a nearby layby and entered the toilets with a growing sense of anticipation and excitement.

There were already two men standing at the urinals and it was obvious from the occasional groaning noises coming from inside that one of the cubicles was occupied. Page assumed that the noises meant that some sexual activity was taking place, although the accompanying sounds of flatulence should have told him otherwise.

Pages nostrils flared but he resisted the urge to walk out and positioned himself in the vacant urinal in between the two men, who were already openly masturbating.

He smiled at each in turn and then reached out and started to play with the two men at the same time. He entered a world of sexual arousal where the sights and smells around him were completely blocked out. His sole purpose now was to entice at least one of the two strangers into a spare cubicle with a view to having quick, rough, hard sex to satisfy his craving.

Suddenly the door of the occupied cubicle swung open and a smart young man wearing a suit, and in his twenties, emerged, still in the process of tucking his shirt in.

Page liked the look of what he was seeing but completely misjudged the situation, "Do you want to join us?' he smiled.

His intended victim reacted, "You dirty bastards. I wouldn't touch any of you with a barge-pole."

Page smiled, assuming that the man was just engaging in some sort of fantasy – playing 'hard to get', why else would he be in this toilet? Unfortunately for Page, the man was a travelling salesman on his way home to Manchester and had never heard of the unsavoury reputation of Stonebridge Island toilets. In fact, the salesman had genuinely found himself in danger of 'touching cloth' as a result of a sudden bout of diarrhoea and had been forced to make an emergency stop at the toilets.

Page persevered, "Come on big boy – show us your cock."

The man recoiled, "I'll see you in court first you little cunt" and brushed past him and the other two men, out into the fresh air.

The 'penny had still not dropped' with Page who shrugged off the rejection and focussed on the job in hand. Fifteen minutes later he was back outside himself and heading towards his car. As he started to open the front door, he heard someone behind him and turned to see the man in the suit, who was clearly furious, "I've got your registration number you cunt. You can expect a visit from the police, and I'll be making a statement no worries."

The younger man squared up to Page willing him to start something, but Page retreated into his vehicle without saying a word and drove off in a state of panic.

On the way home he stopped at a public phone box and made a call to the police ally that he knew would not be averse to some cash, no questions asked. He needed some 'damage limitation', and quick. The publicity would be disastrous for his political aspirations. It was alright for effeminate pop stars like that David Bowie to strut around professing their bisexuality, and get applauded for it, but the voters of Birmingham would not give Page a jot of support.

The man at the other end of the phone was less than impressed with the Councillor's story, in fact it disgusted him, but he had no problem agreeing a price for his efforts. That price would be five hundred pounds, and the knowledge of Page's 'little secret' would be stored away for future use as necessary.

Within twenty-four hours the officer was able to confirm that a complaint of importuning for immoral purposes had in fact been made and was in the early stages of investigation.

He had two pieces of good fortune. A like-minded detective friend worked at the Warwickshire nick that covered the toilets, and the investigation, such as it was, had been given to a Probationer with six months service.

The officer invested £100 of the £500, and his accomplice had no problem 'taking over' the enquiry from the *'sprog'* officer.

The Warwickshire detective was an old hand at this sort of thing and let the report moulder in his desk drawer for a few weeks. In his experience, once the heat of the moment had passed, many complainants became reluctant to bother when confronted with the possibility of the inconvenience of court.

Eventually he wrote a letter to the effect that unfortunately his enquiries into 'this serious matter' had not borne fruit. Either the registration number had been incorrectly recorded, or, more likely, the vehicle had borne false plates. He assured the complainant that the case would remain open and he would follow every possible lead and let him know if anything further transpired. He offered his name and phone number at the office should the victim wish to discuss matters further.

The detective waited for a month for a response, then, with a smile he altered two letters in the recorded registration number and finalised the report, 'no trace, no further enquiries possible'. The crime report joined the thousands of others in a box gathering dust in the archives.

'Easiest ton I've ever earnt', the detective reflected later over a pint.

***

Brenda Doyle was if nothing else a loving mother. She was a formidable figure, both in terms of size, and the ability to give anyone who interfered with her family the most ferocious of tongue lashings or worse. Normally the mere threat of sticking her opponent's heads 'up their arses' as far as they would go was enough to quell debate.

Her hair was normally pinned back behind her

155

ears with grips but although she was worn down and weary, looking older than her years, there remained the glint of a zest for life hidden at the back of her eyes. The new fashion of wearing 'hot pants' were however not an option for Brenda.

Before meeting her two dark lovers, she had initially lived in the rented front room of a neighbour's house in the early 50's, cooking most of her meals on an open fire, before finally working her way up the local council housing list.

Her council house in the middle of a run-down estate in Balsall Heath, although sparse in terms of furniture, was always clean and tidy, and she carried on with both her obsession with tidiness, and being careful with money, even after she had moved into the Handsworth house with Ses and Bud. It seemed to her that there was plenty of cash about, but the 'brothers' seemed to spend it as if it burnt their hands. They certainly enjoyed their 'earnings'.

Brenda's one vice was cigarettes, she was a constant smoker but was trying to cut down on the *'Woodbines'*, which were less than affectionately known as *'coffin nails'*.

One could be forgiven for thinking that she never ate herself but there was always a pint of *'Sterra'* in a glass bottle on the kitchen table waiting to quench Stewart's thirst. Sterilised milk lasted longer than fresh milk and more importantly was cheaper.

As Brenda would often comment, *'water costs nothing',* and no effort was spared in keeping the child, plus Ses and Bud for that matter, clean. The constant presence of a packet of *'Tide'* washing powder, and the line of freshly washed clothes all hung with long wooden pegs, in the cobbled yard

156

outside, were a testament to her efforts as was the rigorous and thorough daily mopping of the front step.

She had done her best to brighten the house by applying bright yellow wallpaper which had massive daisies and sunflowers on it, to one wall.

In short there was nothing *'Cathy Come Home'* about Brenda – she was as solid and durable as the metal dustbin that stood outside the front door, the comparison being that Brenda also spent time trying to keep the lid on her life.

She did however have three other weaknesses – one was a liking for very strong-built Jamaican men, and the second an inability to use any form of effective contraception, "Them rubber Johnnies are no good for me – I want to feel the real thing" she would comment – and she did so on a fairly regular basis. Luckily the complications from Stewart's birth had granted her what she thought of as 'divine contraception', It was God's will. Her regular attendance at the local Bingo Hall was the third.

Brenda was well aware that some of her white neighbours called her a 'slag' behind her back and on one occasion she had dog excrement pushed through her letterbox. Unfortunately for the individual they couldn't resist gossiping about it and when Brenda found out she didn't hesitate to drag the woman by her hair out into the street before rubbing her nose in the offending deposit which she had saved specially.

Brenda's thought it another blessing from above that her two lovers shared a mutual love for the child and indeed doted on him – when they were home. Their duties and zeal for spending their gains meant that they were absent more than present. Brenda was happy with the situation. They provided for her and Stewart, and clearly loved him. She loved her time alone with the boy, in her 'palace'. It was as much, and more, than she had ever expected from life.

Stewart always had a twinkle in his eyes, loved his mother dearly, and had elected himself to be her eternal protector. If any man should raise a voice in the Doyle household Stewart would take his place at his mother's side – young fists clenched he would brook no threats towards the woman who loved him unconditionally.

As the child grew so did his propensity for trouble, and Doyle started to come within the radar of the local police.

His light brown skin made him a target for the local 'bully boys' who would usually lie in wait at the end of their road. He suffered for his 'difference' from the local white kids and Stewart learnt that bullies needed confronting, even when bigger, and would often take the fight to them.

Brenda's run of divine luck came to an abrupt end one day in 1972 when, during one of these confrontations, Stewart, at the tender age of thirteen years, found himself fighting a much larger boy who through sheer size was starting to get the better of him. Stewart found himself pinned to the floor with the boy straddling him and in a choke hold. The proximity of the boy made him feel claustrophobic and he started to panic.

"Your mum's an Irish whore" the boy spat phlegm into his face.

At this point Stewart reached out instinctively and found a large stone which he promptly battered his tormentor with. Blood pouring from a head wound, the boy ran off screaming whilst Stewart dusted himself off and headed for the sanctuary of home.

Three hours later Brenda Doyle heard a knock at her door and through the frosted glass saw the silhouettes of uniformed police officers. She opened the door and filled the door frame with her body as she surveyed the three officers, two in uniform and one CID. Their paths had crossed before and she knew the one in plain clothes to be a good Protestant and Unionist.

She was alone, Ses and Bud had taken the latest arrival and his cargo to another safe house. She steadied herself for a confrontation, "I don't know what you cunts want but you can get off my clean doorstep and fuck off unless you've got a warrant."

The CID officer smiled thinly at her. Quietly enjoying himself, he spoke in a soft Irish accent, "We've come to arrest Stewart, so either shut your mouth and put the kettle on so we can chat or we'll arrest you for obstruction as well and still take him out on his arse. Then I'll come back and go through this house like 'a dose of salts' and I promise you I'll find some stolen gear here, or even a bit of 'black'." He winked slowly at her – she knew exactly what he meant when it came to drugs, and it wasn't her two lovers. Although a smoker she refused to touch cannabis herself but was aware that this did not extend to Ses and Bud.

Brenda's head was reeling – knock his lights out now, and get arrested, or buy time and hear him out. She decided on the latter.

She turned on her heel and they followed her inside, "Take your fucking hats off in my house," she ordered the uniform officers, as they entered the living room where Stewart was sat in front of the TV.

They meekly complied as Brenda wagged her finger at Stewart and said, "Keep your mouth shut son. I don't know what's going on, but we'll sort it out."

The Irish detective followed her through to the kitchen and shut the door whilst she reluctantly made him a cup of tea. Unfortunately, the opportunity to spit in it failed to materialise as she battled to keep her temper in check.

Cup in hand he finally came to the point, "Your kid's done a wounding and he's well in the shit. Looking at some time away from home I'd say. We've got a kid in hospital with a head the size of a balloon and stitches. He says your lad attacked him for no reason." he paused for effect, "There are bigger fishes to fry though if you get my meaning?"

Brenda looked at him with open disgust – she knew what was coming.

He went on, "Your two boyfriends are up to lots and becoming a bit of a pain for us. We want them out of the way. They fancy themselves as some sort of 'Yardie' gangsters and we're not having it. So, it's simple Brenda, it's them or Stewart. You've been living with em, sharing their bed for years. You know everything, including stuff about their boss, now he's a prize worth having. It's a simple choice. You start talking to us and I'll find a way around young Stewart's problem. There could be some cash in it for you as well. What you doing here amongst these darkies anyway Brenda? You might be a left-footer, but you should stick with your own kind."

He drank deeply from his cup and put it down, "You know what Brenda, you should try a good white 'Protty' Irish cock one day – it might not be so bad."

Brenda spat out the words, "I doubt you've

even got more than an inch you bastard. Now you listen. I'm not a grass. Not now. Not ever. So, go and fuck yourself."

She gambled that he was trying his luck and lost.

The officer smiled again, "You know what Brenda, I told my gaffers that you'd say that. It's your choice; your son or your boyfriends. It looks like you've made it."

He turned his back deliberately on her and returned to the living room where he instructed the two officers to take Stewart to a car outside.

Brenda screamed, "Leave him alone – I'll fucking kill you if you touch him."

"Make my day Brenda, I'd love to stick your fat grubby hands into a pair of handcuffs so be my guest." The detective smiled.

The goading bought her to her senses, and she rushed for a coat to go with them.

Her humiliation however became complete as they refused to let her go with them in the police vehicle. Stewart stared pitifully out of the rear window as she was left standing in the middle of the road. She threw her coat to the floor in a rage.

Stewart made the short journey to Thornhill Road police station, and in double-quick time was booked into the custody block, before finding himself alone in a locked Juvenile Detention Room.

Brenda had returned to her house, frantically trying to think what to do. Trying to contact Ses and Bud would be impossible so, mind in a whirl, she headed off down the Soho Road to the 'Hole in The Wall' and banged the door until she got to see Joe. He did the best he could, but by the time his solicitor was on the case her son had already been interviewed with an appropriate adult present.

The CID officer had worked a flanker and told the custody officer that no-one from the family was available. A willing volunteer who lived locally had come in to sit next to the boy. He was an upright citizen who gave his time freely to support the police, for whom he had profound respect. His job was to be present to ensure fair play but not to intervene.

The interview was short and sweet, and Stewart put his hands up to hitting the older boy, signing a statement written by the detective to that effect. What the boy failed to spot was a choice of words which were well beyond his intellectual reach, but which effectively ruled out any possibility of claiming self-defence. Basically, he had been, 'done like a kipper'.

Brenda and the solicitor found themselves fretting, being kept waiting in the public reception area of the station. Finally, the protestations of the solicitor about being denied access to her client reached the point at which they were both taken through to the custody block where Stewart stood completely bemused in front of the custody sergeant's desk.

The solicitor tried in vain to exert her authority but failed at the first post, "I want to make an official complaint about my client being denied access to a solicitor."

The custody sergeant was in no mood to tolerate her, and in any event disliked defence solicitors immensely. They made his life difficult and he always reciprocated if he got the chance.

Leaning forward from his chair, he swivelled the large white-papered custody sheet around in front of her and pointed to an entry where Stewart had declined the offer of having a solicitor present, "You will note," he said, without looking up at her, "that the entry was witnessed by an appropriate adult so please don't waste any more of my time."

The only thing left to do was to witness Stewart being formally charged with an offence of inflicting grievous bodily harm with intent to do so – commonly known as GBH.

Brenda had already been strongly advised to keep quiet by the solicitor and not to risk making matters worse. She stood there watching the world of her 'pride and joy' falling apart, and felt helpless.

Stewart was granted bail with conditions not to approach the victim and was placed on a curfew. But the real nightmare was only just beginning as a Social Services referral was submitted by the detective who wanted more than his 'pound of flesh'. Personal rejection required retribution and Brenda Doyle was going to get it in spades, he smiled to himself, 'to match the two she lived with'.

Her life was now under the spotlight of social workers who would examine every aspect of her family looking for dysfunctionality, abuse, neglect or risk.

Being a single parent, with two 'fathers' of less than reliable and salubrious lifestyle for the child, Brenda was a prime target. Whilst the social workers naturally erred towards the 'left' of life, in terms of their opinions about social order, they were faced with hard evidence from the police that Brenda was struggling to maintain order within her family group. The police also stressed that the child was being regularly exposed to contact with individuals who they knew to be engaged in serious crime. Even for liberal social workers, the concept of black and white cohabiting took some getting used to and placed an extra burden on the boy.

Behind the scenes the vindictive detective held several informal meetings with some key social workers; in fact, he even managed to cajole one female into having a few drinks with him after work, and he laid it on thick. He was enjoying himself and even saw the potential for a 'leg over' if he played his cards right.

Stewart duly appeared at the Juvenile Court in Newton Street, Birmingham, and was advised by his solicitor to plead guilty. Despite her outwardly aggressive stance towards the police she picked up a lot of casual legal aid from a select number of officers who would phone her 'out of hours' to represent people in custody. This case had no potential and she didn't see any point in rocking the boat and risking the loss of her 'unofficial retainer'. It was important to enjoy good relationships with police and criminals alike.

Brenda sat next to her son as the facts were read out to the magistrates in court by an equally disinterested solicitor appointed by the police to present the case. The detective sat at the back, a picture of seriousness and quiet authority, waiting to give the boy's antecedent history. He was the law and fighting to protect society – a man whose words held authority.

They made Stewart out to be a burgeoning local 'hard knock', and the look of contempt from the Chair of the Bench as he peered over his glasses in the oak-lined room said it all. Stewart's fate was sealed. The Magistrate had very fixed ideas about mixing the races and knew for a fact that the progeny of such relationships turned into 'bad sorts'.

The case was duly adjourned for three weeks for social enquiry reports to be prepared, due to the serious nature of the crime.

Brenda expected the worst but in fact the outcome was disastrous.

When he reappeared at court he was made the subject of a probation order for two years but running parallel to this the Social Services determined that Brenda was not a fit and proper mother, and that Stewart was at particular risk given his mother's association and residence with two known criminals.

Stewart Doyle was to be placed into the care of the Local Authority.

The departure from home was always going to be a painful process, but to dig the knife in deep the detective arranged for uniform officers to be present on the day that social workers called to take him away. Brenda was outgunned and no amount of abuse or threats would affect the outcome. Her boy had been taken from her.

Stewart was a problem from the start, rebellious and resentful, and after being passed from 'pillar to post' in various residential homes in Birmingham he found himself outplaced at Richmond House in Redditch, which had a reputation for instilling discipline.

***

Paul Evans looked on with interest as Stewart Doyle stood before him in his office, with his personal belongings in a simple cardboard box, containing not much more than a few precious black and white photos of his mother, and some clothing that had seen better days.

Stewart had been collected from a home in Birmingham by John Baxter who had pointed him towards the rear of the Transit van and travelled back in silence to Redditch.

He had studied the boy through the rear mirror as they drove – he liked what he saw and was relishing what was to come. He rather enjoyed 'breaking in' a difficult customer.

Evans started the easy way – it was a well-rehearsed process, as with soothing words he explained the rules and regulations to Stewart. They were there to look after him, to support him, to stand next to him, and to help him. They would be the closest thing that he had to parents.

The words tripped off the tongue, meaningless phrases that were designed to put the boy off balance.

Stewart was already becoming institutionalised and dying inside a little bit at a time as the weeks and different Homes went past. His mother struggled to get to see him on a regular basis and he was feeling more and more alone – at odds with a world that was constantly punishing him for the colour of his skin.

At the end of the speech by Evans it was the turn of Baxter.

He took the box gently from the boy's hands and placed it on the table in front of him, "We just need to check that you don't have any drugs, cigarettes, porn mags or knives on you. We run a tight ship here."

Stewart Doyle already knew enough about the system to keep his mouth shut.

Baxter tipped the contents of the box onto the table and with one finger disdainfully shifted the contents around. He spotted a photo of Stewart with his mother. Carefully he held it in front of Stewart's face and then in a flash he ripped it into pieces and let them drop to the floor.

Baxter said, "You don't need that crap here. We are your family now."

Stewart snapped "You fucker. You can't do that."

He bent down to pick up the pieces at which point Baxter deftly gripped his hair before slapping him hard on the face, "We don't tolerate violence here boy, or bad language. You might have got away with it with those soft tossers in Birmingham, but you won't here. There's just one way to survive and it's our way. Now pick up your things and follow me."

Evans remained seated and motionless watching the scene play out – just another boy – just another victim – just another day in paradise.

Stewart fought back his tears and anger and followed Baxter to the 'matron's' room – a grand title for a woman who was well-past her sell-by date and enjoyed a regular afternoon tipple before sleeping it off as the world passed her by.

After a cursory examination, which included gripping his mouth in a vice-like hold to examine his teeth, like a farm animal being bought, he was despatched with Baxter to one of the dormitories where his bed was allocated, and his box secured.

Baxter hadn't quite finished, "Right Stewart. Next stop the shower room. We pride ourselves on cleanliness here so look sharp and follow me."

Stewart felt a sense of dread envelop him – this man was strong, powerful and in control. He was beginning to sense that there were no boundaries here, and it was disquieting.

Inside the shower-block Baxter closed the door behind them, flicking the catch down to make sure that they wouldn't be disturbed, "Strip off" he ordered, "Get yourself in the shower. I want to see plenty of soap going in the places you normally miss."

Stewart hesitated before being prompted, "Come on we don't have all day. I've seen loads of little dicks before so one more isn't going to make any difference. Get your kit off."

Stewart stumbled out of his clothes under the watchful eye of Baxter. As he stood shaking with a mixture of cold and embarrassment Baxter nudged him into the shower – all the time carefully noting the contours of the boy's body. This was turning out to be a good day.

Once the humiliation of the shower process had been completed Baxter proceeded with the first steps of the boy's initiation.

"Last thing then Stewart, just bend over and face the other way. I just need to check that you're not hiding something up your arse." Baxter smiled.

Stewart complied and felt Baxter's ugly large hands remain on the cheeks of his bottom, where they lingered for an eternity before he was dismissed summarily and told to return to the dormitory.

Feeling a sense of mounting relief Stewart went back to his bed and sat down mentally exhausted. As he did so he fell through the mattress onto the floor – someone had removed the base supporting slats.

Two other older lads in the room that had been specially briefed by Baxter smiled cheekily at Stewart - just two more tormentors to add to the growing list. They were part of the Home's cadet detachment and in a normal environment they would have been regarded as 'school bullies' but having been subjected to grooming for months, both were now willing participants in something much more evil.

***

For Stewart Doyle there was to be no respite. After fixing his bed and a fitful first night he woke up to something wet splashing on his face and upper body. One of the older boys was standing over his prone body urinating.

As Doyle came to his senses and struggled to get out of the bed he lashed out and landed a lucky kick in the boy's groin, sending him crashing to the floor gasping for breath.

Doyle got to his feet, urine dripping from his hair, as the second lad advanced on him adopting a boxing pose. Stewart Doyle did not play by *'Queensbury Rules'* and hurled a chair at him from the side of the bed before grabbing him in a 'bear hug'. He knew that he had to deal with this second challenge quickly so as not to be facing two of them at the same time so neatly head-butted him causing his nose to split and blood to spurt out, covering them both.

Doyle surveyed the carnage in the room and bawled at two other boys who had remained transfixed in their beds, "Do you fuckers want some as well?" – there were no takers.

Turning to his attackers he spat out the words, "Leave me alone. I won't take any shit from you and if you manage to beat me once I'll just keep coming back for more. I'll be your fucking nightmare!"

Doyle stumbled from the room and headed for the shower room to wash the blood and urine off his body. He had been at the Home for less than twenty-four hours.

In the days that followed, his tormentors

169

avoided direct confrontation, preferring instead to play on Doyle's nerves. None of his personal possessions survived for long as they were either damaged, or simply went missing. He was constantly on his guard against further attacks and became increasingly tired and depressed. On one occasion he climbed into his bed only to find that someone had defecated in it – he was feeling desperate but knew that he could not show weakness.

After two weeks Baxter switched tactics and moved Doyle's tormentors to another room, replacing them with two quieter boys who displayed some sympathy towards him.

Not long afterwards Doyle returned from some lessons to find a complete Army Cadet uniform laid out on his bed. Doyle opened a sash window and threw it to the ground below. He had no intention of playing any of their games.

Baxter however made it clear that it would be in the boy's best interests to get some discipline drilled into him and he had been selected to join the army cadets. Doyle refused point-blank.

The following day his two protagonists were re-introduced into his room and his life of misery recommenced.

A week later the uniform re-appeared on his bed and it again found its way out of the window.

The cycle of hardship versus the hand of friendship continued until several weeks later when the uniform was physically presented to Doyle with a direct instruction that he be dressed and ready to go with the other cadets by 7pm that day. If he refused, they would ensure that he remained in care until he was eighteen and would not see his mother again. There were to be no further discussions on the matter and at that moment Doyle's resolve crumbled.

At 7pm he duly presented himself at the van which was waiting outside the main door of the Home with Evans and Baxter waiting. He was feeling itchy and uncomfortable in the battle-dress uniform and his dishevelled state drew broad grins from the other cadets. Doyle gritted his teeth and got in.

After a thirty-minute drive they arrived at the Harris Grange Army Cadet Force detachment and whilst the others made their way to the parade ground, Doyle was guided by Evans to the office of the Commanding Officer, Peter Hall.

Hall had already been briefed about the boy but held his sexual urges in check. There would be plenty of time for that in the future. Doyle avoided the instinct to physically wince as Hall launched into him with 'both barrels' berating him for his turn-out. He would have to learn to do better.

Doyle was then taken by Evans to join in a drill session outside where he quickly became the butt of sly jokes from his fellow cadets, as he made a valiant attempt to follow the orders. He heard the word 'coon' muttered from one of the cadets in the row in front of him and choosing his moment he punched the individual hard in the back of the neck. The boy went down like a 'sack of potatoes', hit the ground hard, and stayed there.

Mayhem broke out as Doyle delivered punches and kicks indiscriminately to anyone who got near him. It took Evans and four other cadets to hold him down on the floor until the arrival of Hall who glowered at him, "What the fuck are you doing you little bastard. No-one but me strikes anyone here. Do you understand?"

Doyle looked the man square in the eyes and

171

said, "I was forced to wear this uniform and to come here and if I am forced again, I'll do the same thing every time."

With that Doyle started to strip off and throw the uniform on the floor until he was left standing on the parade in his underpants.

That was the end of Stewart Doyle's tenure with the Army Cadets and despite receiving a beating from Baxter on his return to the Home he felt alive again – they could take his body, but they could never take his spirit.

***

For Stewart Doyle, each day living at Richmond House was one of misery. After the fight at the cadets he had learnt to deflect the attentions of Paul Evans who largely left him alone. Evans was something of a coward and had come to realise that despite all the beatings Doyle had the potential to inflict damage which he didn't want to be on the end of – there were plenty of other smaller and weaker fish in the sea.

John Baxter however was a different 'kettle of fish' and the harder Stewart tried to fend him off, the more the man got off on the brute force he was able to exert.

Baxter's routine was to line up a select group of boys in their pyjamas before deciding who needed an extra shower prior to bedtime. Baxter would play on the boys' nerves until the very last minute, seemingly selecting a victim before changing his mind and picking another.

Mind games were his speciality, and whilst together the boys might have been able to present a united front to resist him, none of them was prepared to take the lead.

Sometimes Baxter would choose two boys

who would be pressured into providing 'a show' before he joined in.

On this particular night Baxter again chose Stewart Doyle who found himself being marched off to the shower block by the scruff of his neck, whilst those left behind shed a sigh of relief with the exception of one boy who literally wet himself through sheer fright and relief at not being chosen.

Once inside, the ritual was repeated as Doyle stripped and entered the shower.

"Plenty of soap boy" Baxter barked, "I'll be joining you in a minute."

Stewart Doyle felt the anger rising in him – all consuming.

His mother had visited him that day, but she knew nothing of his plight as shame and fear had always blended to maintain his silence. He was desperate to go home and desperate for this torture to end – he felt so alone.

Doyle turned to face the wall and gently increased the flow of hot water whilst being careful to keep the jet away from his body.

He knew that Baxter would not be able to resist the view and just as he felt the proximity of the man behind him, he suddenly turned and fired a jet of hot water full into Baxter's face. The man screamed and instinctively tried to protect himself with his hands as Doyle increased the heat to the maximum.

In that moment Doyle neatly punched Baxter hard in the testicles and the man went down hard on the tiled floor, with the boy now towering above him.

As his head hit the floor blood started to spurt from a large cut and Baxter slipped into unconsciousness.

Doyle wrenched the shower from its wall

fitting and used it to pummel Baxter's body several times before finally using the heel of his right foot to smash into the prone man's head.

With blood mingling freely with water the shower room was starting to resemble a scene from a horror movie, as Doyle sensed freedom and dashed back to the dormitory for his clothes.

The other boys looked on, not wishing to get involved as they watched him head for the door with one parting shot, "You bunch of bum-bandits. Go fuck yourselves, I'm off."

***

Stewart Doyle's freedom lasted less than eight hours.

After initially hiding in a void building nearby for several hours, Stewart made his way home on foot through driving rain and arrived soaked to the skin, and exhausted, at the front door just before 6am.

As he was about to knock the door his moment of elation evaporated into desperation when two police officers emerged from the shadows, one of them holding an Alsatian on a tight lead.

"Don't fuck about son. We go quietly or you're going to feel this boy's teeth on your arse." he ordered Doyle, who raised his hands in submission. He was bundled into the back of a dog van, one half shared by the dog and the other his temporary prison.

Upstairs in the house Brenda Doyle stirred for a moment as she thought that she had heard voices. She had been literally yards away from her son and didn't know it. He had not been able to reach her, and she had not been there to tell him that everything was going to be alright.

Later that day Stewart Doyle was charged with wounding with intent on John Baxter and kept in custody.

The evidence provided by Baxter, and supported by Paul Evans, was that Doyle had committed a totally unprovoked attack after being disturbed trying to steal food from the kitchen. Doyle was alleged to have thrown boiling water from a kettle over Baxter, and Evans gave a witness statement to the effect that he had found Doyle standing over Baxter using a broken chair leg to strike him before threatening him and running off.

To add to Doyle's troubles, Baxter was left with a burn mark to his face, the veritable 'mark of Cain' and the loss of one of his testicles following surgery to repair the damage caused by the punch in the shower.

The evidence was compelling, and ultimately, he was found guilty at Crown Court by a jury who recorded a unanimous verdict.

His previous conviction sealed his fate, and as Brenda, Ses and Bud sat despondently in the public gallery, the Judge sentenced Stewart to four years to be served in one of Her Majesty's Borstal institutes.

Nearby, Baxter and Evans looked on, adopting suitably dead pan faces and enjoying every minute of the boy's continuing ordeal.

"Take him down" the Judge ordered after sentenced was passed, and Doyle was flanked by two prison officers. At the top of the steps leading down to the cells below the courts he spotted Baxter and shouted, "Watch your back you bastard I will find you."

He began to struggle violently as he was propelled down the steps and received some short and sharp justice when he was out of the public eye. Inside the court Brenda started screaming at Baxter and Evans. Whilst unaware of the true horror of her son's predicament she understood enough to know that she was looking at two pieces of scum and had to be held back by Ses and Bud as she advanced on the pair.

"Clear the Court!" the Judge ordered two police officers who were stationed at the back of the court, "Any further misbehaviour madam and you will be held in contempt of Court."

Baxter whispered to Evans, "Time for a celebratory drink I think Mr. Evans. No need to rush back to the Home is there? Another few hours and I suspect that Doyle will be getting a good 'rodgering' in a cell later."

***

As Stewart entered the reception area of the Borstal, three burly uniformed prison officers surveyed him with obvious distaste. Another 'Governor Grade' officer took the lead, and after the formalities had been completed he said to Doyle, "We don't like 'kiddie-fiddlers' here so we suggest that you put yourself into the Hospital Wing so that we can keep an eye on you."

Doyle looked aghast; one hell had just been replaced with another, "What do you mean. I've never touched anyone in my life!"

The Governor raised his hand to halt the protest as the officers formed a tighter circle around Doyle, "I've yet to hear anything different in this place Doyle. We have a Borstal which is full of innocent people, so let me add you to the list." He paused and then rammed the point home by waving a folder in his face, "We have reports in here from your previous carers, *'predilection to touch younger residents, whether male or female'* in big red letters. So, I will repeat, Hospital Wing or normal placement

176

– make your choice and be quick."

Doyle made the wrong choice and as he followed a P.O. onto the wing carrying his belongings and fresh bedding, he felt several pairs of eyes burning into his back.

The Prison Officer shouted to one of the onlookers, "We have a new arrival. Make sure he settles in."

"Yes Boss." came the prompt response as the P.O. turned on his heel and left the Wing, leaving the inmates to their own devices. Whether by accident or design no help would be forthcoming.

As Doyle started to arrange his bedding in his cell, he was suddenly aware of movement behind him.

Four inmates hurled themselves at him whilst a fifth closed the door and kept watch.

The inmates proceeded to beat Doyle methodically whilst deliberately avoiding his face. When they had finished one of them bent down and sat on his crumpled body on the floor, "We don't like 'nonces' in here so you can look forward to the same tomorrow," he whispered in his ear.

Fifteen minutes later the prison officer returned to find Doyle vomiting and spitting blood in the toilet, "Solitary or stay on the Wing – your choice Doyle."

***

Stewart Doyle's time in solitary confinement in Borstal shaped him for the rest of his life. He spent his waking hours revisiting the abuse that he had suffered and clinically assessed his abusers repeatedly.

The memories stayed riveted into his brain, every minute of every day, and never left him –

177

Stewart Doyle promised himself revenge every night as he lay in the cell.

After three weeks Doyle was moved from solitary to the Hospital Wing and was actually treated with a degree of kindness by one of the P.Os who seemed to instinctively recognise that there was more to the boy's background than that shown on his records.

Stewart spent his days mopping floors and serving tea in red plastic cups laced with bromide, but he survived as the months passed, and his hatred ate away inside, corroding and destroying the innocent boy that had once been.

Chapter Seven

'Pop Goes the Weasel'

Terry Sharpe, aka *'Angel'* to his friends and associates, was out scouting again around London's mainline railway stations. He was looking for the tell-tale signs of young runaways seeking to escape to the bright lights of London, where the music scene was vibrant and stars like 'Ziggy Stardust' had been breaking the mould and boundaries of a stale society - until Bowie killed him off.

The word *'Angel'* certainly had nothing to do with Terry's character, more it was a reference to the motif that was usually found imprinted on the LSD tablets which he sold in pubs and clubs around the alleyways of Soho.

Terry was a product of Bearwood in Birmingham, and as an established 'rent boy' had spent a number of his teenage years circling New Street Station, looking for clients who he either took to the public toilets on the station overbridge, or the Victorian underground toilets in Station Street, at the junction with Hill Street. For special clients he reserved the area adjacent to the lift-shaft on the upper floor of the multi-story car park of St. Jude's nearby. He was never short of business as 'punters' mixed freely with nearby theatre-goers.

The tampon which Terry regularly inserted into his anus, due to muscle loss of the sphincter, was testament to his popularity among Birmingham's casual gay-sex community, but all good things had to come to an end.

Terry had seen the writing on the wall, as the

attitude of British Transport Police had hardened towards him. He didn't do civility very well, and several times his inability to keep his mouth shut and to comply when asked to leave the station had led to his arrest for 'trespass and refusing to quit'. Whilst the court appearances and fines were a relatively minor inconvenience, he was aware that the spotlight was starting to shine brighter, and hotter, on him.

The final straw came as one of the CID officers on the 'railway police' gave him an ultimatum – sign up to being an informant with the promise of some degree of protection, or find himself getting locked up for importuning for immoral purposes with the prospect of some serious jail time.

Terry, now in his early twenties, decided that, all things being equal, he was getting a bit old to be exploited, and it was about time he made a fresh start and built something a bit more lucrative. Like many before him, he was drawn to the allure and promises of London and after a few days hanging around Victoria Coach Station, employing his 'skills', he had found an older 'queen' in his late fifties, who was prepared to put him up on the promise of a couple of 'blow jobs' a week, and a bit of 'arse smacking'. It was the sort of rent that 'Angel' was happy to pay.

As Terry became an established figure on the 'rent boy' scene in London he started to build his connections. Everyone wanted drugs and everyone he knew wanted male company – in most cases the younger the better. He was nicely placed to provide both.

His scouting expeditions to the railway stations frequently produced *'fresh meat'*, young lads who were cold, hungry and without shelter who could mostly be manipulated and groomed with the promise of a warm bed and food. Once they had entered the spider's web of vice that Terry was creating, few ever made it back out again, with some becoming drug or alcohol dependant, whilst others were merely beaten into line. Sex and violence were opposite sides of the same coin for Terry, and he revelled in both. There was a market for sadomasochism in London and he serviced some of its needs.

The only shadow on his fast–growing operation was the local competition. He knew that he was being watched and assessed. There had been a couple of run-ins with some street dealers and there was a pack of local hyenas, both young and old that circled the prey at the railway stations. Terry's view was that there was plenty for everyone, but he misjudged the situation, thinking he was just one of many lone dealers and pimps.

He did have an ace up his sleeve that he thought gave him an advantage over the others, provided by one of his regular clients in Birmingham, a local Councillor Ernest Page, who had a particular attraction to very young boys in uniform.

After Terry had announced his departure for London, the Councillor had provided him with the name and phone number of a man whom he was sure would be able to make good use of Sharpe's services, one Charles Redmund. It was only after their first meeting that Terry had realised that the man was in fact a Member of Parliament.

Terry quickly found himself mixing in exalted circles and he liked the feeling. He was oblivious to the fact that his enjoyment with his newly found 'connections' was creating waves in a pool in which he was a very small fish. His presence also brought with it interest from another quarter – the

Metropolitan Police Drug Squad.

***

Detective Sergeant David Rigg and his partner, Detective Constable John Parker, had already chalked up more than twenty commendations for good work between them, and after three years on the Central Drug Squad in London they had obtained a fearsome reputation among some of the local criminal networks.

DS Rigg managed a network of informants who were mainly drugs dealers operating at street level. They gave him information to keep him off their backs and also to take out the opposition, whilst at the same time the two officers took a monthly cut of their drugs profits in cash.

Rigg and Parker were as bent as a pair of *'Fife'* bananas and had the perfect set-up. As the dealers gave each other up to the officers, Rigg and Parker won regular plaudits from their bosses for their arrest and conviction rate. The two also made sure that brown envelopes containing cash were regularly left in the drawers of their immediate supervisors who asked no questions – after all it was just 'beer money' and no harm done. It was how their world worked.

The two detectives also maintained their own stash of drugs for 'rainy days', hiving a little bit off after each raid for when the odd drugs warrant started off with an unexpected blank. They thought nothing of being creative with the recovery of controlled substances, but always made sure that it was one of the youngest and most naïve officers involved in the bust that would find their stash – after all they would know where to tell them to look.

It didn't take long for Terry Sharpe to appear on their radar, more so because he wasn't a Londoner, and the word on the streets was that he was a 'cock-sucker' with a bad attitude and an even worse Brummie accent.

Initially, Rigg and Parker just completed an intelligence report on the newcomer and created a 'flag' on the subject on the Police National Computer. As a 'person of interest' the flag ensured that they would be notified should he come to the attention of another police officer. It gave them a degree of ownership on Sharpe whilst they considered their options, but as his name kept appearing in reports it wasn't long before they decided to act.

Terry's world came crashing down one morning as the front door of the house he lived in with his 'queen' was caved in by Drug Squad officers using a sledgehammer. The officers, accompanied by a couple of uniforms, surged through the ground floor and up the stairs to the shared bedroom before Terry was able to get one leg out of the bed. The room stank of stale farts and the contents of a 'piss-pot' under the bed.

The older 'fat-bellied' man started screaming hysterically in high-pitched tones as he was dragged naked from under the covers but was silenced with a sharp slap across the face by DC Parker. Terry struck a slightly ridiculous pose as he tried to get to his feet wearing just a bright pink pair of skinny underpants, before being handcuffed and made to face one of the bedroom walls. In the intensity of the moment Terry had pissed himself and urine slowly trickled down his legs – humiliation complete.

Once their two prisoners had been secured, DS Rigg waved a search warrant under the older man's nose, which specified that they were looking for controlled drugs, and a search commenced. The corrupt officer had his standby stash with him should they face any difficulties but an informant had already placed an order for a large quantity of LSD tablets, which were to be picked up at the house later that morning, so the detectives were pretty confident that they were going to find some gear. They also had the benefit of knowing that Terry always kept his drugs stash in a plastic bag tied to a pipe behind the toilet cistern in the filthy bathroom on the first floor.

Rigg always did his best to protect his sources until they had outgrown their usefulness, and so they went through the charade of starting a search of the ground floor first.

Apart from piles of magazines depicting gay sex they found nothing, and the glances exchanged between the uniform officers indicated their displeasure at being tied up at this veritable 'shit hole'.

Twenty minutes later that view changed as they moved upstairs, when one of them found Terry's stash and proudly presented it to Rigg, "Sarge we've got the gear!" waving a large clear plastic bag which contained hundreds of Terry's speciality LSD tablets, all of them bearing 'Angel' motifs.

After the two prisoners had been booked into custody the two detectives dismissed their uniform colleagues and went off for a full English breakfast at a local café near to the station. There was no harm in making the prisoners sweat for a bit and the officers functioned better on a full stomach.

Terry was the focus of their attention and the fate of the old fat man rested in his hands. Both men had been denied a solicitor by a friendly custody sergeant who had been on the same recruit intake with Rigg and had shared a few wild nights out

184

together in the past.

Terry was interviewed first by the two officers and was presented with a stark choice – either he rolled over and became an informant or he would be charged with supplying controlled drugs and finish up serving at least five years in prison. He went back into a cell to think things over whilst the officers turned their attention to the 'queen'.

The fat man sat shaking in the interview room as Rigg dumped the plastic bag containing the drugs in front of him, "Your house, your drugs my friend," was Rigg's starter for ten as the shaking intensified.

Despite his denials, Rigg forced the man to open the plastic bag and to examine the contents, "We're not looking at sweeties here my friend, and we are looking at some serious time. Go on have a good look at the filth you're peddling." Parker deliberately ensured that some of the contents were tipped onto the table and the prisoner, hands shaking, was encouraged to put them back into the bag. A spot of forensic linking never did any harm.

At this point the smell in the interview room indicated that the man had lost control of his bowels and the interview was suspended.

Terry was brought back into another interview room. Decision time had arrived. Rigg went for the jugular. "What's it to be then Terry, work with us, make a few quid and have someone watching your back, or a remand in custody and a long stretch. They'll love you inside, but you'll be having your arse fucked for free of course."

Terry had already decided that he wasn't going to prison and put up no resistance. He did not however expect to find himself tested quite so quickly, as Riggs made it clear that the deal was

185

dependant on a sign of good faith before he left the station, "I need a name Terry, and a good one, just to show that we can trust each other. Don't piss about. You will be surprised how easy it becomes once you let go." Rigg paused, "We've got some stuff to do so you'll be going back into a cell for a while and then it's decision time."

To make his point Rigg leant across the table and gripped Terry roughly by the jaw, looking deeply into his eyes, "Do you understand my friend?"

Terry nodded furiously as Rigg released his grip before Parker led him from the room.

It was all part of a well-oiled approach as to how Rigg and Parker dealt with their prisoners, and Terry was left to 'stew' again for a while whilst they went for a 'liquid lunch'.

In the middle of the afternoon Terry was back in the interview room and facing the question again from Rigg. "It's decision time Terry. See if you can whet our appetites. Give us a name."

Terry drew a deep breath, "Charles Redmund. I can give you Charles Redmund the MP."

Suddenly he had the interest of both officers.

After a lengthy discussion, Rigg and Parker wrapped things up as Terry was released on police bail for six weeks 'pending further enquiries', the threat of prosecution remained hanging over his head.

The older 'queen' was persuaded to admit storing the drugs in the house for an unknown friend and was charged. Despite his initial protestations he was reminded that he was the householder, where the drugs had been found, and that a forensic examination of the plastic bag would, if necessary, reveal his fingerprints, whilst hand swabs would reveal traces of the drug. He had been 'royally fucked', but this time there was no pleasure in it for him.

Events moved swiftly after Terry's first encounter with Rigg and Parker, and he did indeed find it easier to provide information as time went on. The officers had made it clear to him that they wanted Redmund on a plate, but in the interim he started removing the local opposition. Terry was paid on results, and as each street dealer was taken out Rigg would make a cash payment which was witnessed by a senior officer. After the paperwork had been completed Rigg would then take Terry away and extract half of the payment to be split between him and Parker. There were never any arguments and Terry knew that he had no choice in the matter. Terry was sanguine about the position he found himself in, after all he was being paid to remove his competitors. He failed to think through the possible 'downside'.

In a matter of weeks, the perfect opportunity presented itself. Redmund had instructed that Terry should arrange for an 'orgy' for himself and some friends, drugs and 'fresh meat' were the order of the day. Little did Terry know, but Redmund was playing a risky game of his own, going outside the 'rules' he was supposed to comply with.

Rigg and Parker were kept abreast of the arrangements at every step of the way and even sourced a cocaine dealer so that the needs of Redmund's associates could be serviced. With up to twenty people attending this was going to take some sorting but the officers knew that a good result was in the offing.

As the day of the party arrived, Terry was given his final instructions. He was to provide a signal to waiting officers by coming to the door of the house that had been rented for the weekend, once the guests had partaken of drugs and the sexual activities had commenced. The lighting of a cigarette and a door left slightly ajar would be the signal to move.

Terry had already been told that he would find himself being arrested, but that this was just to provide him with some cover.

As the party got underway Terry duly gave his signal, and forty officers, mostly in uniform, stormed through the building, securing prisoners and exhibits in their path, as Rigg and Parker brought up the rear. As part of the charade Terry was obliged to punch Rigg whilst the search was underway, before being arrested in a 'violent struggle' which was witnessed by some of the others in custody.

Charles Redmund was found in the act of having anal sex with a twelve-year old boy, who was himself under the influence of drugs and alcohol supplied to him by the MP. Within hours the man faced formal charges, and ruin, as some selective phone calls went into the media. Reporters on some of the London-based dailies paid well for exclusives, and Rigg and Parker were happy to assist.

A number of other people, including Terry, were released on police bail pending further enquiries.

Elsewhere in Whitehall and in other equally 'hallowed' places, as the news spread, the telephones went into overdrive as detailed analysis commenced to assess the potential for collateral damage. Those who operated within the shadows went to work. They had been endangered, without profit to themselves, and damage limitation laced with retribution was on the menu.

***

Charles Stoppard had been a solicitor for more than twenty-five years. Now in his late fifties, whilst small in stature, he had retained the military bearing which had been drilled into him during his service in the Army during the Second World War. Charles had done well, and his potential had been spotted by a senior officer who had tutored him through the ranks. By the end of the war Major Charles Stoppard had a bright future in front of him and a row of medals which indicated that he had smelt death and blood and come through it.

Stoppard had qualified as a criminal lawyer after being demobbed from the Army but regularly wore his regimental tie, was a prominent figure at military reunions, and maintained his contact with the senior officer, long retired, who had set him on the path to success and fulfilment.

He ran his own practice and had a steady supply of criminal cases, many of which found their way to the upper courts for trial. Well-known for his no-nonsense approach, he was respected by the learned counsel whose job it was to secure acquittals for his clients.

Charles Redmund MP had been referred to Stoppard by those he thought friends and protectors, but it was clear to Stoppard's paymasters, that from the weight of the evidence it was a lost cause. Stoppard was under instruction to let the wheels of justice punish Redmund for them. Stoppard made it known in private consultations that their only hope was to obtain a reduced sentence based on mitigating circumstances, and a quick guilty plea.

Redmund was a man of influence who was not used to being directed but he was frantically trying to work out the route of least damage and was facing a stark choice – health or reputation. He had been left in no doubt by Stoppard as to what was expected of him.

The solicitor also had other pressing matters to sort out. He had already commissioned a private investigator, a retired police officer, to look at the circumstances leading up to the raid.

It didn't take long for the investigator to report back. The man had been 'around the block a few times' and quickly identified Terry Sharpe as being the potential police source. He was also able to confirm through the 'old pal's act', that Rigg and Parker were on the radar of Complaints & Discipline for corruption, although nothing had ever been proved.

Armed with this information, Stoppard used the man as an intermediary to set up a meeting with Rigg and Parker in the 'snug' of a pub well away from their usual 'watering holes'. The two detectives, driven by a sense of curiosity, greed and survival, duly attended, although they insisted that prior to any discussions taking place they would be allowed to search both men for recording devices.

The meeting was cordial but short. Stoppard wasn't a man to waste words and he laid out two options to the men who listened intently.

Option one was to make sure that no charges would follow in respect of any other public figures who were still on police bail following the raid. For that they would each be paid two thousand pounds in cash with a promise that Redmund would plead guilty at court, and there would as such be no trial.

Option two would be that Terry Sharpe would be exposed as a police informant and that evidence would be put before the Complaints Department that he had been used by the officers as an 'agent provocateur' to basically 'fit up' Redmund and the others. Redmund would plead not guilty and there would be a full trial during which the defence would call a number of witnesses to support their case. Stoppard also made a couple of allusions to corruption, leaving the two detectives under no illusion that their 'dirty washing' would be aired

Stoppard gave the two detectives just twenty-four hours to provide him with a response, brought them both a double whisky, and then left with his ex-police minder who had earnt himself a bonus.

Rigg didn't take any persuading and Parker followed suit.

Option one was implemented in full and the private investigator met them in due course to deliver two brown envelopes, after confirmation that all the other attendees at the party had been released with no further action taking place and a piece of paper in the form of a cancellation bail sheet to prove it.

Charles Redmund duly appeared at court and pleaded guilty to buggery and possession of controlled drugs. The Judge who sentenced him made a long speech about the horrors of Redmund's despicable acts and how he was going to make an example of him.

As the packed court listened intently, and reporters scribbled furiously away in their notepads, everyone waited for the big one – a crushing sentence that would send a clear message to people in public life that only the highest ethical standards would do.

The message never came, as despite the build-up, the Judge then sentenced Redmund to three years imprisonment. With at least a third-off for good behaviour Redmund would be free within two years to pick his life up again. Disgraced as an MP, he nevertheless had a number of business interests which would be protected whilst he was away. There was the slight trace of a smile on his face as he thanked the Judge for his mercy before being led down the steps of the dock. He quietly congratulated himself on his choice. There was far worse than a spell in an open prison.

Rigg and Parker subsequently received a Commissioner's commendation for professional conduct in relation to the arrest, and less than twelve months later were arrested following a 'sting' operation which uncovered their drugs business. Their aspirations of achieving fame and success as portrayed in the ITV series *'The Sweeney'* in 1975 had ended in disaster. The days of *'Dixon of Dock Green'* had reached an end both on the TV and in reality, as they faced the prospects of a long 'stretch' in prison where 'bent' coppers got marked for special attention.

It wouldn't be long before the Metropolitan Police would be focussed on other priorities as Notting Hill erupted into major street riots, with sixty-eight arrests being made and three hundred and fifty people injured.

For his part Charles Stoppard received grateful thanks from several high-profile figures and enhanced his personal reputation within his circle of friends who paid for him to enjoy a well-earnt holiday in Thailand.

*

Terry Sharpe was really beginning to enjoy himself. In fact, he couldn't believe his luck since landing in London. Here he was, not only protected by the 'Old Bill', but able to use their devolved power to see off his rivals – and get paid for it.

He had begun to get cocky and overconfident, lording it around the honeypots and cornering the best of the young talent. He had been able to develop his lucrative drug network and employ more protection.

There had been a few 'run-ins' but by the time the festive season dawned, Terry was looking forward to a successful New Year.

One December evening he was sat in a café near to Euston Station enjoying a coffee when he saw one of the last irritants on what he was beginning to think of as 'his turf, chatting to two young recent arrivals.

He was tall, thin and gaunt, with hollow cheeks, and looked like a smack addict to Terry's eyes. There was nothing attractive about the effects of heroin use. The most striking thing was his dark hair, spiked like a cockerel's comb and redolent of Rod Stewart.

They had crossed paths on several occasions over the past few months. The problem was, they seemed to be in the same line of business, and this 'Mickey' had proved remarkably resilient, and resistant to the normal methods of removal, to whit being fitted up by Rigg and Parker.

Terry had put him in for pimping and dealing on two occasions and awaited his usual instruction to sell him drugs, which would be speedily followed by the execution of a warrant, Mickey's incarceration, and removal from Terry's path. But there had been silence. At the last meeting he had asked Rigg, who had made it plain that he decided who was locked up, and Terry was to, 'keep his nose out of it and stick with flogging his arse which was what he did best'.

As Terry watched through the steamy café

window, he saw Mickey give the two boys something, then engage in animated conversation. He knew the patter; next they would go off together and the boy's introduction to the seamier side of London life would commence.

'Fuck this' he thought. 'If those two twats can't sort him out, I'll do it myself.' He beckoned two of his cronies across, tearing them reluctantly from their plates of egg and chips. He watched with satisfaction as they disappeared from sight, trailing Mickey and the two boys.

*

Rick Foster surveyed the wreckage that was Mickey Reynolds. He didn't employ Mickey for muscle. He was reliable, loyal, good with the girls and boys, ran a tight ship dealing in the clubs, and most importantly, Rick owned him, lock, stock and barrel.

Rick was not having a good year. Which was a pity, because the previous years, since he had 'signed up' to the 'club', had seen his inexorable rise through the ranks of the underworld. He had successfully harnessed their shadowy power to his information dossiers and contacts. He had also had the most amazing piece of luck in getting in at the basement level of Bowie's rise to fame. Foster had begun working for the controversial and beautiful young man organising logistics, but this had quickly spread to security, tour planning and the provision of just about any legal and illegal desire of the whole entourage. And they had a shedload of desire.

Once he had a foot in the door of that world, he had been used by other rock stars. The money had flowed in torrents and had been put to good use. But it was working for Ziggy Stardust that had proved to be the real coup because the 'Starman' drew teens, especially fascinated boys, like moths to light, and Rick had the keys to his door, for a price. The arrangement had allowed him to harvest for both himself and his employers.

Then it had all come crashing down on the night of July 3rd, 1973. Bowie had unexpectedly announced his 'retirement' on the stage of Hammersmith Odeon, Rick found himself 'no longer required', and other unsavoury events had caused him to circle the wagons and review his status.

And now some tosser from Birmingham was lording it around Rick's 'manor', interfering with business, and daring to give one of his own a kicking. Rick knew all about Terry Sharpe. The instruction had been to let him run whilst Foster handled the fallout from Redmund and pulled the strings of those two bent coppers. Terry had been controlled without knowing anything about it. But now it seemed he had grown confident enough to strike out on his own. Rick had grown in the organisation and made a phone call. His advice was accepted.

Rick picked up the phone again, Mickey Reynolds wasn't employed for his savagery, but Greg and 'Pancho' were a different matter.

*

Terry liked the look of the man. He oozed wealth, and it looked very much like some of it would be coming Terry's way. Despite employing his growing network of boys, Terry wasn't averse to earning the old way, so long as it was worth his time, and this guy was flashing the cash. Its smell had attracted Terry, and two bottles of expensive champagne had appeared at the table they were sharing. When the expected proposition came, he

195

followed the man and wasn't disappointed when a dark, chauffeur-driven Mercedes with tinted windows drew up. The driver got out and opened the rear door.

Terry had a moment of unease when he saw the man's ugly face, but the allure of cash drew him forwards. A push in the back propelled him into the rear seat and the door slammed behind him. Terry found himself eye to eye with a knife held by a swarthy, moustached man whose smile was one of enjoyment, not friendship.

The wealthy 'client' walked away as the Mercedes glided off. An hour later he was on the train out of London enjoying a gin and tonic and reflecting on a good earner. Free travel, a night out in London, a new suit, and five hundred quid. Nice work.

Rigg and Parker had known better than to rock the boat when Terry's body was washed up on the Thames Embankment two days later. Just another tragic accident after a drunken night out. He had served his purpose and no-one, except perhaps for a fat 'queen' would miss him.

***

Irene Loveday sat at her kitchen table and re-read the article in one of the national tabloid newspapers that had covered the Redmund case. Not renowned for its intellectual reporting, the story focussed on the former MP's abuse of young children in London. The picture of a beaming Redmund, taken before his arrest, holding a cigar in one hand, and a glass of wine in the other, taunted her from the paper, dredging up guilt which she had tried to bury deep.

She still vividly remembered the day that she had stopped outside Richard Brent's room at Avon House where she worked as a Care Assistant and heard the sound of Shirley being beaten. She had only narrowly managed to disappear into an adjoining room as Brent had left and had later left food outside her room.

Irene had been haunted by the young girl's screams ever since then, but as a single-mother struggling to make ends-meet for her young daughter, she simply did not have the inner-strength to report her encounter. She told no-one at the time of the investigation, she didn't want to get involved, she couldn't afford to get involved.

Now, as she read the story again, and recalled Redmund's visits to the Home, she realised that she was in possession of a piece of a puzzle which might be of value to the police, but still she agonised. Irene was not a strong woman and pushed the newspaper to one side as she stood up to prepare her daughter's evening meal.

The resolution to her predicament came from an unexpected quarter later that day as she chatted with her daughter, now ten years of age and wise beyond her years, in the kitchen. The child was drawn to the newspaper on the table and read the article whilst her mother washed up. Finally, she looked up at her mother and said simply, "I'm proud of you Mom that you look after children like me and keep them safe from people like this man. He's a bad person Mom, and it's good that he's been caught."

Irene's heart skipped a beat, but as she looked at the innocence of her daughter, she was visibly touched, and knew that it was time for her to do the right thing – she was about to become a 'whistle blower'.

The next day she walked into her local police station and asked to speak to a CID officer. She was referred to a young detective who was already carrying a heavy workload, and whilst he listened to Irene with courtesy, his brain was already computing as to how he could avoid increasing that workload. It had the distinct feel of being a 'bag of rats', a stone best left unturned. This was a young man who could 'bat things off' better than the England cricket team.

It didn't take long to establish that the original officer in the case for Richard Brent was one Detective Sergeant James Hargreaves who was currently seconded to a project team at Force Headquarters pending his promotion to Detective Inspector.

After a couple of phone calls, Irene was sent on her way with a promise that she would receive a home visit from DS Hargreaves within twenty-four hours.

Later that evening Hargreaves duly turned up at her house. Immaculately turned out, and charming from the outset, he settled down in Irene's living room with a cup of tea and listened carefully to her account. Irene was both impressed and perplexed. She found it reassuring that he was attentive but confused that he had come on his own and was only making rough notes, rather than taking a formal statement.

Finally, Irene came to the point, "I know that Richard Brent was sent to prison but I'm really worried that other children were assaulted, and that other men might have been involved." She hesitated. "I saw that vile man, that MP, here a lot. What if...?"

Hargreaves sought to reassure her, "We most certainly will investigate Irene, but it's really important that you speak to no-one else about this. There may be powerful forces at work here, and we need to make sure that you are protected – and of course your little girl."

Irene was taken aback, "Do you really think that someone might hurt us?"

Hargreaves leant forward and spoke with sincerity, "I promise you Irene that I will protect you, but you must do exactly what I say. I will not be taking a statement from you. I will be treating your information as information only, and I will be speaking to my bosses to make sure that we have people who will keep an eye on your place. You won't see them, but they will be there. We are going to look after you Irene, but you must only speak to me if you have any concerns. Do you understand?"

Irene nodded – she had done her public duty and reported her concerns to the authorities. She was frightened. It was now up to the forces of good to do their job.

Hargreaves provided Irene with his telephone number and promised to maintain contact. He subsequently made several follow-up visits, always on his own, and always the perfect gentleman, although Irene did feel on one occasion that he was mildly flirting with her.

She was flattered but confused until, on his last visit, Hargreaves announced that as a result of her information several people had been arrested and charged. She had done a great service for which his senior officers were very grateful, but it had been decided that her identity would remain a complete secret. Her job was done. He assured her that her public–spirited actions had protected children and that those who had been victimised had been counselled and given special help.

Some months later Irene was made redundant from her job following a restructure of staff at Avon House. 'To be honest', she thought, 'I'm not sorry,

I've had enough of this work and place.' She tried never to think of Avon House again.

Chapter Eight

'Who Killed Cock Robin?'

They were years of shortages and strikes for most. Not for the rich and powerful. They carried on as usual. Some of them worked for the benefit of their fellow humans, most worked for the benefit of themselves. It had always been thus.

Ted Heath gambled on an election after 81% of miners voted to strike, and on 28th February 1974, Harold Wilson returned to 10 Downing Street as the head of a minority government. He called and won a second election later in the year.

An Arab oil embargo forced the price of oil up ten-fold, decimating 'First World' economies as the oil producers began flexing their muscles. In Britain the price of a gallon of petrol rocketed to Fifty New Pence.

Zeus noted that war and death continued unabated. He shook his head, marvelling at, in his view, the iniquity of the world's capacity to accept mass murder and death, but condemn his own 'minor' peccadilloes.

Israel and India went 'nuclear'.

In Vietnam, destruction on an epic scale continued until the Americans found an ignominious way out, and the last helicopter left the roof of the Saigon Embassy on 30th April 1975.

Almost unnoticed by the West, Pol Pot's Khmer Rouge took control in Cambodia, 'Year Zero' would soon be announced there.

Turkey invaded Cyprus in 1974 and the island

was partitioned.

In England a vicious IRA bombing campaign was in full flow, culminating in the slaughter of twenty-one innocents in the *'Mulberry Bush'* and *'Tavern In The Town'* pubs on Birmingham on 21st November 1974. Bombings stopped in the city thereafter, but continued unabated elsewhere.

Zeus was the type of man that constantly reviewed and re-assessed. He hadn't survived as head of *'OK'* for over two decades by being complacent. The Redmund business had caused a few tremors, but had been successfully contained and as always, from adversity came lessons and opportunities.

That such a fool had been able to set up his own group, with the risk it entailed, without detection, had come as a shock. Yes, Redmund had been careful to keep its membership isolated from the *'OK'* organisation, but it should have been picked up before the risk became too great, and heads had rolled.

The head of 'security and enforcement', codenamed *'Ares'*, after the God of War, had left for a quiet and anonymous exile in Thailand, where there was an unending supply of young fodder to keep him amused. Zeus blamed himself, the man had been getting too comfortable and complacent. He had failed by allowing sentiment to cloud his judgement. It would not happen again. He should have acted sooner, especially as there was an ideal replacement available in Foster.

Zeus had never met Rick, but he knew everything about him, had tested him in many ways, and always he excelled. He was clever, ruthless, kept secrets well and had both a 'reputation' and a network of just the sort of contacts that *'OK'* needed to facilitate any 'dirty work' they needed. Foster had handled the Redmund issue with tact and diplomacy, had demonstrated initiative, good decision making, and the ability to implement the 'ultimate sanction' in the case of Sharpe. He was a man that would have risen through the ranks in the war, Zeus' kind of man.

Foster had also become rich, not super-rich as yet, and he had no access to the sort of power that the top echelon of *'OK'* wielded, but Zeus had decided that the time had come to groom a new generation for command of the group. Foster was the natural replacement for the newly exiled 'enforcer' for the group and was approached and duly inducted into the highest level of the group. A new *'Ares'*, was christened.

As the year of drought and floods petered away, Zeus could survey his dark empire with satisfaction and confidence. The secure and 'policed' wall he had put in place around himself had weathered all storms and emerged stronger. The power they wielded continued to grow.

***

The 'Summer of 76' was the year that the earth was baked. The streets of London melted as the temperature hit 35 degrees Centigrade in June. Rick was on a high that matched the thermometer.

There had been dark times. The loss of the Bowie work, and the bastard hadn't really retired, just gone off in another direction, ditching all the *'Ziggy Stardust'* accoutrements, including his group, *'The Spiders From Mars'*. That regrettable business with the boy – and Redmund and Sharpe to sort out.

Foster was a special type of criminal. The type that doesn't get caught. Clever and careful, and brilliant at taking and maximising opportunity. The more he worked for *'OK'*, the better it had been. Doors opened, business opportunities appeared, lucrative information was gathered. But ingrained in Foster's DNA was the experience of his youth. He was quite happy to work for and alongside others, and his respect for, and knowledge of the capacity for retribution of the *'Olympus Klub'*, informed his decision making.

He was under no illusion as to why he was of value - the unique 'fixer' service he provided. To begin with he had been a 'procurer', one of many, but his talent for organisation, and contacts in places that nobody of 'status' would have, or want to have, had led to his rapid rise through the shadowy organisation.

Now he bore the *'OK'* mark tattooed on his shoulder. Had thrown in his lot completely. Why wouldn't he? It was going to make and protect him for life, enable the satisfaction of his appetites without the risk of prison. In Zeus, Rick had met his match. And Rick's character and experience was such that he would always co-operate rather than compete.

He had thought deeply about his future path following his ejection from the 'rock circus' around Bowie. Had extricated himself from the whole thing. Begun to move towards 'legality'.

He re-organised, distancing the drugs, prostitution and protection rackets from himself via intermediaries, learning lessons from how *'OK'* operated. He invested in corrupt cops, continued to gather information about the 'weaknesses' of the powerful that his people came into contact with. Empowered by his backers, he began to build a different type of empire.

He set up a property development company,

buying up vast tracts of derelict land and sub-standard housing in London. He rented the houses out and enforced payments ruthlessly, or received 'services in kind' in the form of recruits to his prostitution and drugs operations. The land was 'banked'. He could see that London was growing fast, and gambled that the value would go up. Even he underestimated. It would make him millions.

He kept Mickey, he was too valuable, too loyal, to cast off, and no risk.

Rick shared Zeus' optimism. The worst was past.

***

For Ses and Bud, life went on much as before. They never felt the need to live apart from each other, or Brenda. They were, in essence old-fashioned 'hoodlums. They were hard men, who dealt drugs, but not all bad, there remained a streak of decency from the old days. They felt the injustice of Stewart's incarceration as keenly as she did, and did their best to support Brenda. They would never leave her.

She had been inconsolable, and her visits to Stewart hadn't helped. She could see and hear the effects of his ordeal on him as the years ticked by. He looked gaunt, and there was a dullness and lifelessness about his manner and speech that she knew, as only a mother can, was merely a symptom of some deeper malaise.

Her rage had remained, but changed in nature, from raging hot to icy cold. Rage at a theft perpetrated by the law, the theft of Stewart's youth, and probably any chance of a decent life. She knew he would be marked by society forever. In her experience there was little in the way of understanding or forgiveness for such as her son. But she was powerless. Only time elapsing could release him, and she counted every day, as if she were in a cell herself.

Maturity and age had bestowed upon the 'brothers' a veneer of both wisdom and respect within the local black community. They 'went back' to the early days. The name *'Windrush'* carried an aura. They had been subjected to and shared all the bad times, and remembered the good. Joe and the club, the gradual evolution of a culture and identity in Handsworth. They were an essential part of the local 'family'.

But in some ways nothing had changed. Prejudice was worse than ever. The difference now was that the community were no longer willing to shrug their shoulders and carry on. They had something, a shared identity and a 'place', and they weren't about to let what was hard-won be taken away by thugs and the ignorant.

Thus it was that they fought back. In 1976, they were at Notting Hill for 'business' purposes but ended up in the riots. Back in Birmingham, when Robert Relf was jailed for refusing to sell his house to 'Blacks', Ses and Bud were there, on the streets of Winson Green, attacking the 'Fascists' alongside the 'Anti-Nazi League'.

But Brenda and her 'husbands' never forgot Stewart, and what had been done to him in the name of justice. They were thankfully oblivious as to what had happened since sentence, but that was about to change

***

For Rob Docker the last three years had been full of ups and downs, and the downs were best forgotten. After being promoted to Detective Inspector in 1973, he'd been posted to Special Branch in 1974, as the IRA bombing campaign in Birmingham reached its sickening crescendo.

There had been repercussions, personal repercussions, that had forced him to cross a line, and once done, there was no going back. So, when he had gone back to Steelhouse Lane in 1975, and the whole football thing had blown up, involving hooligans affiliated to the *'Blues'* and the *'Villa'*, he had little problem in sorting things out in a way that no other cop, and not many non-cops would have contemplated.

If Docker had possessed a conscience, he would have struggled to live with himself. But he discovered that he was untroubled by his deeds. There was something fundamentally human missing, or buried deep and capped with concrete. All he knew was that, having gone so far, nothing was ever going to get in his way. He had 20:20 vision. Life was shit, life wasn't fair. You made your own luck, took what you wanted, and fought to the death if challenged. That was Docker's way.

Still, something positive had come out of the football job. He had been promoted to Temporary Detective Chief Inspector, for what it was worth. The more power you wielded, the better the payoffs were, and the easier to 'lid' stuff that was going 'wobbly'. He had also been able to get rid of or 'move on' some 'dead wood' that had been hanging around far too long, and in their place, had uncovered two gems in John Burrell and Sally Jones.

Despite himself, he found that he liked both of them, a real surprise in the case of Jones. A woman in CID. Not his 'type', a bit too 'chunky', although with that came a splendid pair of 'top bollocks'. He liked the way she handled herself. She brooked no nonsense and gave back more than she got. She'd clearly been through some tough times, she had a hard 'core' that showed out occasionally. Docker thought she would be a bad person to cross, the type that wouldn't give up, which is why he kept her close and 'under his wing'.

Burrell was a different 'kettle of fish' entirely, yet the pair seemed to have hit it off and become a bit of an 'item'. Docker had been suspicious of Burrell to begin with, another one that wasn't his normal type. Young, bright ambitious – dangerous, and like Jones, better to have in his tent 'pissing out'. There was something more to Burrell though. He wasn't the 'run of the mill' 'bright young thing'. He was grounded, useful in a fight, and not afraid to dish out a bit of 'instant justice' when required. It didn't fit, and Docker sometimes wondered how both types could be present in the same head, but he hadn't been able to solve the conundrum, despite plenty of sessions on the 'pop' with him.

Burrell had done well out of the football enquiry, and was now a Detective Sergeant. As 1977 dawned, Docker was thinking that perhaps, at last, he would have a straightforward year, with two team members he could rely on to shoulder some of the burden.

***

Autumn 1976, and England had gone from desert to flood. Denis Howells MP had been appointed 'Drought Minister' in late August, but had worked some voodoo and was now 'Minister for Rain'. It hadn't stopped for weeks.

Sally was in contemplative mood too. She was sat in Steelhouse Lane bar cradling a pint, one eye on the TV which was showing the motor racing, and James Hunt on the brink of becoming World Champion.

Although the bar was crowded, she sat by herself. She wasn't unpopular at 'The Lane', and she was certainly respected, but she often found herself alone in a crowd. It was as if there was an unseen force field around her. That was the subject of her contemplation.

There were two reasons, she felt, one simple, one that currently defied her own understanding.

The first was that, as the result of Uncle Jim, a failed marriage, and the baptism of fire she had received in the police, she knew she was considered 'formidable', an 'ice-maiden'. Her 'put-downs' and acid tongue legendary – viewed and recounted with some fondness by those not on the receiving end.. She had no doubt that, until this year, it had been common opinion that she 'swung for the other side'. Sally had been happy at this state of affairs, as it had allowed her to concentrate on her career, without the distractions of sex.

It had gone well, all things considered. She had set her stall out to become a detective, and had achieved her ambition, thanks to the assistance of an enlightened Detective Superintendent, who for once hadn't wanted to get into her pants. He had arranged an attachment and Sally had worked hard, harder than any of the men had to.

She had been transferred into CID, a true ground-breaker, and into the not so tender care of Docker. On first meeting she had expected the worst from his reputation, and indeed, he was hard and self-absorbed, but somehow she had struck some chord within him, and he had proved to be an ally.

She was under no illusions, he demanded hard graft, absolute loyalty and he was a ruthless bastard, but at least he treated her the same as everyone else, and watched her back. It wasn't perfect, but it was the best 'deal' she had found since joining.

And it allowed her to realise her dream. To be a detective, To be in the role that would enable her to hunt down the abusers, the perverts, the exploiters. Not yet, though. She had to learn her craft, and they lurked in the shadows and had to be 'winkled' out. But she had time, plenty of time.

The second reason for her isolation, and the cause of her own surprise, was John. Everyone knew she was screwing the DS.

Sally had thought that no man would ever again breach the wall she had erected. How could she ever trust one again? It had crept up on her unseen. After her transfer to CID she had immersed herself in the work. Her arrival had been met with a mixture of hostility, indifference, her every move being scrutinized for errors or weakness.

John had only just arrived himself, so there was some sharing of the load, as he was suspected of being a 'bright young thing', the kiss of death in a CID that favoured age, experience and the 'old boys' network. He was the only one who showed kindness without a hidden agenda – she genuinely didn't think he was trying to 'pull' her. It seemed to just suddenly register with both of them at the same time–that there was a possibility of something more.

He definitely wasn't the norm. A curious mixture. Shy, yet able to handle himself. Clever, but with the ability to mix it with the others, and the biggest coup of all, seeming to have Docker on his side. Sally was no fool. She could see that Docker distrusted John to begin with, and she had a feeling he kept him close so he could keep an eye on him. But that had changed during the football job, and John, now a Detective Sergeant, was clearly on Docker's 'in' list, if there was such a thing.

They had begun cautiously. She was wary, and he seemed too good to be true. Caring attentive, witty. He didn't push things and it was several months before they consummated the relationship. The act had awoken feelings in Sally that she hadn't experienced since her childish adoration of Uncle Jim had been corrupted and tainted. She kept them at bay for a few months more, but there was a submerged vulnerability about John that awoke deeper emotions, perhaps the mothering instinct. The more she knew him, the better she liked him, but he was an iceberg, with hidden depths that she knew would take years of trust to uncover.

So here she was, thinking. Could she make the investment he required, after all that had happened to her? It would be a leap in the dark, overturning the past resolutions she had made. It could bring her happiness and completeness, or destroy her.

She downed her pint as James Hunt cracked open the champagne on the podium. She had made her decision, she didn't want to be alone.

**

The seemingly endless waiting was over. The glorious day of Stewart Doyle's release came towards the end of 1976.

Brenda had been to see him every time she had managed to get a *'VO'*, a *'Visiting Order'*, and was at the gatehouse to pick him up with Ses who, as usual, was wearing his black wide-brimmed trilby hat and belted raincoat. Bud would have been there, but

211

some urgent business had come up in Jamaica, and he had flown out to renew some friendships and re-establish some connections.

Doyle had grown up and grown inwards in Borstal, no longer a boy, but a man who had been shaped and fired by injustice. His mother recognised the change in him and tried to keep him close to her.

For two weeks Stewart never once left the house as he brooded and pondered. Brenda tried to talk to him but she couldn't get through. There was no reaction. He ate, he watched the TV, he lay on his bed, staring at the ceiling whilst his LP's played over and over, but he didn't sing in accompaniment like he used to. He barely spoke. He was elsewhere, lost inside himself, but Brenda could see the rage in his eyes.

At the end of that period he got out of bed one morning, dressed and didn't return to the house until after dark, but not before secreting the Ford Cortina car he had stolen earlier in a nearby disused garage.

Each day he went out early and came back after dark. His mother asked no questions of her troubled son, desperately trying not to put him under any pressure, and no explanations were offered

Brenda made sure that a hot meal was on the table every night for her son, and didn't pry. Having just got him back she wasn't going to do anything to lose him again, and she instinctively felt that he was on a knife edge; the slightest push could send him tumbling one way or the other. She was frightened.

During the course of one of his outings Doyle acquired a flick knife and a brass knuckle duster, which he kept in the vehicle that by now had been put onto false plates.

After two weeks he was ready. He was calm

and cold, drawing from the block of ice inside.

On his 'outings', Stewart Doyle had returned daily to the vicinity of Richmond House where his torment had begun, and monitored the movements of John Baxter. The sight of his tormentor threatened to fan the fire that Doyle held within, but Doyle remembered a saying he had heard once, 'Revenge is a dish best served cold'. He would do it when he was ready.

It didn't take Doyle long to establish that Baxter was a creature of habit. Every lunchtime Baxter would take the van out from the Home to visit his preferred 'watering hole' for a few pints before returning to work in the afternoon.

Luckily for Doyle, the combination of lunchtime drinking and being in charge of kids wasn't one that Baxter wished to advertise. He had found a country pub with good beer down a country lane near Studley, far enough away, and in a different County to the one responsible for the Home, but within a fifteen-minute drive.

The regime at Richmond House was lax, and Baxter 'part of the furniture', so nobody was bothered about, or in a position to challenge his lengthy lunch breaks. He always reasoned to himself that he put the hours in overall, and who was really going to rock the boat? He knew he was protected in his role, so long as he didn't do anything stupid in public. Thus, he took precautions against any 'nosey-parker' do-gooders by parking away from prying eyes in the same corner of the rear car park, surrounded on three sides by a large privet hedge. The car park was invariably deserted at lunchtime.

*

Baxter finished his third pint – life was still good, and the livid red mark on his face, plus the use of just one testicle, had not interfered with his sexual appetite. Apart from taking the 'chosen few' to the cadets that evening he had an easy day planned, with plenty of time to satisfy his needs later.

He drank up and said his goodbyes to the lone barman and the only other two customers in the bar – two elderly men who were part of the 'fittings' in the pub and always occupied the same corner seats.

At the door he hunched his collar up as the cold air struck him and headed for the rear car park. Even from a distance he spotted the problem straight away. "Fuck" he exclaimed, as he spotted that the front offside tyre of the van was flat with the rim resting on the ground.

He continued cursing and muttering under his breath as he struggled to get the spare wheel and a jack from the back of the van and started to remove the wheel nuts.

Braced against the cold, he tried to move quickly and was soon winding the jack handle to get the tyre clear of the ground. He lifted it up and dropped it to the floor making a mental note that the tyre appeared to have been slashed rather than punctured. 'Bastard kids – need a good dose of discipline', he thought as he angrily wound the jack.

Breathing heavily, he was just about to refocus his energies on the task in hand, rather than punishing the jack handle, when he was conscious that someone was behind him and heard a click. "Can you give us a hand, mate?" He half-turned and broke off mid-sentence as the flick-knife plunged into his neck.

Baxter let out a scream muffled by gurgling as

blood entered his windpipe. He pitched forward and hit his head on the bodywork of the vehicle.

Stewart Doyle pounced on Baxter and the rage consumed him utterly.

His memory would be that he had stabbed the man perhaps two or three times, whilst in reality in the frenzy that followed it would prove to be more than thirty when a post-mortem was carried out.

A number of the wounds were defence wounds to the hands, as Baxter feebly attempted to fend off some of the blows, but others severed arteries in the neck and legs – it was a blood-bath.

During the latter part of the attack Baxter rolled onto his back, and with his life ebbing away he looked up at Doyle. He was defiant to the last, "Doyle you bastard," as blood seeped from his mouth and a bubble formed. He made a vain attempt to grip an arm but his strength was gone.

Doyle was fuelled with pure hatred, lost in the moment, "You piece of filth. You're a dead man," and smashed him full in the face with the knuckle duster.

Brass crunched against teeth and brass won.

Doyle got to his feet and for a moment stared at Baxter, who was not long for this earth. He aimed a violent kick at the man's groin and then dropped onto the man's chest and drove the knife in once more. Amidst the sound of breaking ribs, Baxter died.

Stewart Doyle pulled a piece of paper from his pocket and stuffed it into one of Baxter's bloodied hands. The note said simply, *'This man raped boys. He got justice.'*

Although it had not been in the plan, Doyle reached into Baxter's jacket pocket and removed his wallet, which he pushed inside his own.

In a final act, Doyle kicked away the car jack and the front part of the van crashed onto the lifeless body beneath it.

His internal fire extinguished, the ice returned, and Doyle walked calmly away to the Cortina, parked further up the lane, as an ever-growing pool of bright red blood seeped out from underneath the vehicle. He was oblivious to the fact that his hands and chest were drenched in blood.

He still clasped the knife and knuckle duster firmly, and in truth at that point would have killed again if anyone had tried to stop him. Fate however decreed that he would make it back to the car unseen.

Before driving off, Doyle wrapped the knife and knuckle duster in his jacket and put them on the seat next to him. After catching sight of his face in the rear-view mirror he made a half–hearted attempt to wipe some of the blood from his face.

As the shock and enormity of what he had done set in, he drove robotically home, parked outside, and picked up his blood-stained bundle.

He tried several times to put the key into the front door of the house but try as he might his hands would not stop trembling.

Eventually Brenda heard the noise and emerged from the kitchen together with Ses to answer the door. She found her son gripping his rolled-up jacket and close to collapse. He looked like a refugee from a horror film.

Brenda was made of stern stuff and went into auto-pilot. The time for talking would be later.

Ses took charge of the bundle from Stewart, and took it upstairs to his room where he hid it under a large pile of bedding in an airing cupboard, but not before noting the presence of the bloodstained knife and knuckle duster.

Brenda guided her son into the bathroom and emerged thirty minutes later holding the remainder of her son's blood-stained clothing, "Burn those in the garden now Ses," she ordered.

Stewart sat at the kitchen table shrouded in a large towel, and stared into space.

Brenda thrust a mug of hot tea with three sugars into his hand and gently said, "When you're ready Stewart, just tell me what's happened."

The man, who, what seemed like an eon ago had once been a boy and was now a murderer, spoke slowly for thirty minutes whilst Ses retrieved Stewart's jacket from the airing cupboard, leaving the weapons hidden, and busied himself outside with the garden incinerator.

Brenda sat in absolute silence, struggling to come to terms with the horror of what she was hearing. Her world slowly collapsed, sentence by sentence.

At the end of his story of abuse and vengeance, starting with the Children's Home, the Borstal, and ending with the murder, he simply said, "Where were you Mom? I just wanted to come home. Why did you leave me with these people?"

The weight of the guilt felt by Brenda at that moment crushed her soul.

They both burst into tears as 'Ses' returned to the kitchen to find them inconsolable. It was time to make himself scarce – he felt like an intruder between mother and son, but just as he was leaving, Brenda gave him one more task. "Ses, the car outside needs to be torched. Take it up to Edgbaston Reservoir and do a good job. Bud is back tomorrow, you go get him first thing from the airport and tell him what's

217

happened."

*

Stewart slept fitfully that night, and when he emerged next morning Brenda had already made some arrangements – he was to be taken by Bud to Brean in Somerset, where the family had a relative who would swear if necessary, that Stewart had been working with him on one of the caravan sites since his release from Borstal. This was to be Stewart's life for the foreseeable future as the police investigation got underway. Ses and Bud knew that, in a case like this, the police would throw the kitchen sink at it, and they were worried, not only for Stewart's liberty, but their own. Assisting a murderer was not a trivial matter.

As the shocking details of the frenzied attack splashed across the headlines, certain eyebrows were raised, brows furrowed and phone calls made. Optimism as to the future in certain quarters was shaken, and Rick Foster was once again put to work. Baxter's routine of crossing the County border proved to be an incredible piece of good fortune.

The Senior Investigating Officer for the case, Detective Inspector James Hargreaves, was relatively new in post and inexperienced in command of such an investigation, and not helped by a Scenes of Crime team that were overworked and under pressure.

Some of the officers on the enquiry team expressed great surprise that Hargreaves was managing a such a high–profile murder, but Hargreaves let his ego do the talking and the doubters soon realised that their views were not welcome, nor carried any weight. The promise of overtime in return for compliance shut mouths.

During the melee that always consumes the

early days of any major incident the handwritten note found in Baxter's hand was logged as an exhibit and within the incident room, an 'action' – a line of enquiry to be progressed, created for it to be chemically treated for fingerprints.

For some inexplicable reason it was never submitted to the Forensic Laboratory for ninhydrin testing and an action/allocator in the incident room, who would later claim to have been drowning in a sea of paper whilst suffering from the effects of long hours, and the collapse of a relationship, closed the action off. The action was dismissed at a subsequent briefing with the words 'nothing has come back from forensics regarding the note'.

Baxter's room was searched, but nothing found. Not surprising, as it was the second 'search' that day.

The enquiry crews were impressed and somewhat relieved that Hargreaves opted to handle the delicate enquiry required at Richmond House. They were happy to let the new 'gaffer' tip-toe through that minefield. Social-worker wankers and scumbag kids, an unattractive proposition.

Hargreaves dutifully spoke to all the staff and boys, but no complaints were received. It looked as if anything Baxter had done had been in his own time. Social Services' hierarchy were happy to go along with that assumption.

Opinion amongst the team, and thus the wider force, was that Baxter had accosted someone whilst inebriated, and picked the wrong one. If it was 'passing trade', then they were long-gone and finding them would be near-impossible. It was felt that Baxter had received summary justice, was no loss to society, and little further effort should be expended in a fruitless search.

With no suspects and no witnesses, the enquiry struggled to make any headway and Stewart Doyle's fingerprints on the paper remained hidden.

The enquiry lumbered on, going through the motions of following leads, but soon it faded from public consciousness and there were other, more deserving needs to be resourced.

Baxter had been a loner, unpopular, and not much missed if the truth be known, so there was nobody to be his champion for justice. The situation was monitored, and any hint of awkward questions was assiduously attended to by Hargreaves. He found no need to request help in heading off busybodies, there were none.

As the Silver Jubilee year dawned, it seemed to those who knew what Baxter really did for his living and kicks, that once again a threat had been mitigated. But they remained alert, and in Foster, had an instrument of ruthless efficiency.

Chapter Nine

'One, Two, Three Four Five'

Bob Williams was Editor of the *'Stratford On Avon News'*. He knew he was just a big fish in a little pond, but it suited him. He was good at his job, and at one time had harboured ambition to go to one of the nationals. But he liked Stratford, liked the 'feel' of the office, and had gradually realised that he never wanted to work in the cut-throat world of the tabloids. He was a decent man and believed that his job was to support his local community and uncover the truth for the public good.

And so, the years had passed. The chance of a *'Watergate'* in Stratford was as likely as the local football team winning the FA Cup. His fodder as a journalist had comprised the small doings of the council, charity events, local sport and the odd bigger crime story. He had reached his current position through a mixture of competence, popularity and durability. He was looking at a comfortable last few years as a pillar of the community with some satisfaction.

Bob looked at the excited person in his office with a mixture of fondness and humour. Sunil reminded him of an eager puppy. Bob was pleased he had given the lad a chance. The elder child of a family expelled by Idi Amin in 1972, Sunil was intelligent and spoke English better than most of the indigenous population. He was also hard-working, good company, personable – and absolutely convinced that he was going to win a Pulitzer prize for investigative journalism. So far, the closest he had got was uncovering a local vicar having an affair with the organist, and they weren't even the same sex.

Sunil was bouncing on his heels and struggling to put a sentence together.

"Sunil, for God sakes, sit down and take a deep breath." The slim Asian did as he was told, but seemed to be sat on an anthill.

"Ok, let's have it then, but slowly." Bob smiled reassuringly. He didn't want to crush his enthusiasm.

Sunil did the first but not the second as his voice gathered pace, "I've got a scoop boss! Biggest story ever. You remember that murder, the Social Worker stabbed in the pub car park?"

Bob did. It had been a big story and filled a few pages. But interest had waned as the trail went cold. Bob also knew that the suggestion the victim had been 'queer' and punting for 'business', meant there was a view locally that he 'got what he deserved', and perhaps the Children's Home was better off without him. Bob suspected the police weren't exactly pulling out all the stops.

Bob tried an open question, "Yes of course. But it's a non-story now isn't it."

Sunil looked triumphant, "Not anymore. I've been contacted by an ex-resident. He's alleging this Baxter, the dead man, was involved in, well, some pretty nasty business with the kids."

Bob began to focus, "Have you met him Sunil?"

Sunil began to wonder if Bob was testing him, "No, not yet, I've made some notes. It sounds genuine, he was crying as he spoke to me, sounded pretty upset and angry. Here."

He handed the notes over and Bob scanned

them. He sat back in his chair. When Sunil went to speak, he was silenced with a finger. Bob turned it over in his mind. He was no fool. This needed careful assessment.

Finally, Bob said, "Is he willing to meet?"

Sunil was anxious to please, "I think so, but he doesn't trust the police, kept saying they were bent and all in it together. He was very nervous, sounded scared."

Bob made his mind up, "I think you had better set it up then. Both of us for this one. I want to see him. If this is a load of bullshit it could ruin us. If not, it needs handling properly, and that means involving the police, like it or not, otherwise we could be in trouble too.

Sunil looked as if he had lost a pound and found fifty pence. He visibly deflated. Bob got up and patted him on the shoulder, "It's good work, and we'll run it if it pans out, but we aren't the *'News of The World'*. We are a responsible part of the local community. That is why we are still successful. The way we handle this can make us friends or enemies, and I'd rather have the story and the support of the proper people locally. I promise you, if it needs airing, we will do it, and you'll get the credit."

It took some time to coax the frightened caller into a face-to-face situation. Bob made his assessment.

The next day he picked up the phone. He knew the Chief Constable from many civic events, and they had a good relationship. Bob trusted him. But he made it clear in the subsequent conversation that whilst he preferred to work with the police, he intended to print the story at some stage. He wanted a 'scoop' but an officially supported one was preferable. He was bluffing a little and covering his own back. He had no hard evidence, and the informant was reluctant to 'get involved, but was convincing. If what he implied was true, kids were being subjected to unspeakable horrors, and Bob wanted something done about it.

*

The Nation was anticipating a celebration. The actual Silver Jubilee date was 6th February 1977, twenty-five years to the day since Elizabeth ascended the throne. Consensus was that she had made a good job of it. Even the 'reds' and Republicans had to admit she had brought stability and wise counsel, weathering a number of 'storms' within the House of Windsor along the way. June 7th was going to be a public holiday and plans for 'street parties' abounded.

It meant nothing to Docker. The majority of police officers were unswervingly loyal to the 'big boss', the source of the 'Office of Constable' and their powers. Docker had loyalty to nobody but himself, and reasoned that he would never meet the Royals, they would never assist him, and he would never be able to 'use' them. Thus, he ignored them and did his best to avoid anything relating to them. There simply wasn't an 'earner' to be had there.

The phone rang, and as was his custom, Docker answered it immediately.

The day took an immediate turn for the worse. He recognised the voice of the Assistant Chief Constable who had previously encouraged him to join Special Branch, and a frown spread across his face, he hadn't got any time for the man. Another 'chinless wonder'.

"Rob, are you busy for the next couple of days."

It wasn't a question, more of an introductory statement, which indicated that the ACC wanted something doing, usually the dirty work he needed to delegate. It didn't do to say no, and before long he was being directed towards one of the newer Chief Superintendents in the Force with some less than reassuring final comments from the ACC.

"He's a decent guy Rob, and something of a 'rising star'. He's not a career detective so this job will tick a few boxes on his CV perfectly with your help. I expect you to look after him. This is something of a sensitive enquiry, so we don't want to go in like a herd of elephants if you get my meaning. Don't you get throwing your weight around or pulling any of your stunts"

The following day, Docker met the man who was going to be the figurehead of the enquiry that Docker was going to run, do all the work on, make all the decisions and take any risks. That was always the way. Rob knew he was on a hiding to nothing. He mentally shrugged his shoulders, you never knew, there might be an 'angle' or two he could profit from. As a minimum he would share out the overtime to his own cronies, knowing they would not be averse to keeping him in drinks and food in return, for as long as it lasted.

Rob had plenty of experience of these 'quick jobs', and when a reputation and career was at stake had found that they could run for as long as it took to satisfy the CV of the person in charge, and remove any risk to reputation.

He was to be proved correct. Those *'couple of days,'* would turn into six months, and the enquiry would see Jubilee Day.

Operation *'Damocles'* was born.

225

*

Docker had decided to practice his listening skills and to give the Chief Superintendent his head. It didn't really matter to him what this 'numpty' said, as Docker would in the final analysis be doing things his way.

Rob Docker had already made his pitch to have Detective Sergeant John Burrell on the team and that request had been accepted. This was not a job where there was going to be a cast of thousands, and he wanted someone next to him who was totally reliable and trustworthy. Apart from currently being a bit misty-eyed over Sally he was an excellent detective and as straight as a die. It suited Docker's work ethic perfectly to have a man like Burrell next to him, although their actual ethics could not have been further apart. He'd added Sally to the team after deciding that her skills outweighed the risk that she would deflect Burrell from what he did best – hunting.

The Chief Superintendent showed him a document which had been signed off at a very senior level, which made it clear that they were conducting an investigation on behalf of the host force.

Docker read the terms of reference. *'Following both confirmed and unsubstantiated allegations of child sexual abuse which are alleged to have been committed at a number of institutions, over a period of years, the enquiry team is tasked with establishing the scale of any such abuse and determining the appropriateness of police actions in response to those allegations.'*

Docker read through the mundane administrative aspects of the document and then spotted something of interest, *'and to facilitate the*

226

smooth access of the enquiry team to both staff and documents within the host Force, a liaison officer will be appointed to work alongside the investigation team. The nominated officer to fulfil this role is Detective Inspector James Hargreaves'.

Docker sniffed loudly – he knew what that meant, a spy had been placed in the camp. "Are you happy with this sir? It seems a bit unusual to have an officer from the Force being investigated working within the team that's actually investigating them."

The Chief Superintendent waved the comment away with a smile, "We're all on the same team aren't we Rob? All in *'The Job'* together. Anyway, James comes highly recommended by his Chief Constable and has intimate knowledge of the murder case which forms part of the investigation. I met him yesterday for lunch actually and he seems thoroughly decent. He's Bramshill senior officer material by the looks of him."

Docker got a bit more interested. Murder was something worth investigating at least, he knew plenty about that. He decided that there was no point in pursuing the issue as the Chief Superintendent continued his descent in Rob's estimation. "I like a bit of classical history Rob, so I've decided on a suitable operational name. We will call the job *'Operation Damocles'*. It's from an ancient parable attributed to the Roman orator Cicero. Bit of a moral tale actually, but everyone's heard of the hanging sword – reminds me of the sword of justice." He'd realised he'd lost Docker's attention and came back to the present. "I'm just in the process of preparing an Operational Order – a bit of practice will do me good. Got a Command Course coming up. I'll let you have a copy when it's done and then really, I would like you to get on with it and keep me in the loop with any developments. Is that okay?"

Rob Docker felt a sense of relief that at least the idiot was not going to be standing at his shoulder at every turn, "Of course sir. Leave it with me and I'll make sure that you're kept fully up to date."

Almost as an afterthought the Chief Superintendent concluded, "One more thing, here are the broad details of the various allegations. I've not given them much scrutiny, more your job, I think. Just let me know what you propose to do. This needs sensitive handling. There may be something in it, but it has the feel of unsubstantiated gossip and our Chief is a good friend of theirs, so no 'bull in a china shop' stuff."

Business concluded, Docker left the man poring over the Operational Manual, a tome Docker had never opened. "Saints forbid," he muttered on the way out.

***

Docker arranged his first team meeting two days later for 10am at Bridge Street West Police Station in Summer Lane – a quiet sub-station where the front-office men reigned supreme and there were fewer prying eyes.

It was a relatively small team of investigators and Major Incident Room staff, but he had hand-picked many of them and was pleased with the outcome.

At 10.20am the door of the room they were occupying, which had a *'do not disturb'* sign on the outside, was opened and a tall smart man sporting a brown leather briefcase, strolled in.

All eyes in the room turned on him. He held out a hand which Docker pointedly ignored, "I do apologise for being late. I am Detective Inspector James Hargreaves. I'm afraid I got a bit lost and then couldn't find a parking space."

Docker motioned to him to take a seat and then continued – one second in the room and he had already taken a dislike to the man. He hadn't told Hargreaves about the briefing but clearly someone else had. He was going to need 'eyes in his backside' to get through this.

Once the briefing had finished, Docker indicated for Hargreaves to follow, and took him into one of the side rooms.

Docker began. "I just wanted to get a couple of things straight. I'm the boss here and you're on my turf so you do what I fucking say. I decide what you know and see, and don't let me catch you poking around. I know why you're fucking here."

Hargreaves seemed slightly rocked, "Why am I here?" he asked. He seemed nervous. Docker could smell something 'off' but didn't know the man well enough to work it out.

Docker was nothing if not direct, "You've been put here by your Chief. He probably had a 'little chat' with ours. No doubt to report back on what we're up to, how we're doing. Whether we are finding anything 'embarrassing'. Getting too close to the truth. That sort of thing. And if we are…. then you'll do whatever it takes to nudge us in a different direction, up a blind alley. You're the conductor of the cover–up when it happens."

He expected Hargreaves to fold, but the man almost seemed relieved, and bit back, "They tell me that you've been an Acting Chief Inspector for a little while now, so in theory I suppose we are the same rank. I'll play your little game for now, but I take

229

what you've said as an insult to my integrity."

Docker's dislike of the man intensified. He didn't like it when he couldn't read a situation, and the back of his neck was prickling, "Listen carefully. You might be up the arse of your Chief Constable, or perhaps he's up yours, but that counts for fuck all to me. Go and introduce yourself to the team outside. It looks like there a few 'fuck-ups' to sort out and I'll be interested to see whether your fingerprints are on any of them."

He watched Hargreaves all the way out of the room. Alarms were ringing but he didn't know why, and Docker didn't like that one bit.

***

In the days the followed, Rob Docker came to understand that this was to be no ordinary enquiry. As part of the protocol drawn up by his Chief Superintendent, he had been required to meet with senior CID officers from the Forces on which the Children's Homes affected were located.

He had attempted to arrange individual appointments but found himself summoned to a meeting with a number of them where it was made collectively clear that his presence within their spheres of influence was unwelcome, and that if he stepped on any toes he would find life uncomfortable. Docker, alive to his own survival, could smell fear, and backs being scratched. He knew he could win battles, but he wasn't sure about the war. He could be outgunned.

Docker was not one to be cowed by such behaviour, least of all by a bunch of fat-bellied 'has-beens' who had spent too much time having 'liquid lunches'. That said, he practiced his diplomacy skills and promised to keep them in touch with

230

developments. He had no intention of keeping that promise.

The scale of Docker's challenge started to manifest itself as investigators started to return to the Incident Room with outstanding 'actions' that could not be finalised. In one instance Docker had despatched officers to collect a number of police pocketbooks from an archive relating to officers who had been involving in investigating previous historical child abuse. The investigators found on arrival that without exception the notebooks were missing, and no-one had an explanation as to why.

The same investigators approached the officers in question. Many of them had since retired, but to a person repeated the phrase, *'I have no recollection of the investigation referred to and would need to rely on my notebook for an accurate record of what took place.'* It was clear that individuals had been carefully briefed and that the investigators were being stone-walled.

John Burrell was tasked with making enquiries in relation to Richard Brent. It was quickly confirmed that the prosecution file had been shredded due to an 'administrative error'. Shirley had since left the care of the Social Services and her whereabouts were unknown, whilst Brent had been released from prison, having served his sentence as a model prisoner, and had apparently gone to live abroad. He had sold his house and not left a forwarding address. Rick Foster was nothing if not thorough. After his elevation in *'OK'* he had gone back through the years looking for potential risks and had employed a few 'investments' and threats.

Docker personally reviewed the Baxter murder, but when he requested a copy of his personnel file from Social Services, he was informed that following his death the file had been shredded on the instructions of the Director.

When he asked for details of any discipline issues relating to abuse by social workers during the previous decade, he was told that there were no records of any such reports in existence.

It felt like doors were closing around them, but Docker persisted. He was at his best when working under pressure and the very presence of all these obstacles told him that there was something out there to find. He didn't like being treated like a twat. It was getting personal, and Docker wasn't a loser.

Docker requested from Hargreaves, lists of all the children who had been resident at Avon House and Richmond House over a ten-year period, as well as the names of all staff members. Hargreaves came back, outwardly helpful and willing, with reams of paper. Everything was fed into the incident room and prioritised for actions to be allocated. Hargreaves had however used his initiative and his first list of staff members was exclusively male–they were after all investigating male paedophiles, weren't they?

The enquiry team was facing a mammoth task, but Docker kept them focused and led from the front, working long hours and taking calculated risks to reduce the workload wherever possible.

As far as Hargreaves was concerned, Docker had dismissed the information from the *'Stratford-On-Avon News'* as 'total bollocks'. He had made sure that Hargreaves had seen his entry in the Policy Book to that effect, describing it as un-evidenced 'tittle-tattle' from someone who wasn't prepared to stand up and be counted. Docker might be a corrupt policeman, but he was a good detective. He secretly despatched Burrell to see the Editor. His 'nose' was twitching.

*

Burrell assessed the man opposite him. More of a boy really, 'Shane' was in his late teens or early twenties. They were in a transport café near Coventry, and Burrell watched as his guest demolished a full English with all the trimmings. He looked like he needed it, gaunt with skin stretched tight across his face. It spoilt what had clearly been elfin looks, there was a haunting beauty beneath the ravages of whatever demons haunted him. He would have been attractive to predators, Burrell concluded.

It had taken weeks of promises and missed meetings to arrive here. Burrell knew that the fragile figure in front of him would never appear before a court giving evidence, but he was determined to hear the story.

'Shane', clearly not his real name, began haltingly, and the tale came out in bursts punctuated by tears. He recalled in detail the catalogue of abuse he and others had suffered at the hands of Baxter and others, and how finally when he became too difficult to handle Baxter had taken him for a long ride in the van one night and dumped him unceremoniously in the middle of nowhere. Told in no uncertain terms that Baxter would kill him if he ever returned, he began a nomadic existence surviving on the streets. From that point on he was just another 'Misper' report.

What he said shook the tough Detective Sergeant to the core.

*

Burrell knocked at the door, sniffed, and waited. If he had learnt nothing else, it was to be courteous and patient. It always worked well for him and whilst some of his colleagues believed in a more 'direct' approach he was comfortable that his style paid greater dividends.

Today John had an 'attached man' with him who he didn't much like – a young guy with just four years' service who wore floral 'kipper' ties and was full of attitude. He had been put onto the enquiry under the pretext of gaining experience on a major incident but in truth his local senior CID officer didn't think much of him either and wanted rid of him out of his office. Such people could often find themselves moving upwards or sideways as a means of moving a 'problem child' on.

Burrell had seen it all before, the favoured alternative routes were that you were either a member of the *'Welsh Mafia'*, *'The Scottish Mafia'*, the *'Irish Mafia'*, the Catholics, the Freemasons, the Buffalos, a golf club, or just good at buying rounds of drinks for the gaffers to get a good posting. Officers had been recruited to police Birmingham from all parts of the United Kingdom to make up the shortfall in numbers needed and they quickly formed alliances based on religion, and social background.

This attached man definitely fitted into the 'Billy no mates' category.

John Burrell made a mental note to make sure that the kid had got plenty to do. He was either going to 'make him' or 'break him'. He turned to his colleague, "Let me do the talking."

The door opened and Brenda filled the door frame, arms folded, "What do you pair want?"

Burrell produced his warrant card and said soothingly, "We're from the police. I'm John Burrell."

Brenda snorted, "I know who you are. I could smell your stink from the end of the road."

"No need for that attitude missus" the attached man blurted out, as Burrell shot him a withering look.

Burrell persevered, "Mrs. Doyle, we are making enquiries of a very sensitive nature and I would be really grateful if we could talk inside, perhaps over a cup of tea? I don't want to talk on the doorstep. You know how nosey neighbours can be." Burrell had already spotted the curtains twitching next door as they had made their way up the path so tried to hit a sensitive spot.

Brenda Doyle disliked police officers intensely, more so after what they had done to her son leading up to his first conviction, but she knew that she needed to be cautious. In any event she didn't want to give the nosey old cow next door something to crow about when she met up in the snug of her local with the local 'nosey parkers.'

She ushered them inside, "Wipe your bleeding feet on the way in and tell boy wonder here to keep his 'gob' shut", she instructed Burrell.

In the kitchen, Ses and Bud were sat at the table. Brenda exchanged a look with Ses which did not go unnoticed to Burrell's trained eye, whilst his trainee was totally oblivious to anything other than the apparent grease mark on his favourite tie.

Brenda's two lovers were despatched to the living room, where they busied themselves hiding a bit of 'bush' under the sofa, and in plant pots, whilst Brenda put the kettle on. It was a bit like a comedy sketch as they tripped over each other and swore constantly calling each other a *'bloodclart'* in strong Jamaican accents.

Brenda reserved her comments exclusively for

235

Burrell, steadfastly refusing to acknowledge the presence of the younger officer.

Over tea, Burrell provided brief details of their investigation, and stressing that they were merely working their way through a list of children who had been in the care of the Local Authority during a specific period – Stewart fitted into this category and they needed to speak with him to see if he had any information which might assist. He made no secret of the fact that they were investigating allegations of child abuse but chose his words carefully, was caring and measured.

Brenda listened intently, and at one stage Burrell could have sworn that he detected some tears welling up in her eyes.

Judging the right moment, he enquired as to Stewart's whereabouts and again stressed that they had been allocated a T.I.E (Trace-Interview-Eliminate) action and that it was nothing more than a routine enquiry.

Brenda composed herself, her emotions a mixture of fear and anguish, as she faced the reality of the horrors she had seen in Stewart's face, "Stewart's been working away since he got out of Borstal, so I don't see much of him. He says I let him down and we've had a fall out, so he doesn't phone much. You know how these things happen. If you leave your phone number though I'll tell him to get in touch next time he calls."

The attached man shuffled his feet and stared at his tie before fiddling with it, which for some reason irritated Brenda, "What the fuck's wrong with you. You shit your nappy, boy?"

Burrell was becoming increasingly vexed by his colleague's lack of ability to read situations. He had deliberately not responded to her statement as he wanted to keep her talking, but the moment was lost.

"Thanks Mrs. Doyle, you've been very helpful." He held his hand out to shake hers and it produced an involuntary response. A first for Mrs. Doyle, as she held his warm hand. Burrell took the opportunity to peer into the depths of her eyes. Something in that look warranted further exploration. Brenda also thought she saw something, genuine sympathy, but reproached herself for nearly falling for the oldest police trick in the world.

The officers went outside, and as Burrell occupied the front passenger street of the car the man who couldn't read signs said, "Another fucking waste of time Sarge. This enquiry is an absolute bag of rats. I'm bored to fucking death. Who cares about these little scumbags, they get what they deserve."

Burrell snapped, "Every time you open your mouth, shit comes out, and its pissing me off. Drive this fucking car back to the nick and drop me off. I want you to go to the Central Information Unit and start going through some box files. I want to know all about Stewart Doyle and don't come back until you've done all the checks starting with the date that Doyle was released from borstal. Do you understand, you gormless little twat? It's time to get back to basics. You spotted nothing back there? You're no Sherlock fucking Holmes."

The attached man blushed and drove in silence.

Two hours later Burrell was sat at his desk thinking about Sally when the attached man returned carrying a batch of papers. His face was red but this time it was flushed with excitement. He was about to redeem himself.

237

It wasn't long before the two of them were in Rob Docker's office discussing a plan of action.

Doyle's CIU file had revealed that he was out at the time of Baxter's murder and that the offence for which he was in borstal related to an assault on the same man.

There was also a piece of confidential information in the file from the prison officer who had treated Doyle well. The officer had recognised that Doyle was keeping a well-guarded secret and whilst he had never been able to find out what it was, it was clear to him that it was an obsession that continually simmered below the surface.

Under normal circumstances these were facts which would have been researched prior to their visit, but they were simply overwhelmed by the lists of names provided by Hargreaves, and Doyle was just one name buried within hundreds, a lot of whom had criminal records or were untraceable.

Co-incidence, or part of a missing piece of the puzzle? They would soon find out, and now Rob Docker was taking a personal interest.

Docker liked to keep his staff happy, and the attached man's reward before they booked off-duty was to 'spring' for a curry at *'The Jarna Curry House'* in Digbeth which was a favoured watering hole for the CID.

***

It was a 6am start. Docker did not want to overplay the information to hand but there was no point in taking risks and they knew that they could be facing up to four people on the premises. He briefed the other CID officers who included John Burrell, the attached man and Sally, as well as two 'uniforms' and a police dog handler. Hargreaves had also 'wormed' himself into the group.

They all sat around the CID office casually drinking mugs of tea but most of them were seasoned detectives who knew the drill and were well aware that things could always go wrong if they didn't work as a team.

Docker reminded them that Stewart Doyle had two convictions for wounding and was clearly a violent young man. If he was found on the premises he was to be handcuffed quickly and secured – no time for niceties.

The 'dog man' would go around the back of the house with his dog and another officer whilst the rest of them, led by Docker would go through the front door.

Thirty minutes later three police vehicles made a silent approach and pulled up fifty yards short of the house before the officers got into position.

Docker knocked loudly several times as one of the officers stood next to him with a sledgehammer in his hands. The sash bedroom window above them opened and Brenda Doyle looked out. She recognised Burrell among the sea of faces and her heart sank, "What do you fuckers want at this time of the morning?"

Docker shouted back. "Open the door Brenda, or we'll put it in."

Brenda's reaction only confirmed to Docker that he was on the right track. She responded by throwing the contents of a 'piss pot' out of the window which missed Docker but made a considerable splash over the flared trousers of the attached man who recoiled in horror. "You dirty slag," he shouted up at her, as Docker ordered the front door to be smashed in. Burrell could not avoid a

239

smile. A little entertainment was always welcome in such moments.

The officer with the sledgehammer was adept with using its power, and after two massive strikes the wooden frame splintered and cracked as the door fell inwards.

They piled inside and bundled up the stairs just as Ses was coming out of the bedroom shirtless and clearly ready to defend Brenda. As he raised his fists Burrell pre-empted him by punching him square in the stomach. As he collapsed winded on the floor Docker said, "Cuff him, he's nicked for assault police." He added, "Nice one John, those boxing lessons do come in useful at times."

They left Ses to the uniforms, clambering over the groaning figure into the bedroom where Brenda was brandishing the empty crock 'gazunder'.

Docker smiled broadly, he loved policing, and he loved these occasions, the wildness and the fury of confrontations fuelled his adrenalin, but it was all about winning.

He stood back from Brenda, "You could do a bit of damage with that Brenda, and you'd have to walk all the way to the outside 'Kharzi' as well. You're already in the shit so have a day off and don't make it any worse."

He allowed her a moment. She was a powerful woman and Docker didn't fancy that thing wrapped around his ear. Sally and Burrell were circling around Brenda, who saw the hopelessness of her situation and threw the pot at the wall in rage and frustration. "Fucking bastards. You're all bent, I hate you."

Docker affected an aggrieved air - on behalf of his colleagues, knowing that Brenda had him down to 'T'.

240

He moved to gain control and calm the situation. He produced the search warrant that they had obtained the previous day from a magistrate at the Victoria Law Courts and instructed Sally to stay in the bedroom with Brenda, who was also told to get dressed.

Downstairs, Bud, who had been sleeping on the sofa, had attempted a sharp exit via the rear door and was now regretting his actions as blood oozed from a dog bite to his right ankle. A rather large and satisfied Alsatian surveyed him curiously across the room hoping perhaps that he might try to run again. The pile of small plastic 'poly' bags, each containing a quantity of herbal bush cannabis, which now sat on the kitchen table, added to his misery as the dog sat waiting, ears pricked and ready to go again.

A quick search of the remainder of the house revealed no sign of Stewart Doyle and Docker set his team to work to conduct a detailed search of the premises. He told Hargreaves to stick close and positioned himself in the hallway, directing operations. He didn't want Hargreaves poking around on his own.

Burrell and the attached man were allocated Stewart's bedroom to search. The damp smell of the room, which had not been used since Stewart's departure, was not to the younger officer's taste, and the large splashes of urine on his trousers left him feeling anxious to get the job done so that he could get home and change.

Burrell found a photograph of Doyle in a bedside cabinet together with a writing pad which appeared to have some pages missing. He went off to check with Brenda that it was a recent photograph – no warm handshakes on this occasion.

241

The writing pad was of greater interest due to the indentations on one of the unused pages which appeared to bear the word *'paedophile'*. He placed it in a bag and in his pocket. He had special instructions from Docker and had been looking for something like this.

After a few minutes the attached man sat on the bed and lit a cigarette, "Fuck all in here Sarge. The place stinks."

Burrell looked around him mentally ticking off the possibilities. He stopped at the airing cupboard, "Have you looked in there?" he asked.

The attached man pretended to be offended, "Of course - just a pile of old smelly bedding and clothes. You can hardly get in there for crap."

Burrell fought to control his anger at this little upstart, "Empty everything out onto the floor. We're wasting time, and Docker will have your 'guts for garters' if the job's not done properly."

The man knew better than to argue and reluctantly started to remove the contents onto the floor. Rolled up blankets, sheets, old pillows, a couple of old toys, and several items of clothing, the pile grew larger.

As he reached towards the bottom the attached man stopped in his tracks, "What the fuck!"

Burrell pushed him to one side and there in front of him lay a knife and knuckleduster both seemed bloodstained."

"Get a Scenes of Crime Officer and photographer here and tell Docker – quietly though, we don't want Brenda cracking off again." Burrell ordered.

Burrell was an inherently decent person and subsequently laid the credit for the discovery at the door of the attached man who positively glowed at being in the limelight.

The number of police officers at the house increased as a forensic team arrived and photographed the weapons. They had hit the jackpot.

Ses couldn't look Brenda in the face. He had said he'd get rid of the incriminating items but had been called away to some urgent 'business' the day after Stewart fled and had forgotten to do it. He'd meant to sort it out upon his return, but things kept cropping up and he'd thought that as the heat had cooled, and they were safer where they were. It was a disastrous error and would prove to be like a stone landing in a still pond, spreading ripples far and wide.

Docker marshalled his troops together. Since being left in the bedroom with the female officer Brenda had steadfastly refused to answer any further questions as to Stewart's whereabouts. It was time for a different tack.

Bud was despatched to a police station to be charged with possession of controlled drugs with intent to supply, and the officers dealing were given strict instructions that he was to be denied bail by the custody officer.

Brenda was conveyed to a separate police station after being arrested for harbouring an offender, allowing her premises to be used for the supply of cannabis, and attempting to pervert the course of justice. Docker also made sure that Brenda wouldn't be getting any phone calls from the cell block in a hurry. He delegated the job to Hargreaves, confident that Brenda would tell him nothing on the journey. Hargreaves tried to protest, but Docker made the point that he was giving him the prime prisoner. He couldn't help himself and added, "If you'd done your fucking job properly, you'd have been here weeks ago."

With the house quieter and only Burrell present in the room, Docker turned his attention to Ses who was now dressed and seated in the living room, "I don't have much time so listen up. I want Stewart and you've got twenty-four hours to bring him in."

Ses looked up at the man who had got the better of him once, but not again, "Go fuck yourself you honky bastard."

Docker dragged him upright by the collar of his shirt and went to punch him once more in the stomach. His punch never landed. Ses might have been getting on a bit, but he hadn't forgotten his boxing skills. He feinted and hit Docker with a left that rocked him back several steps. Burrell stepped between them and Ses stopped his advance. He recognised the stance of another boxer.

Burrell looked Ses in the eyes, "Think about it before you take another step. You are deep in the shit, don't keep digging."

Docker appeared at Burrell's side, rubbing his jaw, "John, leave us for a moment, it'll be ok, wait outside the door if you want, but shut it – go on, it'll be fine. I want to have a 'man to man' chat with our friend here."

Burrell, hesitated, but complied. He had some thinking to do. For the second time in a few weeks his stomach was churning.

Ses and Docker emerged ten minutes later.

Docker smiled reassuringly, "Come on John, all sorted. Let's get this shithole sorted out, I need a drink. That little wanker with the piss on his kegs owes you for letting him grab the glory of finding the stuff."

Burrell looked quizzically at Ses, but the man just nodded and turned away. Docker saw something in Burrell's face and mentally noted to ask later, but there were too many things to sort out and it went out of his mind.

"What did you say to him?" he asked Docker.

Docker purred, "Just spoke to him in a language he understood, about a few things I know about him. He doesn't care much about himself, but everyone's got a weak spot, and our mate Ses, well he really loves Brenda, and his 'brother'. I made it plain what would happen to them if he didn't come across."

Thirty minutes later the police team left on cue, and Ses watched them go from the doorstep. He prepared himself for the drive ahead and left the house, first making a phone call from a public call box, before heading for Brean. His mind was racing, playing all the permutations – and none seemed to end well. He had decided to ask Stewart what he wanted to do. It was his mother facing jail after all. He truly believed that Docker would manufacture enough evidence to put them all away for a long time. Docker had unnerved him. He knew far too much detail about Joe Docker, 'The Hole in The Wall' and all their related 'business' activities.

What Ses didn't know was that up to ten other individuals were also making the journey with him.

Docker was not a man to leave anything to chance and the time spent at the house had given him time to get authority for a full surveillance unit to be deployed. From a static observation point the officer with 'eyes on' gave the team the code number for a target on the move and away they went.

This was a group of men and women who

245

lived in the shadows of policing and were real experts in their trade. A mixture of bikes, cars and vans cocooned Ses on the long journey south, and the man was oblivious to their presence as layers of clothing and other accessories were regularly changed to maintain the deception.

It took four hours for Ses to reach Brean. But he continued to Burnham before finally turning onto the car park of a large white-fronted pub near to the seafront. As usual, the sea was 'out' and the sands stretched to the horizon.

He went inside and made straight for a corner of the lounge.

Two of the surveillance unit, a man and a woman, ostensibly a courting couple, followed him whilst the rest of the team covered all of the escape routes.

After five minutes the team leader received a message through his covert ear-piece – two clicks in quick succession followed by another two clicks – the game was on, and the officers, having previously had sight of the photo found in Doyle's bedroom, had confirmed his presence.

Ten minutes later, six local uniform police officers stormed into the lounge of the pub and found Ses deep in conversation with Stewart at one of the tables, his helpful relative a passive bystander, already wishing that he had not got involved in 'accommodating' the refugee from justice.

All three were arrested and bundled into separate police vehicles before being taken to a local police station. Back in Birmingham it was smiles all round in Dockers office – it was time for the attached man to buy a couple of rounds in the police bar. Docker was no fool and already had the measure of the wannabee detective. He was inconsequential, there would be plenty of time to sort him out at a more convenient time.

Docker had just one job to do before heading for the bar. Observers could be forgiven for thinking that he was running the show, but the truth was that he still had an Assistant Chief Constable and a Chief Superintendent to keep up to speed, so two phone calls were necessary. They were still happy to manage from a distance and he told them as much as they needed to know.

Despite himself, he was beginning to get interested in this job. There might be something in it for him after all. Burrell had filled him in on what 'Shane' had said – or at least much of it, and it had a ring of truth that events were beginning to fit. Docker didn't like 'kiddie-fiddlers' one bit and he could sense something here that might have some mileage – and if it involved powerful people it could be to his advantage as well. A win-win.

The ACC in turn briefed the neighbouring Chief Constable – suddenly people were sitting up in their chairs and paying some interest. This result had not been expected.

Back in Burnham, ten large portions of fish and chips were being served up before the surveillance team headed home to Birmingham. The Unit had a reputation for great skill and professionalism which unfortunately included 'navel-gazing' debriefs, that went on for some time and scrutinised the performance of each operative in minute detail. It would be hours before they would be allowed to go off duty – no alcohol for them.

*

Dockers list of 'hostages' was growing, and he was

247

confident that he would be able to use them to press sufficient levers to sort out the evidence against Stewart Doyle.

He arranged for the three prisoners at Burnham to be detained overnight, and for Burrell, together with the attached man and four uniform officers, to travel down first thing in the morning to bring them back.

*

Next day they returned in three vehicles in convoy with Stewart Doyle firmly ensconced behind the front passenger seat of one of the cars, handcuffed to the attached man, whilst Burrell drove. It was the 'golden rule' never to let the prisoner sit behind the driver unless you wanted to risk them being strangled whilst behind the wheel.

They went back in almost complete silence apart from the odd forced pleasantry between the two officers. Burrell was tired from the drinking session the previous evening, and the turmoil of his inner-thoughts which he was at times struggling to contain, but the younger officer had a habit of chirping up every few miles as if he liked the sound of his own voice.

Stewart Doyle stared to his left out of the car window and steadfastly refused to engage. He had not spoken a word since Burrell had formally arrested him on suspicion of the murder of John Baxter. The words had hit him like a sledgehammer, and he had withdrawn into himself.

On arrival back in Birmingham Docker started to cut the evidential cake accordingly. Hargreaves was given the important role of working with Sally, leading the preparation for the interviews with Brenda and Stewart. The task was designed to keep him out of the real action, but he couldn't think of a reason to refuse.

Docker and Burrell got to work. They knew their business and worked together like a well-oiled machine, much more complex than one simply being 'Mr. Nice' and the other 'Mr. Nasty'. The very nervous relative from Brean was quick to make a witness statement confirming the date on which Doyle had actually arrived in the resort. He didn't have much choice in the matter, as it was made clear that the alternative was a charge of 'assisting an offender' followed by a remand in custody. He was released without charge and given directions to New Street Station – no free ride back home, just a sigh of relief from a man who was glad to be getting out of the 'big city'.

Ses reluctantly made a witness statement indicating that the room that the weapons had been found in was Stewart's room and that no-one else had used it since his departure to Brean. He failed however to mention that it was actually he who had hidden the items there, nor of course a small matter of a stolen car being set on fire.

Ses received a caution for obstructing a police officer in the execution of his duty. He was escorted from the station by Burrell. It seemed to him that the officer was about to say something, but in the end, he just opened the door and motioned for Ses to leave.

Ses didn't hang about to resolve a nagging feeling that he'd seen Burrell before.

Arrangements had been made for Bud to be produced by means of a *'Production Order'* from H.M.P. Winson Green, having been remanded in custody the day before for drug offences. He likewise made a witness statement denying all knowledge of the weapons after being promised that bail would not be opposed at his next court appearance.

That just left Brenda Doyle and Stewart Doyle.

Brenda Doyle had requested the services of a solicitor, and given her previous experiences of useless 'briefs', was happy to have one nominated from the Legal Aid list. It was not difficult for Docker to make sure that it was a 'friendly face' and he 'briefed the brief' before the interview.

Docker had already decided that he wanted nothing to detract from the recovery of the items at the house, nothing for a jury to get distracted by. The guidance that Docker provided was that he wanted a 'no comment' interview and that's exactly what he got after Brenda had finished her private consultation with the solicitor.

She followed his advice to the letter and Docker put on a show of being frustrated by her silence – so far so good.

Brenda was released on police bail for a month pending further enquiries. Docker wanted to keep her on the end of a hook for the time being.

In the meantime, Stewart Doyle sat in his cell waiting for the inevitable. He had also been offered a solicitor but declined. He trusted no-one in authority anymore, let alone some stranger who was just making money from his misery.

The hours dragged by, and with no watch and no natural light he had no idea what the time was. Every hour the flap in the cell door would drop down and a face would peer inside checking on his welfare before an officer slammed it upwards and firmly shut again. Outside he could hear voices, and the odd shout from adjoining cells, but otherwise he was completely isolated.

Finally, in the middle of the afternoon, the steel door to his cell in the Central Lock Up opened and Burrell beckoned him out.

Doyle followed Burrell across the metal grilled landings, as several uniformed officers bustled about with long key chains dangling from their belts. They were mostly seasoned officers who had swopped the mean streets for a place where they just dealt with mean people.

Entering one of the interview rooms, Docker was already seated, looking intently at some papers. For moments he deliberately ignored Doyle's presence and then looked up and motioned for him to take a seat, "Stewart. I am Detective Chief Inspector Docker, and this is Detective Sergeant Burrell. You have been arrested on suspicion of the murder of John Baxter. You are already under caution. Do you understand that you are not obliged to say anything unless you wish to do so but what you say may be put into writing and given in evidence?'

Doyle nodded and fixed his eyes firmly on the table in front of him.

Docker then proceeded to go through Hargreaves' detailed interview plan, to which he had made one addition, whilst Burrell made contemporaneous notes. Docker had spent years cutting corners and 'fitting people up' but he knew that this one could be played straight – it was already in the bag and didn't need a leg up in the interview.

To each and every question Stewart Doyle proceeded to reply, "No comment."

Docker remained patient and matter of fact throughout, asked each question, waited for the expected response, and then moved on to the next question.

He produced the jacket, the knife, the knuckle duster, the notepad and then just as he was about to finish said, "Just one more thing before I finish, Stewart. I'd like you to have a look at this note and tell me if you have ever seen it before."

It was Sally that had found the note. Docker had quietly instructed her to go through the original murder enquiry without letting Hargreaves know. He had told Hargreaves she had gone on leave for a couple of weeks, instead she had been sat at home working her way through boxes of papers recovered from a damp basement at Leek Wootton, the fading stately home that functioned as Warwickshire Police Headquarters.

It had been a week of shuffling papers, the words swimming across the pages, before Sally found a Scenes of Crime Officer's reference to a note recovered from the murder scene. She had painstakingly traced its path to the exhibits store and disinterred it. The document had been misfiled and as Sally faced box after box of exhibits a lesser mortal might have given up but that wasn't in Sally's nature. Three hours of mind-numbing searching, and plenty of choice language revealed the document – bingo!

Docker had been incensed when he had first seen it, and had it fast-tracked through Forensics. Yet another 'balls-up' which needed to be looked at in due course, or perhaps more than a mistake. His instinct had told him to keep the discovery to himself, Sally and Burrell.

Now he held it in front of Doyle's face in a plastic exhibits bag - it appeared to have been extensively dyed a light red colour. The writing was still clear though.

Doyle studied the note and said, "No comment."

Docker smiled and raised his eyebrows. He paused and said, "Just for your information Stewart, this paper has been subjected to something called, ninhydrin treatment. It's a way of treating the paper chemically to reveal fingerprints. Guess what – if you look carefully on both sides you will see a thumb on one side and a forefinger on the other. One hundred per cent provable fingerprints Stewart – and they are yours."

Doyle's heart sank, along with any hopes of freedom. "No comment", he responded, as Docker closed his notebook and invited Doyle to sign Burrell's contemporaneous notes.

After they had finished Docker asked Burrell to step outside for a moment.

Docker had got what he wanted in terms of the interview and now he made one final effort to find the truth, "Stewart it's just me and you in here now, no notes, nothing recorded, I will deny we ever had this conversation but I'm giving you a chance. What the fuck's going on here. Why did you stab a man more than thirty times? What's really going on?"

Doyle desperately wanted to tell Docker his story, to unburden himself of the guilt and the shame he felt but he couldn't. His life and his faith in authority was shattered, and he certainly didn't trust Docker. He remained silent. He desperately wanted to cry. He felt the tears well up in his eyes – he vividly remembered the moment that knife had been in his hands. He choked and put his head in his hands distraught, "Take me back to my cell now please." He had thought many times that he had reached his lowest point in his life, but this was simply too much

253

for him.

Later that day Doyle was formally charged with the murder of John Baxter and returned to the cells.

He appeared before the Birmingham Stipendiary Magistrate next morning at 10am and was remanded in custody after Docker stood in the witness box, took the oath and gave evidence as to the circumstances of the offence before asking for the remand.

Brenda sat at the back of the court, subdued, just managing to exchange a brief smile and a blown kiss with her son before he was taken down.

Docker briefed Burrell to keep in touch with Brenda. He knew he was giving him a difficult task, but Burrell was an exceptional detective and had a way with people. He wanted to be able to use this woman in the future and sensed that through her entanglements with Ses and Bud she had connections into the criminal underworld that could prove useful. He was also aware of their connections to Joe and it never did any harm to know what his brother's empire was up to.

Three months later, Stewart Doyle appeared at Birmingham Crown Court and pleaded guilty to murder. His defence barrister offered no mitigation on his behalf and after Docker had provided his antecedents, which included his two previous convictions, and social enquiry reports had been considered, the Judge sentenced him to life imprisonment.

Brenda remained strong for her son as the sentence was announced – no time for tears or emotions, she would not break now. She swore vengeance quietly to herself and had time now to find out who the real culprit responsible for her son's destruction had been.

For his part Docker had put a murderer away and there were a few plaudits to be handed around and received. But Doyle had just been a side-show, almost a distraction from the enquiry that he had been posted to. Docker's nose wrinkled – he could smell something rotten in this job and his focus was no longer on getting it done quickly.

Following the conviction Docker sat down in his office with Burrell with the door shut for several hours. He almost trusted the man, as much as he could any human being, and although he didn't occupy a place in his darker side of the world, he enjoyed working with him.

Docker needed to find a way of breaking away from the endless lists of names they were wading through and find his way to the heart of this mess. He also needed to keep Hargreaves at a distance whilst he did so. He had run jobs with a hidden cell within them before, and there were only two people who qualified to be in it.

Chapter Ten

'Tinker, Tailor, Soldier, Sailor'

Hargreaves didn't like it one bit. He knew that Docker and Burrell were up to something, but he couldn't get a foot in the door. He tried to keep tabs on them, but they were too close, there were too many opportunities for them to meet without his knowledge. He had tried to gain Burrell's confidence, but had been rebuffed, and Docker wouldn't give him the time of day.

Hargreaves was worried. His Chief was asking difficult questions, but that wasn't his main concern. He had been tasked from elsewhere, and he knew that he was failing. There could be serious repercussions. He usually worked subtly, but the unexpected progress of the enquiry team was making him increasingly desperate and he was taking chances. He didn't know how, but Docker and Burrell clearly knew more than they were saying. It must have been Doyle who had spoken, off-record, he decided.

Following the Doyle business, the enquiry had, on the face of it, settled back into the routine of ploughing through the haystack of paper he had so carefully provided, making little headway. Hargreaves didn't believe it. He had even tried to get the enquiry quashed at a high level, but had been told that, because of the success with Baxter's murder, it was impossible. He had been curtly reminded of his position and responsibilities and summarily dismissed from a meeting with his superior, who was clearly not happy with him one bit. His initial enjoyment at baiting Docker had quickly faded, and he had begun to feel he was being outmanoeuvred.

* * *

Alan Richardson turned up at the gates of ACF Harris Grange in Rubery fifteen minutes before his fixed appointment to see Peter Hall. He was wearing a smart suit with a waistcoat and black highly polished shoes that you could virtually see your face in. A wiry individual who nevertheless walked with his shoulders erect; he had responded to an advert in a local newspaper for an Adult Instructor to set up a Corps of Drums within the Unit.

From inside the Nissan hut adjacent to the gate, Richardson could hear the bellowing of a man who was clearly not holding anything back.

Eventually, Staff Sergeant Paul Evans emerged from the hut and welcomed the newcomer inside, where the volume of bellowing increased. Peter Hall was in the process of berating a number of cadets for the state of their uniform and was bawling at the top of his voice. With a puffed-out chest, he gripped his leather stick firmly with a brown gloved hand under one arm – a vicious man who effortlessly exchanged his daytime salesman suit for the power of the uniform.

Alan watched with interest as the man stood, eyes bulging, tearing strips off the youngsters, the occasional spit landing on their battle-dress tops, their khaki webbed belts with brass fittings that required constant polishing.

Finally, Peter Hall handed over to Evans and ushered Richardson into his office.

Peter Hall had never seen any real military service, whereas Richardson was an ex-serviceman with campaign medals to his name. Now working in a

257

shop in Longbridge since his discharge he nevertheless retained a huge sense of pride in his previous life.

They went through the formalities of an interview which confirmed that Richardson was proficient in playing the bugle and the side drum, which augured well for the establishment of a new band.

Hall probed a bit further, "We expect a lot of commitment in this Unit. Lots of hours put in, and nothing but the best will do. How do I know that your wife is not going to get fed up with all the time that you spend here?"

Alan had clearly not lost his sense of discipline. "Well sir, there's nothing to worry about in that respect. I am new to the area. I don't have a wife or a girlfriend. I don't like having some woman hanging around my neck. I can be as flexible as you like, and I enjoy working with youngsters. It's nice to see them develop isn't it?"

The deal was sealed – ACF Harris Grange had a new Staff Sergeant and Drum Major.

*

Alan Richardson didn't waste time getting to grips with the Corps of Drums. He was a natural at working with the youngsters, who responded well to his mix of discipline and supportiveness and were keen to please. A talented musician, when he was playing, he carried a bugle on a red cord over his left shoulder, and a side drum fixed from the belt on his waist. As he drummed out various military tunes, and added the blend of bugle calls, the cadets were in awe of his skills. He also taught them how to tap their sticks between each other, as they stood in lines, and in between the drumbeats.

Peter Hall watched from a distance and was suitably impressed.

He was normally a vain man who courted attention to his own achievements but if he could use Richardson to promote his detachment then so be it. He also had an interest in the new man's personal life. He suspected that Richardson was going to fit in perfectly, never mind his musical skills. Hall had an eye for like minds.

After one of the cadet evenings, Hall invited Richardson to go for a pint at the nearby local pub. Hall was well-known in there and treated with a degree of deference – the man was after all an officer. One pint became three, as Hall insisted on paying, and before long they were chatting quite openly, "Still no good lady to rush home to yet then Alan?"

Richardson paused and then declared with a degree of reverence, "Sir I don't have a woman to rush home to" he paused again, "Can I be frank with you sir. I feel I can trust you, but I also understand that I might be giving you some problems."

Hall's level of interest increased, "Alan you must call me Peter when we are socialising. I insist. The formalities are for when we are wearing the Queen's uniform. Fire away. I am not easily shocked."

Richardson tentatively ventured further, ignoring the invite to be over-familiar, "Well you see sir, I am not really one for girlfriends. Not my style. I can assure you though sir that I am totally trustworthy. I don't let my personal preferences cloud my judgement or affect my behaviour. I've a reputation to protect."

Peter Hall smiled broadly, it was music to his ears, "Don't worry Alan, your secret is safe with me.

You are among friends. We are fellow soldiers and I respect your honesty - one for the road?"

They did and after a whisky chaser again paid for by Hall, they were off.

A week later they went for a pint again, this time Paul Evans came along as well. By the end of the evening it was clear to all three that they were of a similar 'persuasion', although nothing more than double-entendre and oblique allusions were made. At the end of the session, Hall announced to Richardson that he was having a small gathering at his house that weekend and that he was invited, "We'll have a curry first at a place I know and then get back home for some beers, a bit of cadet business, a bit of banter among friends – male friends only of course." Hall laughed. Richardson readily agreed and showed his gratitude by insisting on standing a final round.

That Saturday evening as arranged, Richardson met Hall in the *'Anna Purna Indian Restaurant'*, on the Bristol Road, Selly Oak.

Hall already had a table for six in a corner and greeted Richardson with a handshake and a smile, "You used to be able to get a chicken curry in here for forty-eight pence, but the prices have gone up a bit now." he joked.

They sat down with a pint each, but Hall made no effort to order. Fifteen minutes later Paul Evans entered the restaurant with three army cadets, dressed in casual clothes, in tow. Hall watched Richardson's face for any adverse reaction and saw none. He was adroit at 'grooming', whether it be adults or children.

None of the three cadets were members of Richardson's Corp of Drums, but he recognised them as being regular attendees from Richmond House Home in Redditch. They didn't look particularly happy at their good fortune, but Peter Hall announced that it was common practice to acknowledge good work by taking the boys out from time to time – after all they came from under-privileged backgrounds and were not used to 'fine dining'.

Although they were under-age, bottles of beer were placed in the centre of the table and they were allowed to drink freely.

Paul Evans ordered for the three youngsters, and Richardson chose to order a particularly hot *'Vindaloo'*, which he attempted to assuage by downing more beer, but soon there were beads of sweat on his forehead.

With the meal finished and the small talk over, Peter Hall paid the bill and left a good tip. The boys and Evans left for Hall's home, whilst Richardson followed Hall in his own vehicle.

They gathered as a group in the kitchen where more cans of beer were available.

Richardson also noted the presence of a number of pornographic magazines in a well-thumbed pile on the kitchen table which the boys were encouraged to examine, as cigarettes were passed round.

The boys were also encouraged to try and keep up with their elders in drinking, and it was obvious that two of them were already extremely unsteady on their feet although they were still strangely compliant for drunken youths.

Thirty minutes later Peter Hall announced, "Time to relax in the living room I think…." again he scrutinised Richardson looking for any signs of disquiet and saw none. A good evening was in prospect, he thought. After tonight, Richardson would be fully drawn into his web.

The atmosphere changed, as the three boys were ushered to the front living room where the lights had been dimmed and the curtains drawn. The magazines went with them.

Hall and Richardson were paused for a moment in the kitchen, finishing a drink, when suddenly Richardson let out a loud groan and belched at the same time, "Fucking hell. I think I'm going to shit myself sir. I need to use the toilet and quick. I'm touching cloth here."

Somewhat irritated Hall responded, "It's at the top of the stairs on the landing. Get yourself sorted out and join us. We don't want your arse on fire, do we?"

Richardson needed no second bidding and bounded upstairs two at a time farting loudly on the way up. Hall's nose wrinkled as he made his way to the living room.

Fifteen minutes later Hall suddenly remembered that one of his guests was missing and left the room, which was by now hot, stuffy - and unbearable for the three unwilling occupants.

Hall shouted up the stairs, "Alan are you okay?"

From the toilet he could clearly hear the sounds of vomiting, 'useless tool' he reflected and went back inside.

Five minutes later Richardson appeared at the living room door and peered inside, flecks of vomit still visible in his mouth and down the front of his shirt. The smell of regurgitated curry fought with a faint smell of what Richardson took to be 'weed'.

The sickly-sweet odour made Hall's stomach do a lazy flip as Richardson mumbled, "I am truly sorry sir, but I need to go. I must have had a bad curry. I'm going to be shitting through the eye of a needle all night."

Richardson had a clear view of the living room where by now the three boys and Evans were sat naked on the sofas leafing through the porn. A precursor to some 'special love'.

Hall had other things on his mind, "Never mind, there's always another time. Best you get yourself off. I'll leave you to see yourself out."

Richardson groaned again and clutched his stomach; "I will sir. I just need to go again before I leave." He ran for the stairs and Hall gave up and went back into the living room.

After another visit upstairs Richardson stumbled off into the darkness without any farewells. From the sounds emanating from the living room, nobody would have heard or responded.

The following week Alan Richardson turned up bright as a button and immaculate for the next cadet evening. Prior to the usual parade Hall summoned him to his office and left him standing whilst he observed the man from behind his chair.

Hall adopted a formal approach, "Alan I have been giving it some careful thought and I am not sure that we are going to continue with the Corps of Drums. It's not that popular with the cadets and I am considering other options. As it's your speciality I think I will have to let you go. I am sorry to disappoint you but that's the way it is."

Richardson knew the real reason. He had made a fool of himself and was not about to be forgiven. He had failed the 'test'. He left without protest – Hall clearly perceived him to be a total embarrassment and a loser. He left without a word of protest – he had never been that keen on officers anyway even when they weren't proper ones.

*

Hargreaves was correct in all his assumptions. Docker not only didn't trust him but was fast cultivating a level of dislike that boded ill for the Warwickshire man. Docker was, as they often said in the police, treating him like a mushroom. 'Kept in the dark and fed shit'. Hargreaves was oblivious of what Burrell had learnt from 'Shane'. If he had known he would have been panicking, because the trail led from Richmond and Avon Houses to Harris Grange. There was no actual proof, no witness willing to stand up and be counted, in fact there was a 'wall of silence', but a little thing like evidence had never stopped Docker.

*

Rob Docker had considered taking Peter Hall out whilst the man was in full uniform during one of the cadet training evenings, but in the end, he decided on the more traditional approach. The 'fallout' from on high if he had engineered such a public spectacle made it too risky.

After sorting out the search warrant via his 'friendly' magistrate, Docker did what he had done so many times during his service and dragged himself out of bed one morning at an ungodly hour for the early morning briefing.

As he entered the office, he spotted the usual tired faces, some of it self-induced from excessive alcohol consumption the night before, but the rule was 'never be late next morning' and they rarely were. It mattered not what state you were in, but it did matter that you didn't get a reputation for letting your colleagues down.

Amongst the officers sat James Hargreaves,

looking immaculate, like something out of a 'Burtons Tailor's' shop window. Docker had once again tried to resist having him on the job but the man who managed from a distance, Chief Superintendent Rackham, had already insisted that Hargreaves was not to be excluded and reminded Docker yet again that they were, 'all on the same team'. The man's attraction to Hargreaves talents bordered on the ridiculous and Docker had pondered briefly on which team he was actually 'batting for'.

Docker mentally notched up another reason to make Hargreaves and Rackham suffer at some point.

Apart from the four uniform officers and a civilian police photographer, Docker had John Burrell, Hargreaves and the struggling attached man with him. It would be more than enough for Hall, a man who Docker knew was a spineless coward, and now lived on his own.

Docker had already decided that he would make the arrest himself, with the attached man alongside him, whilst Burrell and Hargreaves would focus on the upstairs bedrooms and one room in particular.

They already had a good idea what they were looking for. Men of Hall's type just couldn't resist keeping some 'treasure'.

The knock on the door went in dead on 6am, and the light on upstairs signified that their target was in.

The curtains twitched just once, and minutes later Peter Hall answered the door wearing a dressing gown and pyjamas. He was doing his best to look calm and collected but Docker was an expert in body language and could already sense legs paddling away like mad under the apparently 'calm water'.

Docker went straight for the jugular, produced his warrant card and said, "I am Detective Chief Inspector Docker, are you Peter Hall?"

Hall was the very height of politeness, "Yes officer what's going on?"

Docker wasn't in the mood for small talk, "Just listen carefully. I am arresting you for conspiracy to commit buggery and indecent assaults on under-age males over a period of time. You do not have to say anything unless you wish to do so but what you say may be put into writing and given in evidence. Do you understand?"

Hall recoiled, "I think that there must be some mistake officer. I help young people. I can give you the names of some very influential people who can vouch for me...."

Hargreaves uncharacteristically interrupted the man before he could finish, "Just listen to Mr. Docker. We're not here to listen to bullshit." Hall promptly shut up.

'An interesting intervention', Docker reflected, and stored it away for future analysis.

The officers spread out inside, established that Hall was the only person at the address, and got to work as Hall was allowed to get dressed before being baby-sat in the living room by the attached-man who, knowing his alleged background, recoiled from sitting too close to him.

'Dirty little pervert' he reflected, 'he need's his cock cutting off and shoving in his mouth' – the attached man was not the most eloquent of speakers and an even worse thinker.

With the prisoner secure, Burrell and Hargreaves searched the man's bedroom and within moments the suitcase was recovered from its hiding place at the rear of the wardrobe.

Burrell conferred with Docker, confirming the recovery.

Docker uncharacteristically punched the air, "Well done. We've got the bastard now. Get the suitcase photographed in situ upstairs and then log everything separately. It takes as long as it takes."

Logging and recording the items individually took time as the suitcase was full to bursting.

After an hour, Docker decided it was time to get Peter Hall off to the Central Lock Up so that they could get him through the custody procedure and 'bed him down' prior to being interviewed. Apart from asking by name for a well-known brief who had something of a reputation for being adversarial, Hall had said not one word, in contrast to his initial verbosity.

Docker left, along with the attached man and two of the uniform officers, leaving Burrell, Hargreaves and the photographer to get on with bagging up exhibits, whilst the other two uniform staff remained downstairs to deal with any unexpected visitors to the address.

Hargreaves felt his energy levels starting to sap. This was going bad ways and he needed some thinking space. He called a halt for a moment, "Time for a cup of tea and a stretch, John. I need a cigarette and I'll get one of the uniforms downstairs to make a brew." The photographer shared the same passion for a 'cancer stick' and they left together. Burrell didn't smoke but also welcomed some thinking time.

As was usual, when left to his own devices, John's thoughts turned to Sally. She was far too good for him – he knew full-well that he was 'punching above his weight' but she had accepted him for who he was and expressed unconditional love. He was the happiest he had ever been. But he was wracked with guilt. He had been holding back. Their relationship was built upon flawed foundations and Burrell was caught in a dilemma. Sally was the first girl he had truly loved, and he feared rejection if he confessed, but holding secrets was no recipe for a long-term relationship. And this job, this bastard job, had re-awakened buried memories.

Burrell stood up from the bed he had been sitting on, stretched and paced around the room trying to keep thoughts of Sally in his mind rather than the thoughts of what may have taken place in the room, which had the smell of evil about it.

Stretching his tired muscles, he stepped forward and the floorboards beneath the carpeted floor emitted a creak which got his attention.

Burrell lifted his foot clear and then put it down again – another creak.

Hargreaves returned to the bedroom on his own ten minutes later, leaving the photographer and the two uniforms watching TV with their feet up on the sofa, to find Burrell moving furniture and rolling up part of the carpet.

"What the fuck are you doing John?" he asked.

Burrell paused, "I'll let you know in a minute, maybe nothing."

He peered down at the floorboards and it was obvious that a 'hidey hole' had been created. He pulled a loose section of floorboard up and could see that inside the void were a number of letters addressed to Hall.

Hargreaves and Burrell sat on the bed looking at several envelopes, all of which bore Hall's name and address in 'copper-plate' writing and all bearing a stamp with a London post-mark.

As they examined the letters it became obvious that the author was one Charles Redmund, and that he was clearly a close friend of Hall. It was also evident that they shared a common interest – the pursuit of young boys.

Burrell was curious, "Why has he kept these letters hidden and not in the suitcase. What makes these so special do you reckon?"

It wasn't so much a question as a statement, but Hargreaves decided it was time to try and assert some rank, "John let's wrap it up here. I don't know about you, but I need to put some food in my belly. I'll concentrate on these when we get back and you focus on the suitcase. That way we will get things sorted out much quicker."

Hargreaves placed the envelopes in an exhibits bag and hung onto them. Burrell made a quick assessment of what Docker would say and decided that allaying Hargreaves' suspicions was worth allowing him to have the letters. What could Hargreaves do? He knew Burrell had read them. It was time for some police canteen food.

*

Docker had decided to concentrate initially on building up a picture of Peter Hall's lifestyle during the first interview. His solicitor had turned up with alacrity, and as was his right had elected to have a private consultation with his client - a consultation which went on for hours.

Docker had seen the tactic applied before, and there was nothing that he could do about it. The solicitor was trying to buy thinking time and put pressure on the officers by eating into the period that they had available to conduct an interview before having to provide rest periods.

It was late afternoon before they were ready to go, and Docker and Burrell sat facing Hall and the solicitor across a table in a small interview room. It was functional and oppressive. Docker asked the questions whilst Burrell kept contemporaneous notes.

Apart from acknowledging his name to each and every question, Hall responded, "On the advice of my solicitor I wish to make no comment."

After an hour, Hall's solicitor pushed the delay button again, "I would like to consult with my client again please officer." he smiled at the officers. Docker didn't like that smile but held his gaze. The man was a 'little shit' and Dockers look was one of plain contempt.

Once again Docker and Burrell sat twiddling their thumbs whilst the clock ticked away.

Finally, they went back into interview, and Docker started to press home on the contents of the suitcase.

As they reached this point, Hall's solicitor said, "My client has indicated to me privately that he is not feeling well. Clearly, we don't want to be obstructive, but I do feel officer, that he should be seen by a Police Surgeon to make sure that he is both fit to be detained and fit to be interviewed further."

Docker felt the anger rising with him but stifled his desire to inflict pain on the two bastards in front of him, "Do you want to see a Doctor Mr. Hall?"

Hall put on his best pained look and held his forehead, "Oh yes please officer. I have a very bad headache and feel sick and faint."

Docker had no choice. Details were recorded

270

on the custody sheet and they went into waiting mode again.

As usual, it seemed to take an age before a Police Surgeon, a family-practice doctor who performed the function on a part-time basis, attended, after his normal surgery had finished, and declared the prisoner fit to be detained. Privately he confirmed to Docker that in his professional opinion there was absolutely nothing wrong with the man.

Back into the interview once more and they tried to pick up where they had left off. On this occasion however the solicitor indicated that his client wanted to make a prepared statement. Docker had a feeling it wasn't going to be a confession. He had to grudgingly admit that the brief knew his stuff.

The answer he expected came quickly – the statement was merely a reiteration of Hall's exemplary record of public service. Known in the trade as a 'full and frank denial'. A long diatribe which took them no further but wasted more valuable time.

As Hall finished, Rob Docker once again took up the interview reins with a view to getting into detail but was yet again stalled by the solicitor, "Mr. Docker I think I must ask you to take into account that my client was woken from his bed during the early hours and has spent a traumatic and sleepless day in the cells. It's now starting to get late and he is tired. That tiredness might well affect both the quality of his responses to your questions and their value in evidence. I would invite you to allow him to have a proper rest period. That is of course unless you would like to release him at this stage?"

Docker had no choice but to lodge Hall in the cells for the night.

———

The solicitor left the station and Docker sent Burrell home, "You get back to Sally, mate, and try to put a smile on your face. Back first thing in the morning."

Burrell was thankful to get away, and with Hargreaves and the rest of the team long since gone home, Docker sat in his office with his feet up, drinking a large scotch from the bottle in his bottom drawer.

Docker finished a second drink and then on impulse went back into the Central Lock Up.

He knew the night duty custody sergeant well and had also saved the man, an ex-CID officer, a couple of times following minor indiscretions.

Docker asked for the keys to the cells and made it clear that there was to be no record of his visit on the custody record. That would of course be no problem.

Rob Docker turned the key to Hall's cell and entered, pushing the door nearly closed, but not shut.

Hall looked up, startled, from the bench where he was lying with a coarse grey blanket covering him, "What's going on. Where's my solicitor?"

Docker grabbed the man by the front of his shirt and dragged him off the bench. Twisting the open collar violently he started to choke Hall who attempted to cry out but failed as a punch to his stomach took the wind out of him.

Docker kept his grip, "Hall, I just want you to know that you can run, you can hide, you can lie, you can cheat your way through this, but I'll fuckin do you somehow. Mark my words, your days of messing with kids are over. You are finished."

Docker pushed the man, who fell back into a crumpled heap on the wooden bench. He walked out

272

of the cell and locked the door before returning the heavy bunch of keys and bidding his former colleague goodnight. As he banged the cell door shut, he had glanced at Hall and could have sworn the man was actually smirking. What did he know that Docker didn't?

*

Docker had decided to do the application for a three-day remand to police cells himself in order that the numerous enquiries that still needed to be done could be carried out. It would be a formality, but the added weight of having someone with rank standing in the witness box in one of the courts at Birmingham's Victoria Law Courts could only help.

At 10am sharp, the three-man bench emerged from their room at the rear of the Courts accompanied by the Magistrates Clerk, who was one of Docker's 'drinking partners'. One of the dock officers supervising Peter Hall shouted, "Court rise!" and everyone stood up until the magistrates and the clerk were seated.

The business of the day began, and after a short address by a prosecuting solicitor Docker was invited into the highly polished, wood-lined witness box. Docker exchanged a fleeting glance with the Chair of the Bench, a local businessman and another familiar face.

Docker was instructed to take the oath and, as he had done so many times, raised his right hand, Bible firmly grasped within in it, and read from a printed card, "I swear by almighty God that the evidence I shall give shall be the truth, the whole truth, and nothing but the truth." Docker was a well-practiced actor and gave the oath in a passionate yet reflective voice as if it was his first time. Deeply meaningful words that meant absolutely nothing to Docker who stared firmly at the bench, assertive but a pillar of honesty. He was 'The Law'.

Docker was invited to outline why the police required the remand, and the magistrates listened intently as Hall leaned forward from his seated position in the dock, straining to catch every word.

Burrell and Hargreaves sat on the wooden public benches at the back of the court watching a master at work.

Docker concluded his evidence and then waited for the expected onslaught from Hall's defence solicitor, who sat looking dapper and serious, studying his papers and fiddling with his glasses. The onslaught didn't come,

The solicitor stood up and addressed the magistrates directly, "I have no questions for the officer your worships, but would like to address the court." It was a clever ploy by the solicitor who neatly avoided a public spat with a senior police officer in open court. He didn't want to lose the opportunity to win the sympathy vote, and any allegations of assault against the officer could be saved for later use as necessary.

Docker stood down from the witness box and watched the solicitor go to work, effectively trying to demolish the police case in relation to the contents of the suitcase on which so much relied, "Is it an offence to possess pornography for personal use your worships? My client is an officer in the Army Cadet Force – why wouldn't he have pictures of cadets enjoying themselves? Some of the material was confiscated whilst on cadet camps from some of the youngsters – my client was merely the innocent custodian of some of this material."

And so, he went on. The man was clearly 'waxing lyrical' and enjoying himself, whilst stressing the fact that the police had not even put any specific allegations to his client during interview and were merely on a 'fishing expedition'.

The defence solicitor sat down after making one last statement, "My client should be charged today, or released from custody. The police are clearly not in a position to do the first, and if they ever are, my client is more than willing to surrender himself to the police. He has a fixed address, full-time employment, and is greatly respected within the community for his voluntary work with young people. He, like any other citizen, deserves to be considered innocent until a court determines otherwise."

The Chair of the Bench consulted with his two colleagues and the clerk, who then announced an adjournment in order for them to consider the facts. In truth Docker knew that they were just going to sit on their arses in the back room and drink tea for twenty minutes.

Sure enough, at the allotted time they re-emerged. Everyone stood up and sat down again like regimented puppets as the Chair of the Bench put on his glasses and addressed those assembled, "Mr. Hall stand up please. We have considered all of the facts carefully. Mr. Hall is a man of previous good character. He has no convictions. On the balance of what we have heard today we are not minded to approve the prosecution's request for a remand to police cells."

There was some shifting of seats as one of the magistrates to the man's left looked distinctively uncomfortable, "The application is therefore denied. Release the prisoner. We will take a short

---

adjournment again before moving on to the next case."

Docker glared at the three men as they retired from the room for a second time. Docker was used to some 'nobbling' going on, but it was normally done by him and he bit down on his anger. Clearly darker forces were at work, and to pull this off, were to be reckoned with. What had he stumbled upon, and what did it mean for his own well-being? Time for some reflection.

There was silence in the court as Hall was ushered out of the dock and then out of the court by his solicitor, who maintained a cosmetic veil of sternness which befitted the occasion.

Docker followed, and motioned for Burrell and Hargreaves to follow him – they walked out of the court and turned left, down St. Judes Passage, the narrow passageway leading to the police station, in complete silence.

"My office now John – we've got some sorting out to do." Docker pointedly motioned to Burrell only, and Hargreaves took a seat at a desk outside. The office door closed. Hargreaves' attention was drawn to a newspaper opened at a page which provided details on the recent case of the ex-Metropolitan 'Porn Squad' chief Wallace Virgo, who had been found guilty of taking bribes from Soho vice-kings. He didn't notice Docker watching him intently through the window.

*

Docker gave Burrell strict instructions that Hall was to be their number one target and to drop everything else. Docker channelled his anger into reviewing the various lines of enquiry, during which Burrell mentioned the recovery of the letters from their hiding place.

Docker's ears pricked up – this was news to him, why hadn't he been told? Burrell explained that he had assumed that Hargreaves had showed them to Docker. He got a bollocking for his trouble.

Docker concluded, "John you should know better than to trust that tosser with anything. He's tied up in this somehow. Probably getting some back-handers and a promise of the next rank."

Before dismissing Burrell, he made one final point, "John I want the surveillance on Paul Evans to continue for seven days and then we'll bring him in. Any new contacts made in that time I want to be told about immediately. Make sure that the flag against his name on PNC is down to you and me only. We need to be told about sightings, vehicles etc. and particularly any meets with Hall. We're in the middle of a viper's nest and I won't rest until they've all been skinned and hung out to dry."

Burrell was despatched, and as he left Hargreaves appeared at the doorway. "I need to speak to you about some letters that we recovered at the house." The man seemed to have the knack of perfect timing.

Docker barely contained himself, "I should have been told about this earlier James. What's going on?"

Hargreaves sat down without being invited and passed the bundle of letters across the table, "John's been up to his eyeballs with the other exhibits, so I just tried to help out a bit. I've read through them and done some research. I think that you need to have a look through them as well Rob."

Docker ignored his attempts at familiarity, "Do you think I've got time to sit reading letters

277

James. What do I need to know?"

Hargreaves persevered, "The letters are from a man called Charles Redmund who is currently serving a prison sentence for child abuse having been arrested by the Metropolitan Police...."

Docker interrupted, "You mean Charles Redmund, the MP?"

Hargreaves frowned, "One and the same. He's in a prison down south but has a house up this 'neck of the woods' and a lot of interesting connections including a local councillor called Ernest Page."

Docker stifled any visible indications that he knew the man that Hargreaves was referring to, but Councillor Ernest Page was indeed quite well-known to him, and for all the wrong reasons. Once again, alarm bells were ringing. This job had layers upon layers, and Docker had just found his own name in one.

Hargreaves continued in a matter of fact fashion, "Page was acquitted some time ago of indecency offences. Got off as 'clean as a whistle', an innocent man falsely accused it seems."

Docker shifted uneasily, "Get to the point. I've got a raving headache and I've still got a fuckin performance report to complete today."

Hargreaves oozed sympathy, "Yes, I know that you have a lot on, but apart from today's blip in court things are going really well aren't they? It would be a shame if anything detracted from that success. I really do think perhaps that you should take a few moments to have a look. They might be just what we are looking for evidentially, or they may be nothing. I think it should be your decision. You are after all the boss."

Hargreaves smiled and thrust the letters across the desk gently before making his excuses and leaving the room.

Docker sat staring at the letters and tried to make sense of what Hargreaves had just said. He disliked the man intensely and disliked him even more when he was trying to be smarmy. Docker reached for the letters – the performance report would wait.

It took him an hour to read through them all, at which point he turned the key in his office door to give himself a moment's peace and reached for the whisky bottle in his bottom desk drawer which seemed to be getting something of a pounding these days. At this rate he would soon need to visit his metal dealer friend for a fresh bottle. Just one to calm his nerves turned into two.

The letters clearly showed evidence of a paedophile connection between Hall, Redmund and Page – prima facia evidence that would add some real weight to the case that they were trying to assemble.

The problem was that the letters also clearly indicated a corrupt relationship between Page and a senior police officer. If that should become a line of enquiry, then it might lead right back to the person currently holding the letters. Docker was annoyed with himself. An easy and seemingly uncontentious 'little earner' had risen from the grave to potentially fatally bite him.

Hargreaves was certainly a man of high intellect and was now in possession of some facts that were a threat to Docker's very existence. He couldn't know for sure though, could he? Docker thought he could, but only if he were enmeshed in this too. Which might explain the sudden attempt at friendship. If Hargreaves' job was to 'cuff' this enquiry, then what better way than to find a bond of self-interest with the lead investigator?

What a mess! The only thing in Docker's favour was that nobody, especially the likes of Hargreaves, could imagine the depths to which Docker would stoop to protect himself.

The only other person to have seen the letters would be no less inquisitive, as good detectives were. Docker would need to deal with Hargreaves and Burrell, but for the time being he was undecided as to how.

The letters went into his locked cabinet – hidden from sight but not from mind.

Chapter Eleven

'Humpty Dumpty Sat On A Wall'

Two days after the release of Hall there was an unexpected development.

Burrell was finishing yet another gruelling twelve-hour tour of duty and had just phoned Sally to say that he was on the way to take her out for a late drink. The last few weeks had been difficult, and he was acutely conscious that their relationship was suffering. He had been unable to hide his inner turmoil and she had begun asking awkward questions to which he had no answers. Fortunately, she had initially put it down to his being affected by the grim details of Operation *'Damocles'*, which was true, but not in the way Sally thought.

But that didn't really fit with Burrell's usual tough persona. After all he had seen just about every type of iniquity perpetrated by humans during his police career, and Sally had clearly begun to ask herself whether it was their relationship that was the underlying cause of his ill humour.

The moment he put the phone down, it rang. Burrell hesitated for a moment. Who would know if he just let it ring and walked off? He didn't have it in him to do it though, his sense of duty always came before anything else and Sally knew it. With an uncharacteristic sigh he picked the phone up.

It was one of the custody sergeants in the Central Lock Up, "John you should have had a phone call earlier, but the officer dealing with a prisoner we've got in doesn't know his arse from his elbow. We've got a Paul Evans in custody for assault.

There's a marker flag on PNC saying that you need to be informed."

From what was known about Evans, this was completely out of character. Burrell hadn't expected any result of from the 'flag' Docker had asked to be put on the man, but here he was, a few steps away. Another demon to confront. Once more he hesitated, then forced his fear down, "I'll be with you shortly."

He rang Sally back to give her the news and got short shrift. Her patience was wearing thin. It was not the moment or the means by which to tell her the truth.

Burrell promised not to be long, but his pleas fell on deaf ears, "You think more of Docker and this bloody job than you do me. I'm off to fucking bed – don't wake me up."

In the custody block, Burrell got a briefing from the custody sergeant. He just couldn't resist the urge to see Evans in his cell. The prisoner was said to be in a highly emotional state and had been bedded down for the night to calm down. Burrell had to know why he had done what he'd been arrested for.

Evans had been apprehended in the act of punching and kicking local Councillor Ernest Page in St. Phillips Churchyard in Colmore Row. The officer who had been sent to the incident had described it as being a bit of 'handbags at dawn' in nature, but unfortunately the Councillor had fallen during the struggle and finished up with a nasty head wound which had required his admission to the Birmingham Accident Hospital overnight.

What the arresting officer did not know was that the incident had been called in by one of the surveillance team following Evans, who had witnessed the meeting on one of the benches in the churchyard, which had then led to a heated exchange, followed by the fight.

Under strict instructions not to blow their cover, the team had made an urgent call for police attendance as members of the public gave the grappling pair a wide berth.

Burrell was too close to this, raw emotions had been disturbed, and both his thinking and judgement were affected. Uncharacteristically he failed to phone Docker for advice and decided to go it alone.

Outside the door were the man's shoes and leather trouser belt – no sense in taking risks when someone was in a bit of a state. Prisoners had even been known to create ligatures with shoelaces and it wasn't going to happen on this custody sergeant's watch.

Burrell found Evans curled up in a ball on the wooden bench, tears streaming down his face. He remembered the man. It had not been so long ago. Thirteen years had barely changed Evans, but Burrell was no longer a young teenager.

Burrell adopted his most sympathetic tone, "I'm Detective Sergeant Burrell" he announced, and went on, "I understand that you have been arrested on suspicion of assaulting a local councillor. You will be interviewed about that in the morning, but I just wanted to make sure that you are okay and to have a chat about some of your circle of friends."

He had got Evan's attention, "You're working with that guy Docker I presume?"

Burrell said, "That's right he is my gaffer."

Evans responded, "Peter Hall told me about how Docker assaulted him in a cell. Is that what you are here for?"

Burrell fought down queasiness and anger at the mention of Hall, "Nothing of the sort Paul. I'm just trying to get to the bottom of what looks like a big mess – a serious one at that. Perhaps I can help…?"

Burrell left his open question hanging in the air and sat down on the bench next to Evans, hands deliberately thrust into his pocket, unthreatening, and relaxed, a friend perhaps.

Burrell spent the next twenty minutes talking about anything and nothing, no probing, no threats, just soothing reassuring words aimed at giving Evans some hope, some comfort, perhaps a way out.

Burrell chose his moment, "Listen Paul, I think that you have a whole weight on your shoulders which needs lifting. I'm not taking any notes, there is no-one else here and I can't use what you tell me against you. This is a moment to trust me and lift that burden so that you can move on with your life. It's up to you. I am happy to walk out of here and leave you alone or I can sit here and listen. It's your choice Paul – what would you like me to do?"

After what seemed like an eternity Evans responded, "I've got something to tell you."

Burrell took a gamble. "Just get your thoughts together Paul, while I go and get us both a mug of tea. I'll be back in five minutes." It was a gamble, but one which was designed to cement the trust between the pair.

Burrell returned to the cell with two strong mugs of tea which he'd made in the CID office and rustled up a couple of biscuits.

Burrell settled down again on the bench, "I'm all yours Paul, take your time and let's just see how we go."

For the next thirty minutes Burrell sat listening to Evans spill his heart out. It had all gone too far. He was, he admitted a homosexual, but he insisted that he had never willingly got involved in child abuse. Bullied by Hall, beaten occasionally by Baxter, bought off with gifts by Charles Redmund MP, the list went on.

Burrell just let him talk. He was well aware that he was already breaking all the rules by not cautioning the man, but he had an irresistible urge to hear the full extent of it. He had been tortured by guilt since speaking with 'Shane'. He knew, he always knew, that there must have been others, but he had buried it deep, and had said nothing, done nothing, even after swearing the police oath. Now he knew for sure what he had turned his face away from. Others had suffered, lots of them, and he could have saved them, at least some of them. How many were there, during the last thirteen years, when he could have said something, done something?

This bloody job. He was too close, too involved. One by one, the ghosts had arisen. Ses, who had sent him to the Cadet Unit because of his boxing prowess. Baxter who had driven the boys from the homes. At least Doyle had done for him. 'He had more guts than me' thought Burrell. Evans, ridiculous even then, and Hall, the worst of them. None of them recognised the boy who had boxed his way to confidence, enclosed within the adult body of the tough, no-nonsense John Burrell. Names meant nothing to these people – just the young bodies they occupied.

Burrell thought he knew the top and bottom of the whole nauseous business, could have told Docker everything weeks ago, but he was wrong. He had never met Page or Redmund. Burrell had been too much of an unknown quantity, from a good, stable family background. Hall had kept him for himself, too much of a risk to pass upwards.

Whilst Evans rambled on, Burrell concluded to himself that he had let everyone down, especially Sally. He had failed in his duty. The shy and bullied boy that he had been resurfaced. He was broken. He attempted to pull himself together, and returned his full attention to Evans, just as matters took a twist for the worse.

Evans had got to the question of Ernest Page, "I always loathed him. He's totally bad just rotten to the core" he asserted, "He struts around as if he owns the place - drunk on power. It was him who was pushing all the time to set up the parties. He was paying Baxter to do more and more. It just all went too far. I tried to tell them to stop, but they wouldn't listen."

Burrell continued to listen, allow Evans to fill the silent void, "And there's one more thing that you need to know." he paused, "He's got a bent one of yours in his pocket who made some witness disappear when Page was facing an indecent assault charge."

Burrell interrupted him, "What's the name of this officer?"

Evans shook his head, "I don't know. All I know is that he's met him in Birmingham. He's a senior officer and perhaps he's not the only one. It shouldn't take long for you to find out."

Burrell called time – he had heard enough. He had things to take care of. "Okay Paul let's leave it at that for now and we'll see what we can sort out tomorrow. You can trust me. I won't let you down. Get some rest now."

Burrell hated the little shit with every bone in his body for what he was, and the harm he had done, but hid it. He needed Evans onside. He was the key to doing something to end this, maybe too late for some, but he could help those to come.

Burrell left the cell clutching his mug, his mind already ten steps ahead. He made for the office and made a phone call to Docker, not quite sure whether it would be another 'bollocking' or a pat on the back.

It turned out to be the latter as Docker concluded, "You've done well John. Keep it pretty tight until we have had time to go through it all again tomorrow. Have a couple of pints on me in the bar and put it on my tab."

Burrell had intended shooting straight off, but with a lot to ponder, and Sally's words still ringing in his ears, he decided on a pint and went downstairs to the basement bar. He was surprised to find James Hargreaves feeding a 'one-armed bandit', with a gin and tonic in his free hand.

Hargreaves insisted on buying Burrell a drink, and two more followed courtesy of Docker. Burrell was careful, but the encounter did nothing to help resolve his racing mind, and he missed wondering why Hargreaves should even be there, so conveniently, at that time of the evening. It wasn't even their normal parade station during the operation. It also didn't take long for Burrell to indicate that he had just been speaking to someone of interest in the cells – not quite as tight as Docker had instructed.

Finally, tiredness caught up with Burrell, who donned his jacket and said his goodbyes, leaving Hargreaves in the bar.

Burrell drove home to a house in darkness. He

287

really needed to be comforted, perhaps to confess all. He keyed the door and stepped inside to silence. Sally had placed some bedding on the living-room sofa – the message could not have been clearer. He just couldn't face any more emotional trauma and curled up on the couch. After an hour of agonising, he found some relief in sleep.

Fifteen minutes after Burrell's departure, as the bar was closing, James Hargreaves presented himself to the custody sergeant in the custody block. There had been a shift changeover, but the previous sergeant had briefed his night shift colleague that Evans was a man of interest to the CID, so he wasn't surprised when Hargreaves requested to see the prisoner on behalf of DCI Docker. Hargreaves had seen the name 'Evans' on the prisoner dry-wipe board and understood the connection.

Whilst the custody sergeant had an inherent dislike of 'county wankers', he complied and left Hargreaves alone with Evans in his cell.

Fifteen minutes later Hargreaves departed the Lock Up. Everyone had a vulnerability, a pressure point, and Evan's button had been pushed. A weak man at his lowest ebb, he had been given a way out with honour, his ageing mother and beloved sister 'looked after'. The alternative was ruin, and worse.

An hour later, one of the custody assistants dropped the hatch of the cell occupied by Evans and peered inside, to be met with the sight of the prisoner slumped on the bench with his head resting on his chest. Evans had slashed both of his wrists and stabbed himself in the jugular vein in his neck with broken pieces of the porcelain mug that Burrell had inadvertently left in his cell. A large pool of blood had spread across the cell floor and blood had actually sprayed the ceiling of the cell from the neck injury.

Paul Evans was dead, and as the staff in the Central Lock Up went into a well-rehearsed drill when someone 'topped themselves', Docker got another phone call at home with the news.

At that stage neither Burrell's visit to Evans nor that of Hargreaves had been recorded on the custody sheet, and the custody sergeants were not about to commit professional suicide by disclosing them. The cell however had been preserved for forensic examination and the Complaints and Discipline Department called in as a matter of routine. They were all over it like a rash – the broken mug was a complication that no-one had bargained for, and the custody staff had no option but to leave it in the cell because of its fatal use.

Burrell was woken on the sofa by a truculent Sally who had picked up the house phone. He was briefed by Docker to take a day's sick leave until C& D had done their work and left the Lock Up. Burrell was beside himself with the thought that he might be responsible for the loss of the crucial evidence to convict Hall and others. He had no feelings for Evans, but he had been 'small-fry'. Docker had to be firm and directive to keep him from throwing himself at the mercy of C & D. The Burrell he knew seemed to have gone AWOL, replaced by a gibbering wreck.

With no knowledge or understanding of what was going on, Sally dressed for work and left the house without speaking. Burrell's pain increased.

On the surface, Docker was being as supportive as ever of his staff, and those around him appreciated the man's loyalty. At that stage he was unaware of Hargreaves follow-up visit to the cells, and the man had also absented himself for the day on the pretext of an urgent call back to his home force.

*

Rob Docker had a more pressing problem than Hargreaves, an unexpected one. Burrell seemed to be disintegrating, and the detective's level of knowledge about some of Docker's activities could pose a threat, especially of Burrell threw himself on the sword of Complaints and Discipline. Docker knew about Burrell's visit to Evans, but not the detail of what had been said. Docker felt vulnerable, and that was when he was most dangerous.

His first task was to visit Ernest Page in hospital. Once, long ago, Docker had arranged for the complaint in the case against the man to conveniently disappear after contact and payment from an anonymous 'middleman'. A 'nothing job' from his younger days. But Docker hadn't left it there, he had made a 'freelance' approach to Page and there had been occasional 'business' between them since, but nothing to do with young boys.

To the world, Page remained an innocent man, but Docker now knew it was far more than a spot of 'cottaging' and corruption that Page was guilty of, and it left a bad taste in his mouth. He had been well-paid for his efforts, but the man made him feel nauseous. He was a dangerous 'loose end'. It had always been a fact that they could take each other down, so discretion was mutually assured, but this investigation would steamroller through that pact if Page were implicated.

Docker's message to Councillor Page was courteous but firm and the man was instructed to keep his mouth shut firmly. He had merely been the victim of a vicious and unprovoked attack from a man who had accosted him in the churchyard, and that was all he was to say.

The fact that Evans was now dead left that version of events unchallenged and Page left hospital later with his head swathed in bandages, steered out of the building by his long-suffering wife who knew nothing about his other life.

Docker's second call was to the owner of a 'sauna' in Handsworth which he visited from time to time. The use of the word sauna was somewhat misleading; rather it was just a conventional label for a brothel. The business was owned by a local criminal who used it to launder his ill-gotten gains from the local drugs trade. He had ten girls on the books who were looked after by a 'madam' – a jovial lady who had been in the 'oldest profession in the world' for years, but was now enjoying her management role asserting on a regular basis to clients that she was 'too old to open her legs' anymore. She always produced a 'belly-laugh' at her own joke but having survived the streets she was no pushover.

The owner of the place had developed a direct line into Docker, who sorted out any issues in relation to difficult clients in exchange for free-gratis visits, and also ensured that the premises were protected from the prying eyes of the local Plain Clothes Unit. Docker had registered the owner as an informant and the intelligence records had been clearly marked *'No action to be taken against these premises without prior consultation with DCI Docker.'*

Docker had a particular liking for a short blond girl who had clearly broken the unwritten rule that you should never have feelings for a client. Despite having shared Docker's affections with one of the other girls, after an unexpected 'tag team' on his last visit, she displayed genuine warmth towards him which was reciprocated. Docker had no problem in displaying warmth as a lover but just not to his wife.

The brothel keeper's role was to concoct a totally fictitious story about John Burrell visiting the premises and trying to blackmail the blond girl into having sex with her under threat of being arrested. Docker, true to form, had decided to ditch Burrell.

Within twenty-four hours, Docker had provided them with a photo of Burrell, which had been taken at a recent leaving function, together with personal details of the officer - just sufficient to give any investigator the ability to form a reasonable assessment that the man was genuinely known to them.

The 'nail in the coffin' was delivered after Docker had a 'heart to heart' with the attached man who had been so much 'under the thumb' from Burrell. Docker explained that the Force was conducting a highly sensitive integrity test on an officer who was suspected of being corrupt. The attached man's job was to tell John Burrell that he had received a phone message from a man claiming to have important information about Peter Hall, and that he wanted to meet urgently at an address in Handsworth.

Docker swore the man to secrecy with the implied promise of a Detective Constable's post in the future. Good things he said, came to 'trusted soldiers'.

Burrell duly got the message on his return to work and turned up at the sauna. After being invited in he was met in a room by a blond woman and two men, "This is the man officers," she said, her voice trembling.

An already traumatised John Burrell found himself in the clutches of the Complaints and Discipline Department.

Within an hour, another team of officers was going through Burrell's desk and locker, from where a brown envelope containing a bundle of used notes were recovered, plus one rather large and partially smoked 'spliff'.

Things were not looking good.

By the end of the day a stunned Burrell had seen his warrant card taken from him and suspension notices served by Chief Superintendent Rackham, pending a full investigation into the allegations.

He turned to the one man whom he thought would help him in his hour of need and after a phone call, met Docker at a pub in the city-centre that evening.

He knew that Docker was bending the rules by agreeing to see him but knew the man would not let him down.

Docker listened intently to the story as it unfolded from Burrell's lips. The man was visibly distressed, beside himself with worry and concern at the prospects of being charged and losing everything. Docker shook his head. He could scarcely recognise the Burrell he knew. He had thought the Sergeant was made of tougher material. He internally reproached himself for such bad judgement. It re-affirmed that he had made the correct decision in vowing to 'resolve' the situation before any damage could be done – to him.

Burrell was pleading for advice, and it wasn't long in coming, "John. You're a good man in my book but that counts for nothing in a situation like this. Even if you managed to get the blackmail knocked on the head, you can't get away from the cash and the cannabis. Mud sticks." Docker paused, "On top of that it won't take long for them to match your prints on the broken mug that Evans used to kill himself with - gross misconduct at minimum, leaving it in a cell for a prisoner at risk to use." Docker paused again for the words to sink in, then delivered the 'coup de grace', "I know someone in C & D. My advice John is that you should try to save yourself from the risk of prison. Offer your resignation and I'll do my best to get them to call it a day – job done."

John Burrell's world totally disintegrated.

*

John Burrell had lost the job that he loved, the job that defined him, had rescued him from the horror, had rebuilt him. But worse than that, he had lost hope. A hope that resided in the woman that was most precious to him. Sally had been the 'glue in his life', kept him sane, happy, and had given him a new purpose. He couldn't bear to lose her.

In the days following his suspension and resignation he had tried and failed to convince Sally that he was completely innocent. But she had known he was hiding something, and, even now, he couldn't tell her about his shame, his weakness at the Cadets. She had thrown him out and then refused to take any of his phone calls. Finally, after begging her to meet, she had relented and arranged to see him in a pub near her home after she had finished work at 6pm.

Burrell got there early and had a double whisky to calm his frayed nerves, and then another, which was a big mistake. By the time Sally arrived he was already well the worse for wear. As she got to his table he stood up, swayed slightly and tried to peck her on the cheek. She avoided his fumbled attempt and sat down, already regretting her decision. It was so sad to see his decline.

John weaved his way to the bar and came back with a 'Gin & Tonic' and another double whisky.

Sally looked at Burrell and thought that she still loved him despite everything. The corruption she could have lived with - he wouldn't be the first to have dipped his fingers into the till, but the prostitutes were beyond forgiveness. And she knew he was still lying. There was something else. She had put him on a pedestal and thought that he was so different from the others. He had made a complete fool of her and she couldn't let it go even though her feelings remained so strong.

Sally did him the courtesy of listening, she thought it would be the last time that they would meet, and owed him that much, but her mind was already made up. She had sought advice earlier in the day from Rob Docker, and whilst he wasn't always to her taste, he had made it clear that as far as he could judge, the evidence against John was overwhelming.

As the effects of the whisky continued to take hold, John's excuses turned to pleadings. He tried several times to grasp her hands across the table, but she was having none of it.

John's emotional state was starting to draw the attentions of other pub-goers and Sally's heart was breaking. She had sworn twice before that she wouldn't let another man do this to her, and yet here she was again. She buckled up her feelings. She had to be strong now.

As the tears welled up in his eyes and started to trickle down his face, she couldn't stand anymore,

"John, this has got to stop. It ends here. You have a label now – you're a bent copper. Worse than that you betrayed me, and I can't forgive that. I hope that you can find your way in the future, but it will be without me. Please don't contact me again." She slid the engagement ring that had cost him a month's wages across the table, got up and left. She didn't look back – if she had he would have seen her own tears.

John Burrell sat staring at the ring and felt numb.

After what seemed an eternity to those still watching, he slipped it into his pocket and went to the bar for another whisky. In the final humiliation of the evening the barman refused to serve him and asked him to leave, "We don't want drunks in here causing trouble mate. Piss off or I'll call the police."

In hindsight that would have been the best thing that could have happened to Burrell.

*

Burrell drove to the nearest off-licence and purchased a half-bottle of whisky, before driving into Birmingham city-centre and parking up by the old railway club in Monument Lane. He had attended a few charity functions with the railway police there and enjoyed their company. They weren't a bad lot and stoically accepted the constant ribbing from their Home Office colleagues that they were not 'real coppers'. Just at this moment he would have died for the company of just one of them – real or not.

The lights were on inside the club, but he made no effort to enter, instead swigging from the bottle and trying to find some answers, trying to find a way forward, trying to break out of the nightmare, trying to envisage a life without Sally. Each thought

---

just led into a dead-end.

There was a public phone on the wall in the foyer of the club and after a while Burrell went inside and tried to phone Sally. The first calls went unanswered and then finally he heard her voice at the other end. Burrell began to plead like a child for her not to abandon him; he couldn't bear the thought of being without her.

Sally had reached the end of her tether, "Go to hell and leave me alone." she screamed before slamming down the phone.

Burrell tried to call again in desperation – he needed to hear the sound of her voice. The phone was off the hook at the other end.

John Burrell made one more phone call to the man he had trusted implicitly. He phoned Rob Docker on his home number. His wife Lilian answered, cold, detached and unfriendly. Docker was 'out'. She didn't know or care where – he was probably with 'that reporter whore'.

Burrell held the phone in his hand for a few moments – he had nowhere left to turn. He had not spoken to his parents since the day he had joined the police. Although totally irrational in his heart he blamed them too for what had happened to him. Placing the receiver back on the handset he staggered into the toilets and vomited on the floor.

Back outside, Burrell returned to the car, his mind made up.

His briefcase was still on the back seat. He fished a pad and pen out of it and started writing. It was meant to be a short note, but the words began to flow as he unburdened himself, as he had never been able to face to face. He carefully folded the pages into his coat pocket before making his way down a slope at the side of the club which lead to the railway track.

There was a small gate at the end which allowed access to the 'Permanent Way' gangs who checked the tracks daily. It was open, and Burrell made a right turn and walked in the direction of the tunnels. He wasn't thinking anymore, he was just focused on taking the pain away.

In his younger days Burrell had chased a few thieves across railway tracks and knew that trying to walk on railway sleepers was a matter of balance and focus. He had neither at that moment so stumbled now and again on the ballast stones before finally reaching the mouth of the tunnel.

A ten-minute walk would bring him to the platforms on New Street Station, but he wasn't going there.

Inside the tunnel, he made his way to one of the alcoves that were dotted at regular intervals along the track. They weren't that deep but gave just enough protection from passing trains. As he sheltered, a train passed through, the lights inside shining brightly, and the draught from the carriages creating a suction which threatened to draw him out from safety. It was a mesmerising feeling. Burrell stood there as two further trains passed him heading north towards Wolverhampton.

As the next train approached Burrell took three steps into the middle of the track and faced the drivers cab his arms raised in the crucifix position. In the glare of the train lights Burrell saw the shock on the train driver's face, but whilst the speed of the train coming out of the station was not high, the driver had no chance of applying the brakes. Death was instantaneous.

The three British Transport Police officers

who responded to the call, the entire shift in fact, were not new to this scenario, but dealing with death was an individual experience that they each handled in different ways. In truth everyone's stomach churned at least a little bit when the call for *'one under'* came over the radio.

John Burrell's body was trapped under the first carriage of the train as the driver's compartment had passed over him. It was instantly clear to the officers that the man was dead, and although the body was not badly disrupted, it took time to remove him to the side of the track.

The authorities were impatient to get the trains running again, but the officers did their duty diligently and would brook no pressure from anyone to cut corners. Surprisingly, Burrell had suffered few facial injuries and, in the torchlights, and darkness of the tunnel one of the officers recognised him, "This guy is a local copper. I've had a drink with him at the club."

They searched him and found the pages he had written, "What a fucking waste of a life." the officer mused as he put the paper into an evidence bag..

One of the officers left to phone a senior officer, whilst the other two got Burrell's remains into a body bag, strapped it together, and with help from some of the rail staff carried him back along the line to one of the platforms.

Shortly afterwards, he was taken by a firm of undertakers, with one of the officers providing identification continuity, to the mortuary at Newton Street, a place that Burrell was entirely familiar with in life, but which was now to be his own temporary resting place in death.

Rob Docker got the call an hour later and was told about the pages found on Burrell. The first thing he asked, was whether anyone had read them. The answer was 'no'. Due to the dark, and respect for the officer, it had been bagged unread. Docker told the caller it was important evidence relating to a major case and nobody was to read it until he got there.

He sat in the BTP office alone and read Burrell's final words. Then he read them again. He ran the permutations in his mind and decided that he needed to do nothing. There was no mention of Councillor Page. He was safe. For now.

Docker never had trouble sleeping, and that night was no different. He had indirectly driven an innocent man to his death, but Rob Docker didn't feel other people's pain. He concluded that he had just tipped Burrell over the edge, so it not really his fault. He regretted losing Burrell, but life wasn't fair, and then you died. That was it.

Sally was informed of Burrell's suicide the next morning, and the notes were released to her with Docker's blessing. She was distraught, her feelings made worse by the content of the pages as she replayed their last conversation over and over. But after a week off sick with stress she returned to work, steadfastly refusing to discuss Burrell with anyone, and buried herself in her job. Docker kept his distance, there would be plenty of time to talk.

How fragile life was. In due course, H.M Coroner for Birmingham recorded a verdict of suicide whilst the balance of John Burrell's mind was disturbed and released the body for a funeral. It made the papers, but suicides were never front-page stuff.

Another victim never got a mention – the train driver never got over the suicide. With the face of

John Burrell in his dying moments imprinted on his brain forever, he went sick and subsequently took a medical pension.

Docker pulled some strings, and despite the cloud that Burrell had left under, he was afforded a proper send-off with Docker mandating that the whole of the CID office should be in attendance. Many of his former colleagues, who had known and respected him, formed a 'guard of honour' and his old helmet was placed on top of the coffin. White shirts and black ties were the order of the day.

Docker performed the eulogy and spoke of the man who had worked with him in glowing and affectionate terms. He actually believed most of it.

Sally Jones attended the morning funeral but left immediately after the service and went home to be alone whilst his colleagues gave him a good 'send-off' leading to a lot of sore heads next day. Docker put some money behind the bar to pay for the drinks – in truth blood money – but well received.

During the afternoon Sally decided to start clearing out some of John Burrell's remaining possessions, which he had not taken with him after she had ordered him to leave.

She spent time bagging some of his clothing and then started on the desk in the spare room they shared. In the drawer he used were several folders and a pocketbook. With tears streaming down her face she thumbed through some of the papers – memories, painful memories. Why was life so shit?

Her attention was drawn to one particular folder and she began to read several pages of handwritten notes that Burrell had made directly following his conversation with 'Shane'.

As the enormity of what she was reading

enveloped her, Sally stopped crying and her inner strength returned. Coupled with the final letter he had written to her everything now made sense. She couldn't and wouldn't ever be able to forgive herself for failing him when he needed her most, but she could do her best to put some things right.

There were things to do.

Chapter Twelve

'Atishoo, Atishoo, they all fall down!'

Sally had rebuilt herself around seeking revenge for
John Burrell. Not justice. She knew what she could
expect from justice, and it wouldn't be enough for
what Hall had done. Ruined John's life and ruined
their future together.

John's notes had been sketchy, done from
memory, but they clearly showed that Hall was guilty
as hell, had been John's prime abuser, and was now
free. With Operation *'Damocles'* over, and that was
suspicious in itself, Hall was free to carry on. But it
was worse than that, there were others involved,
'higher ups' with power and influence. No names,
just descriptions of parties, of horrors where older
men preyed on the young.

*

Rob Docker went to see Brenda Doyle at her
home address. He knew that matters could not wait.
He hadn't liked Sally's demeanour after the enquiry
had been put to bed, and she had made a couple of
allusions to 'knowing more'. He had a nasty
suspicion that Burrell may have said something to her
before ending it all.

After making contact he had insisted that
Brenda be on her own at the house.

Just weeks after the winding up of Operation
'Damocles' and the demise of John Burrell, it was
past time for Docker to tie up some other 'loose-
ends'. With Baxter and Evans dead, his 'to do' list
had helpfully grown shorter, but there was still work

to do.

Hall had been released from bail without charge, after the meeting with the local Chief Constable where the enquiry had been quashed. Clearly strings had been pulled somewhere. But Docker wasn't only tidying up, he also sought revenge, and had the extra imperative of covering his back.

Docker sat waiting in his car in the darkness for a few minutes before knocking the door.

He was a meticulous planner, and the caution he applied in making sure the area was clear of any prying eyes was routine and normal for a man who was a born survivor.

Docker finally approached and knocked the front door. Brenda ushered him in silently. She had been told about Burrell's death and although he was a 'Copper', she had recognised something decent in him. She doubted that he was corrupt, which meant that he had probably been 'fitted up'. In Brenda's experience that was the norm.

They sat at the kitchen table facing each other - the only thing on Docker's mind now was to get things sorted and to move on.

Brenda Doyle was a woman full of anger and distress in equal measures – she had been unable to save her son; she had failed him, and she wanted revenge, but she had nothing in common with Docker, and didn't trust him. Docker had no intention of becoming trusted so that wasn't a problem.

Docker felt his way forward, "I know how you feel Brenda and we need to put things right...."

Brenda snapped back, "You have no idea how I feel. How Stewart had to struggle through life because of you racist bastards. You lot put him where he is now."

Docker spoke quietly, "But I do know Brenda.
I do. My father was a black man and my twin brother
was black. I know all about it, and I know how my
family suffered at the hands of my step-father."

He produced a faded black and white
photograph from an inside pocket, the only one he
had showing his brother and himself when younger.
The boys in the picture looked happy, arms around
each other, Joe smiling broadly. Docker knew it was a
fraud, there had been no such happiness as far as he
could recall, but he now had her attention.

Docker was a showman and could have easily
got himself an 'Equity Card' for theatrics, but on this
occasion he actually let his real feelings show as he
recalled the violence of his step-father, the forced fist
fight with his twin brother Joe and the consequences
of the sacrifice made by Joe, who like Stewart had not
deserved the cards that life had dealt him.

After sharing part of his life-story he finally
concluded, "This is our chance to put some things
right Brenda, but I need to know whether you are in
or out. If you are in, I'll do my best for Stewart, see if
there are grounds for an appeal against sentence. I
know a lot of people, a lot of lawyers, and I have an
idea about how to do it, but it can't happen without
your help."

Docker went on to outline a possible plan and
then concluded, "If you are out then you are on your
own and I won't be seeing you again. You know in
your heart that we aren't the ones who destroyed
Stewart. Some of them are still running around free,
living the good life, and they will be doing it again, to
other boys. We both know the so-called justice
system has failed, but I have my own system, and I

need your help."

Docker had another card to play, a fact gleaned from the notes Burrell left.

It was his Ace card, "I also think you should have a chat with Ses. Apparently, he knew John Burrell when he first started boxing – and was the one that referred him to the Army Cadets – into the clutches of that bastard Hall. It was that which drove John over the edge – his abuser walking free. I'm guessing that Ses didn't know – he doesn't strike me as a 'kiddie fiddler'."

Brenda was drowning in a sea of information yet desperate to get her son out of prison and to make somebody pay. She was in, and knew without question that Ses would be too – and where Ses went, so did Bud.

She did a spot of bargaining on their behalf and struck a satisfactory deal. It cost Docker nothing. The 'brothers' were more useful to him on the outside of prison and 'on the payroll' for future use.

Brenda and Docker parted – promises to be kept – actions to be taken.

Docker stepped out into the darkness – a familiar environment.

*

Ses needed no other motivation than his anger and guilt. The thought that he had been duped by Hall, had sent a boy to him, and that he was one of Stewart's abusers, was enough.

The 'brothers' were once again united in support of each other, and Brenda. They were old hands at this sort of thing and quickly fell into the groove. They engaged some 'help' from the club to watch Hall, noting his movements, looking for an opportunity. He appeared to be keeping his head down, barely moving from his flat, except for shopping trips. No safe option presented itself for several weeks, then one day Hall acquired a rental van and spent several hours loading it with cases and boxes. He was clearly on the move.

*

Hall had tried to enjoy his moment as he left court on bail. He had caught that bastard cop's eye and given him a big cheesy grin. The look that had been returned had been unsettling, and Hall had broken eye contact first. Still, what could Docker do? He was bound by the rules, and there were people backing Hall who made those rules. And Hall knew a lot, one of the reasons he had kept those letters from Redmund hidden, instead of destroying them. He had thought that they might come in useful. He didn't know why, but it seemed he had been right.

A few weeks later, after his bail had been cancelled, Hall had received a visit. Two men with London accents. One looked as if he were made of granite, the other sported a 'Jason King' moustache. Neither seemed the type to mess with, and Hall was a coward underneath all the bluster. Greg and 'Pancho' were men of few words but none were wasted.

The two visitors had laid down some rules of their own, or at least conveyed them. The price of his freedom. No more 'freelancing. His time at Harris Grange was over. He would be moving, starting anew. A suitable position would be found, and after a reasonable time to allow the dust to settle, he would resume his 'other duties'.

Thus it was that Peter Hall was placed at a children's home in North Wales as a care assistant. Highly recommended, with an impressive CV. He would be an asset, and some of the existing staff knew he would fit in just fine.

Hall was impressed and a little scared by the power his real employers wielded. He had been brought to heel.

*

Hall quickly settled down. He had a room at the Home and was quickly integrated into the routine. He knew that at least one of his colleagues was 'keeping an eye' on him, so he was on best behaviour for a while. But he was an arrogant and vain man, and his fears faded as time passed. He began to resent his enforced abstinence, made worse by the fact that he was living and working in the 'honeypot'. He began to use his downtime to get away, to put temptation out of reach. He sought out isolation, finding it in walking alone. He particularly liked the nearby coastal paths where the forces of nature, in particular, the ever-changing sea, helped to distract his thoughts.

One evening, whilst walking the cliffs, he became aware of two figures behind him, and they were a somewhat unusual sight, in North Wales. As he dawdled, they caught up and their features became clearer. 'I know they all look the same', he thought, 'but that guy looks just like Ses'.

Peter Hall was reported missing the next morning, when he didn't turn up at breakfast and his bed was found empty.

It was several days before his body, bashed and battered by the waves, washed up in a cove near to the cliffs he habitually traversed. Not the first to go over the top. Accident or suicide? It was impossible to say. An 'Open' verdict was recorded at the inquest.

Rick Foster didn't like the position of not knowing what had happened. He liked certainty. You could deal with it, build on it. He added a third possibility, that someone had got to Hall, but who? In some ways though, it did render one thing certain, Hall would be telling no tales. There would need to be another assessment made. He had tried putting a 'fire-break' in place around this mess, but perhaps it was time for 'scorched earth'.

*

Docker put the phone down after the briefest of conversations, pulled his feet up onto his desk, and reached for the bottom drawer once more. At times these days it felt like an involuntary action – a need – but this time it was different, a cause for real celebration. It wouldn't do to drink too much during the daytime, but the demise of Peter Hall deserved just one swift whisky, whilst he put the finishing touches to the recommendation for a commendation that he had put together for Police Constable George Hanley otherwise known to Hall as 'Alan Richardson'.

Putting the undercover officer in to get close to Hall in the Army Cadets had been a stroke of genius.

George Hanley was a highly experienced Level One covert officer who routinely courted danger. He had indeed served in the military, where he had learnt his musical skills, and his medals were genuine, but his subsequent police service had been skilfully erased from all public records and replaced by a phony name and a 'legend' that would be hard for even the most curious to unravel.

Feigning sickness had given him just enough time to discover Hall's suitcase of 'treasure' in the bedroom, and just seconds to literally push his fingers down his throat in order to produce real vomit.

Rob Docker truly respected the man and his

bravery, but he had seen the likes of him before and he knew that he would almost certainly never again be able to fit back into conventional policing. Such officers became so immersed in their roles that wearing a uniform again, and abiding by rules and instructions, just became too much for them. They either became sick, or angry burnt-out men who left with ill-health pensions and a sense of betrayal by the system that frequently deemed them to be dispensable.

This had been a relatively short deployment, but after a break of just a few weeks Hanley had already started working on another long-term 'UC' engagement. With the rise of the National Front after the Robert Relf saga, the previous year, George Hanley was about to swop highly polished boots for a pair of high-laced 'bovver-boots'.

***

At first, it seemed that the end of his sentence might as well be fifty years away. He was ruined and filled with terror at the prospect of prison. But the organisation had kept its promises. An open prison, a 'soft' job in the kitchen garden, and, the 'word' had clearly been passed around, nobody bothered him, prisoners or guards.

And now, suddenly, there was only a month to go. Charles Redmund had even allowed himself to begin to plan. To dream of a future where he regained his rightful place. With 'them' behind him, it would only be a matter of time. His loyalty was beyond question.

Charles was in his cell, reading. He had the choice of books from the prison library, and his cell was really, quite comfortable. No other prisoner had seen it, if they had they would have suspected that

Redmund was at minimum, an informant, or some sort of organised crime figure – the latter was closer to the truth.

The cell door was pushed open by a friendly prison officer, "You've got a visitor Mr. Redmund, it's a brief. Follow me please."

Redmund was ushered into the visitor's room. He was intrigued because his defence solicitor had moved on shortly after sentencing. A few of the tables were occupied and two or three Prison Officers stood around the room, looking bored. This was an Open Prison and not much happened to break the monotony.

He was shown to a table where Stoppard sat waiting, whilst his escort wandered off to talk to a colleague.

Redmund went to speak, but Stoppard held a hand up and stopped him, "Just listen Charles. I have instructions for you."

Ten minutes later Redmund returned to his cell. His hopes of a return to power and prestige dashed. But the alternative offered was palatable.

A month later he was collected from the gate by two men and driven to a hotel at Heathrow Airport. Two suitcases containing his remaining possessions and new clothes were waiting in a room, together with a one-way ticket.

Barbados would not be so bad, he thought. It was a much better class of prison to spend the rest of your life in. He was thinking in terms of decades, but accidents do happen, and fat, unfit men regularly drown in the sea.

***

Ernest Page was being stalked, and so were his stalkers. Greg and 'Pancho' had reported back that they were not alone in taking an interest in the Councillor, but Foster had decided to let the situation run. In the meantime, he did some background checks and came to a view as to what was going on. It was the right conclusion, but for the wrong reasons. Luckily for Docker, Foster did not uncover the link to Brenda.

Revenge was the likely motive as pennies fell into place. The lad, Doyle, had finally talked, no doubt to his mother and she was acting upon it. That also explained Hall. The damage could be managed.

A few days later Greg reappeared in London and reassured Rick, "Job done, and we didn't have to lift a finger, just like you said, boss. They did him quick, bonked him on the head once. They looked like pro's to me. Didn't think 'darkies' had it in em to be that good. Very efficient, picked their moment and were careful to set it up to look like he might have fallen. He'd been to a 'do', so no doubt had a skin full, and they put a bottle of scotch in his hand, poured some down his throat. I doubt the Police will find anything to bother themselves about."

A few days later, Foster had to agree with Greg. The case was being handled by a certain DCI Docker – it was no coincidence that Ses and Bud had done the deed on his patch.

Rick had the feeling that Docker would see it as convenient to write the tragic event off as an accident, given his past contact with Page, and that would suit everybody.

***

Sally had been both devastated and satisfied on hearing of the death of Hall via Docker, who had been contacted by the police in Wales. In some ways, death was too good for him. She had wanted him to suffer first, and she had wanted to be his torturer, to put fear and pain into him. She had fantasied about what she would say as she did so. But he was out of her reach now. Probably for the best, she would have sacrificed her career for the satisfaction now denied.

She reviewed what she knew. Hall, Evans and Baxter dead. Brent a minor player and long gone. She didn't know about the letters found in Hall's flat, so Redmund and Page remained obscured from her view. Neither 'Shane' nor Burrell had mentioned them by name. That left one person she could tackle. She had smelt something wrong with him from the start.

*

Sally had invested both her time and body over the last few weeks. A casual meeting in the bar at Steelhouse Lane had developed into a secret affair. She didn't like the man at all but reasoned that the least she could do for John was make this sacrifice.

She had picked the man because she had worked around Docker for too long, had learnt a lot about the ways in which the police operated. And she knew that when the shit hit the fan, truth was the first casualty.

The first Custody Sergeant had cracked as soon as he had been confronted with Burrell's print on the mug shard. He had been given a stark choice. Either he had left the mug in the cell, or Burrell had. He took the lesser option, was busted to PC and was now walking some godforsaken beat in his 'tit hat'. Sally didn't think he had anything left to tell as he had been broken completely.

The night shift Sergeant was a different matter, however. He had emerged with credit due to his handling of the death in custody. He was the man

313

currently snoring in her bed.

Sally had done a spot of asking around, about Burrell's last days, and the incident that had resulted in his disgrace. People had been sympathetic and willing to tell her things that the 'rubber heel squad' from Complaints had never thought to ask. One officer had mentioned that John had been drinking with Hargreaves in the bar that fateful evening. It was odd, and what if Hargreaves had remained at Steelhouse Lane after John had gone home?

The second Custody Sergeant couldn't believe his luck. Although married, he wasn't one to let an opportunity pass, and assiduously pursued the sex on offer. Even better, she was one of Docker's. He clearly trusted her, and the Sergeant trusted Docker's judgement.

He was a bitter man who believed that fate and 'the gaffers' had conspired to prevent his obvious skills being rewarded with advancement. In truth he was a limited ability, time-serving moaner, who treated everyone with sarcasm and cynicism and reaped his just reward in their responses. It hadn't taken long before he had started to tell Sally his tales of woe, both in the job and out, where his wife had gone off sex and, in his view, deliberately got fat to spite him. Sally silently applauded her if it was true.

She skilfully manoeuvred the conversations, encouraging him to prove how clever he was, and how stupid the bosses were, until, that last night, in her bed, he had gleefully told her how he had escaped censure, in fact achieved quite the opposite, on the occasion of Evan's suicide.

"I normally wouldn't protect a wanker like that carrot-crunching DI, but he had a bit of luck having someone like me to cover for him." he

---

314

boasted.

"What do you mean?" Sally purred softly encouraging him.

The man was now in full flow, "Oh, he went in the cell that night, last to see the prisoner. But I had to keep my mouth shut. I was just trying to help the job, been told the prisoner was a CID job. I mean, your boss is in and out of the fucking cells more often than the prisoners are – it's the norm isn't it. Have a bit of a chat off the record and all that. Makes the world go around and gets the baddies off the streets."

That night of passion was the last he saw of Sally. The next person he had to tell the tale to would be a no-nonsense Superintendent from Complaints. Sally had been wired up for the conversations whilst dressed. The rest of the time, she had taken a chance with a cassette recorder under the bed. The Sergeant was such an arrogant fucker that the law of averages meant that he would say something stupid on tape before long – a man immersed in his own flawed ego.

The sergeant's dreams of advancement went into terminal decline. Most were glad to see the back of him.

*

Sally asked to be part of the interview of Hargreaves after he had been arrested for Misconduct in Public Office. She knew he would get off a serious charge, but she wanted to look in his eyes, wanted him to know it was her. Her request was allowed on condition that she remained an observer, and she enjoyed watching him squirm.

It was clear to everybody in the room that Hargreaves was hiding something, but all the evidence pointed to suicide, and only Evans and Hargreaves knew exactly what had passed between them.

There were flagrant breaches of the Police Discipline Code, but Hargreaves was from another Force, and the Complaints file had to be passed back to his Home Force for finalisation, the decision as to punishment resting with his own Chief Constable.

The short Chief with the blonde secretary was not impressed at the revival of anything to do with *Operation Damocles*, after he had spent time 'lidding it', and Hargreaves, who was expecting some benevolence from his own Force, found himself reduced to Constable. It was a disaster for him, all his power gone, his 'usefulness' expired.

***

A group of ruthless men held an extraordinary meeting of *'The Olympus Club'* to discuss recent events and damage limitation. The meeting was held in a private room at one of the many prestigious 'gentlemen only' clubs in Central London, and two men with an unmistakeable military bearing stood guarding the outside door. Their very own *'Greek Pantheon'* in the heart of a city thousands of miles away from a culture that they mimicked. Outside, the sounds of traffic and the buzz of normality, as people went about their daily business.

The man known as *'Zeus'* called the meeting to order.

The group's 'intelligence officer' a former high-ranking serviceman, gave a very precise briefing as to which 'lower order' members had been exposed, those who might still be at risk, or compromised, and those who would say nothing ever again.

Foster, or *'Ares'',* as he was now known in this circle, now took centre-stage, outlining the measures he had taken to protect the 'inner-circle', and the most important assessment, whether any risk continued. It was concluded that he had done very well, and several of the older members noting the approval of *'Zeus'*, looked at Foster anew, realising that he was rising fast, and could go to the very top.

Following this, a retired Judge expressed some views on the potential for any civil litigation to emerge and what the prospects of any criminal proceedings might be. He deferred to his retired police colleague to deal with any questions as to how the police might approach any fresh enquiry into allegations of child abuse.

Twelve men, the principal deities of an organisation that had several layers to it, sat in the room, their power and spheres of influence spanning all of the major political, academic, judicial, military and policing institutes in the land – the *'Gods of Olympus'*. These were not men that frightened easily, and they did not view life in the conventional sense when it came to morality and the rights and wrongs of their actions. They took what they wanted.

They were bound by three common bonds, a predilection for sex with children, a love of power, and a very small tattoo in Greek lettering *'OK'* – short for *'Omikro Kappa'* on the upper part of their left arms to denote membership of the club.

'Zeus' summarised their position and made a number of recommendations from which individuals took actions away with them to complete. The problems had been effectively contained within the Midlands area, and other arms of the organisation remained untouched. The most pressing issue was to ensure that a weeping sore had been effectively 'cauterised' and would not spread the infection any further.

At the conclusion of the meeting there was just one item of 'any other business' as one of the members put forward a motion that one Major Charles Stoppard should be handsomely rewarded and encouraged for his good work.

The motion was passed unanimously, and in a final gesture the members raised their glasses in unison, and as one saluted *'The Olympus Club'*.

Shortly afterwards Rob Docker received an anonymous telephone call. The voice on the other end recalled previous 'favours', including those involving Page and a lad called Danny.

The caller went on to suggest that 'letting sleeping dogs lie' would result in an 'early Christmas present'. Docker chose his words carefully, reserving some local matters, and an agreement was reached.

In December Robert Docker was in fact promoted substantively to Detective Chief Inspector at the age of thirty-four years, in recognition of his good work, and was posted to Force Headquarters. It was a bit of a non-job, but he'd escaped from those before, and would do so again. In the meantime, it gave him the opportunity to conclude some outstanding business.

Operation *'Damocles'* wasn't quite over for Rob Docker.

*

Docker was not one for attending meetings, or training courses if he could avoid it, and the thought of strategic planning or *'blue sky'* thinking turned him cold. Those closest to him were therefore somewhat surprised when they discovered that he had put himself forward to attend a two-day seminar on *'Policing – The Future'* at a hotel in Birmingham.

Docker reassured them that he was just taking

the chance for a pre-Christmas 'piss up' with some old colleagues, from a previous CID Course. Only the misguided amongst them would have remotely considered that he was going soft.

The keynote speech was to be delivered by a Chief Constable, who was already being tipped as a future Commissioner of the Metropolitan Police – the highest-ranking police officer in the UK. It would be followed by a 'question and answer' session from the delegates.

The man with the small stature, whose previous brief meeting with Rob Docker had been less than warm, was making a name for himself within ACPO, (the Association of Chief Police Officer), and Government circles, for his radical thinking and ability to achieve budgetary savings – more for less was in vogue and this man was leading the way.

Just weeks before, the Chief Constable had also received written notification that he would be receiving the Queen's Police Medal in the New Year's Honours List. This was a coveted award generally given out to less than forty police officers UK-wide each year. With specific instructions from the Awards Committee to keep it a secret until the official announcement on New Year's Day he was nevertheless bursting with pride and thanks to the local colleagues and politicians on the Police Authority who had nominated him.

In due course, if he landed the top job, he would be guaranteed a Knighthood and with it the promise of a seat in the House of Lords after retirement – life was brilliant and although there had been a few casualties along the way, he had survived any negative attention – they didn't call him *'Teflon'*

319

for nothing.

Docker duly attended at the hotel where the seminar was being held and collected his delegate pack. He looked around and assessed his fellow attendees. 'Useless wankers – never seen an angry man, or got their hands dirty with real work', he concluded.

During the open session Docker deliberately sat in the front row and did his best to appear engaged and interested. He even made some notes in the full knowledge that they would go straight in the bin at the earliest opportunity. Some 'prat' next to him kept trying to engage him in meaningless chat about policing priorities but he managed to deflect him and eventually the man turned his attentions elsewhere.

Even for a man of Docker's fortitude it had been a difficult twelve months and he was very tired – tired of the cretins that surrounded him within the job, tired of administering his own brand of justice, and tired of his personal life.

Lunch duly followed, and then it was time for the great man's appearance onto a raised stage which at least helped him to compensate for his lack of height. A complete master of his art, he paced up and down the stage and spoke for an hour without any notes.

Hands raised on occasions, with palms outstretched to the audience, he was a picture of eloquence and never faltered once, except for one fleeting second when he spotted a face at the front of the audience who peered at him with quiet curiosity, and the hint of a thin smile. A good memory for faces was a boon if one was ambitious, and he had not forgotten Rob Docker, or his discourtesy.

The Chief Constable was used to people either

320

being scared of him, or in total awe. In this man's eyes he saw no trace of either, and it made him feel extremely uneasy.

The question and answer session duly followed, and members of the audience were invited to tender their questions after first introducing themselves. Docker waited for things to settle then raised his hand and stood to ask his question, "Rob Docker sir – West Midlands Police – like many in the room I am really keen to understand and learn what you as a successful police leader feel are the key attributes required to get to the top?"

The speaker was slightly perplexed as to why a man he had wronged would want to gift him such a question, but Docker had given him a subject that he could *'wax lyrical'* on for a good ten minutes. The words tumbled out: honesty. integrity, leading by example, openness. He went on and on before being politely drawn back into the *'Q and A'* by the chair of the session.

Docker had achieved his aim. At the back of the room Jane Smith sat quietly taking notes, one of a select group of local media representatives who had been invited to attend this specific part of the seminar only. Her newspaper was already holding space for her story the following day and had also negotiated a lucrative option with a national tabloid.

Jane Smith could already smell blood. In different circumstances she would have engineered an overnight stay so that she could celebrate afterwards in Docker's room, but this was pure business.

The evening passed off uneventfully, and Docker even enjoyed the after-dinner speaker as liberal quantities of wine were passed around each of the tables. Maybe there was something to be said for *'hob-knobbing'* with the good and great after all.

The Chief Constable had chosen to stay for the evening, and after the formal dinner he circulated among the delegates, pausing for a few minutes at each table, sometimes longer at others, dependant on the potential for a useful connection to be made.

The man deliberately paused next to Docker and touched him lightly on the shoulder, "Good question today Docker – good to see that you are developing a more strategic approach to your work."

Docker shifted gently in his seat so that the hand slipped away. He smiled broadly and offered his hand whilst remaining seated, "A very interesting day sir. I look forward to you catching more of the headlines in your career."

A few glasses of wine had dulled the Chief Constable's senses slightly and he took Dockers comments as being a compliment of sorts. Perhaps this moron was not such a *'problem child'* after all, he thought.

The handshake concluded with reaffirmation that they had no common secret bond between each other, and the Chief Constable moved on, dismissing Docker from his mind, and life. That was the last time that Docker was to see the man.

The following morning the Chief Constable woke up in his room at the hotel, slightly the worse for wear, but content that it had been a productive exercise. He had achieved his aim and would be leaving after breakfast. He had a Discipline Panel to chair and he was looking forward to stamping his authority on some minor miscreant.

He had just finished shaving when he noticed two newspapers had appeared under his door. An avid reader of *'The Times'*, he was surprised to see a copy of a well-known tabloid – definitely not his 'cup of tea' at all.

He picked the newspapers up from the floor and threw them onto the bed. The tabloid fell open on the front page *'Chief Constable and Secretary – secret hotel trysts at the expense of the taxpayer.'*

It wasn't a pretty story but it was full of dates, places, and even photos of the man and his *'blonde bombshell,'* some of which showed close-up trysts – all courtesy of Jane Smith and a free-lance photographer who was normally an ardent member of the 'paparazzi'.

Jane Smith had done her work well, and the comments she had put together following his response to Docker's question placed almost the final nail in his coffin.

The man froze in fear and suddenly remembered Docker's words the previous night. As he silently mouthed the word 'bastard' the phone rang – the chair of the Police Authority was already chasing him and by the end of the day he suffered the ignominy of being suspended from duty, his career hanging on by a thread.

Two days later Docker delivered the *'coup de grace'* – it was the only way that Docker knew how to operate – complete and utter annihilation of his target – no half measures.

A handwritten letter arrived in the post addressed to the Chair of the Police Authority, signed by one Stewart Doyle, who had recently been convicted of the murder of John Baxter and sentenced to life imprisonment.

Docker had paid him a visit in prison after the sentencing and promised to support an appeal based on manslaughter if he did exactly what he was told.

Brenda had already paved the way for him with Doyle, and it wasn't a difficult task. Docker thought that he had enough evidence of what Doyle had been through to gain the sympathy of the judges and swing an appeal.

Docker dictated the letter which alleged that the Chief Constable had been involved in a cover-up in relation to allegations of child abuse. Docker had the pieces to some of the puzzle and the letter made for authentic reading, given that some of it was a total fabrication.

It mattered not – this was the hammer blow that would ensure that his visit to Buckingham Palace to receive his QPM would be put on hold, and then quietly withdrawn. The 'Awards Committee' took no chances when it came to those that stood before the Queen.

The Chief Constable then received a written discipline notice from another Chief Constable from an outside Force, who had been appointed to investigate him, indicating that he was formally being investigated for Misconduct in Public Office as well as Perverting the Course of Justice, and fraud.

On the same day his wife placed a solitary suitcase at the door of their home and showed him the outside of it.

*

Docker was not finished yet, and within days Chief Superintendent Rackham, who had failed so miserably to support him found himself the subject of an article in the *'Birmingham Evening Mail'* where he was 'outed' as being gay and accused of visiting well-known *'cottaging'* sites in Birmingham and Coventry.

The first statement was true, and the second just pure fiction, but the job found it hard to separate

324

the two issues, and he subsequently found himself posted to an administrative role in charge of paperclips in Force Headquarters where he was to languish for years to come.

These were not the days of liberal thinking and the word diversity had yet to be embraced. These were times when coppers were *'men's men'* who were macho and strong, not *'puffs'* or *'queers'*.

Whilst the man couldn't be dismissed from the service for being a homosexual, and an internal investigation later cleared him of any criminal wrongdoing, he now had a label around his neck which would prevent him from going any further.

In a final twist, Jane Smith ran an exclusive story which won her journalistic acclaim for an investigation into paedophile rings in Birmingham, Worcestershire and Warwickshire. It wasn't enough for Docker that most of those named were either dead, missing or in prison he wanted to see their names and reputations terminally damaged.

One of those named however was very much alive, and Hargreaves, the original investigator, spent some uncomfortable months suspended again whilst being investigated, before he was totally cleared of all allegations of Misconduct in Public Office.

The police investigation into the murder of John Baxter had indeed been a shambles but more by design than accident. James Hargreaves had used the female civilian indexer to file the action relating to the critical piece of evidence. His fleeting affair with the married woman had been both interesting and useful.

The enquiry also tried and failed to link him with others, but the 'old school' closed ranks and the investigators found it difficult to penetrate a wall of silence.

Once again, James Hargreaves narrowly escaped justice. But other eyes were on him, and they were only interested in Hargreaves' personal balance sheet. Was he still an asset or now a liability? The answer would prompt very different outcomes.

*

Just weeks later Docker acted as a 'plus-one' for Jane Smith at the regional news reporters award ceremony, held at *'The Night Out'* at The Horsefair in the city centre, where she was up for an award for her investigatory scoops.

First opened in 1975, with a 1,400-seat auditorium, Docker found no difficulty in merging into the background of an establishment that boasted that it was able to produce 1,000 meals per night and five-hour non-stop shows.

The management however knew him well at the venue, and he had recently managed to place Bud into a senior doorman's position at the nightclub, which had played host to many famous singers and groups including the *'Three Degrees'*. The second of Brenda's lovers was more amenable than Ses, and Docker wanted to keep the man in his pocket for the future.

Docker was aware that the two men dabbled in the politics of racism and had attended a march that year in Rookery Road, Handsworth where cyclists had led the *'Afrika Liberation Day'* rally. Holding banners proclaiming, *'We are our own liberators'*, *'We want Africa freed from imperialism'* and *'Imperials hands off Jamaica'* the *'Pan African Committee UK'* sought to get their voices heard. The children of the *'Windrush'* generation were growing up and Docker was astute enough to know that having

326

good sources on the inside of the Black community would pay dividends in the future.

Docker had kept his promise to Brenda and set the wheels in motion for an Appeal of Stewart's case via a barrister of questionable integrity that he knew. There would be no need for lying in court this time though. Once Docker had recounted what Hall and Baxter had done, he was pretty confident that the conviction would be reduced to manslaughter, and the sentence to a few years. Doyle would get his second chance.

Docker's thoughts drifted momentarily to Burrell during the evening but the warmth of Jane's body in a flame-red figure-hugging long dress sat next to him was enough to distract him.

An experienced criminologist looking at the facts would have been forgiven for thinking that Rob Docker had acted through some sense of *'Noble Cause'* in seeking some form of justice for the scores of victims who had suffered humiliation, and the worst kind of abuse at the hands of evil men.

They could not of course have been further from establishing the truth.

Rob Docker possessed no such sentimental characteristics and was driven only by revenge against men who had crossed him inside the job, and a desire to sweep some more filth into the gutter, outside it.

Normal people might also have suggested that Docker's actions, in respect of his police colleagues, were totally disproportionate in terms of the harm that they had done him personally, but Docker was not a normal person.

He was a ruthless man with no boundaries – this was Dockers law.

***

Hargreaves was, as usual, pounding a lonely beat out in the wilds of Warwickshire. It was cold, and it had been a long set of nights. He plodded along an unlit country lane; head down, seemingly fascinated by the toes of his boots. But inside, he was boiling hot, his mind racing through schemes to get his rank back or get even.

His target could have been Sally, the author of his initial downfall. But in a funny way he respected her. She had supported her man, and she had been punished enough. Let her live without her love.

His target could have been Docker. Hargreaves knew he had underestimated the man's capacity for devious and ruthless dealings. But he actually admired him. Docker was an animal. If you bit him and didn't wound him enough, he just bit back harder. Hargreaves had lost fair and square. There was no way he was going back into that boxing ring.

No, his target was those who could have saved him. Those who had condemned him to this turgid and menial existence. Those who had made it plain that he had to 'knuckle down' for a couple of years, until the dust settled, then something might be done. After all he had done. After all he had risked for them. It had started with blackmail, his being compromised with a boy – a set-up, but it had proved a positive relationship until now.

Now he had nothing to lose, no reputation, no career. Two could play at the game of blackmail, and he knew so much.

Hargreaves, lost in thoughts of imagined victories, stood to one side of the country lane, on the grass verge, as car headlamps approached.

'That car's shifting', was his final thought.

**

Another Christmas, and Sally met Rob Docker in one of the many small back-street pubs in the Jewellery Quarter. To the casual observer they might have looked like a couple having an affair - the older man seeking refuge in the 'snug' with his younger lover. They would not have been more wrong, the potential for romance between the two was as possible as 'hell freezing over'.

Neither was interested in 'small talk' but Docker had requested the meeting and Sally needed to hear what he had to say. He bought the first round of drinks and Sally savoured a 'Gin and Tonic', which felt good.

Docker came to the point and informed her that he had arranged for her to come back and work for him as an Acting Detective Inspector on the HQ Family Protection Unit. The Unit was in a bit of mess and if she did a good job, he was pretty sure that she would be made substantive within six months. Who knows how far she might go?

Sally gave no outward signs of appreciation. She knew that Docker operated on the simple principle that you 'kept your friends close and your enemies' even closer.' Either way Sally took it as a compliment. Even though he hadn't asked outright, she knew from his comments that he suspected her of running Hargreaves down in that lane. She smiled to herself. It would do no harm to let him wonder.

*

On Christmas Day, Sally Jones left her house early and visited the grave of John Burrell's parents, in St Peter's Church, Harborne, where his ashes had also been scattered. By sheer co-incidence the

---

329

graveyard was at the rear of the church where she had got married and the grave was situated towards the bottom of the graveyard which was enclosed by lines of high fir trees.

Fortunately, the 'Bell Inn' next to the church was open and Sally sought solace in a drink, completely alone, but surrounded by people. There was a hint of snow in the air.

Sally was down but not out, and as she faced the prospects of a new year, she was determined to face her 'ghosts' head on. She had been given a job to do and she was determined that she would make a difference. Docker could not have offered her a better role. The Family Protection Units dealt with both Child Abuse and Domestic Violence. She was on a mission.

***

In a plush house in a desirable London neighbourhood Rick Foster raised a glass to himself. He was safe, they were all safe. But it had been close. Only he really knew how close.

A New Year approached, one full of possibilities. *'Zeus'* was getting older, there would be an heir designate.

But the old Rick Foster had to be left behind. The street survivor. If he was really going to aim for the top, he needed to reinvent himself. A new identity, new and legal investments and businesses. Bury the past. He took a long sip of his Malt. 'A good New Year resolution', he thought.

***

Following the demise of Peter Hall, the Harris Grange Army Cadet Force detachment went on to achieve great things, its reputation untarnished. Hall's untimely death had ensured that no further proceedings could be contemplated and as each generation of his victims passed through age and time, they took their own secrets with them to their graves. Wracked with individual guilt at allowing themselves to be groomed by such a monster none could face the torment of public disclosure.

As realisation crept in among the 'circles of power' within Social Services that they needed to get their houses in order, Richmond House and Avon House were quietly closed by their respective Local Authorities and the remaining residents were dispersed to the four winds, with staff members being made the subject of 'early retirement' or placed in other Homes. The end of the story you might say, except that years later some of those residents found the inner courage to make public complaints about systemic child abuse involving those already named, plus a number of previously unknown offenders who worked with children. The tentacles even stretched as far as North Wales.

When the tree is rotten you have to remove more than just a few branches, you need to take the roots out as well. The failure to do so had led to further victims and further abuse which could have been prevented. Fewer 'Stewart's' and 'Shirley's' to have their lives blighted.

But for those at the very top, those with power, justice was a plaything that could not touch them.

Michael Layton and Stephen Burrows 2020

Authors' Comment

Sadly, historical child abuse is now recognised as being both prevalent and widespread in the UK over a period of decades. On occasions it was perpetrated by those in positions of power and influence, within the very institutions that were created to protect them, and the victims were often the most vulnerable in society.

Today's generation have a duty to ensure that those who engage in such evil acts are not allowed to prosper, and are brought to justice.

PLEA FROM THE AUTHORS

Dear reader - thank you for reading this story to the end of the book, we hope that means that you enjoyed it. Whether or not you did, we would just like to thank you for buying it and giving us your valuable time to try and entertain you.

If you would like to find out more about our other fiction and non-fiction books then please visit our website, **www.bostinbooks.co.uk.** Alternatively, search for our names on Amazon. We also have a Facebook page 'Bostin Books'.

If you enjoyed this book, we would be extremely grateful if you would consider leaving a review on Amazon.co.uk (or the Amazon site for your country). To do this, find the book page online, scroll down, and use the *'review button'*.

The most important part of a book's success is how many positive reviews it has, so if you leave one then you are directly helping and encouraging us to continue on our journey as authors - thank you in advance to anyone who does!

Printed in Poland
by Amazon Fulfillment
Poland Sp. z o.o., Wrocław

65117772R00197